STAY WITH ME TILL MORNING

'John Braine goes home again to Yorkshire for
his entertaining new novel, probably his best
work since his first, *Room At The Top*'
The Observer

'The real wonder is the sympathy Braine en-
genders almost against the reader's will'
The Guardian

'Braine's writing is filmish, physically varied
and vivid and everlastingly on the move'
The Financial Times

45/-

John Braine

Stay With Me
Till Morning

MAGNUM BOOKS
Methuen Paperbacks Ltd

A Magnum Book

STAY WITH ME TILL MORNING

ISBN 0 417 01990 4

First published 1970
by Eyre Methuen Ltd
Magnum edition published 1978
Reprinted 1978
Reprinted 1981

Copyright © 1970 by John Braine

Magnum Books are published
by Methuen Paperbacks Ltd
11 New Fetter Lane, London, EC4P 4EE

Made and printed in Great Britain
by Hazell Watson & Viney Ltd
Aylesbury, Bucks

For Jane and Kingsley Amis

One

Clive Lendrick was five foot eleven, at forty-six was only slightly overweight, and hadn't had to consult a doctor for over twenty years. He had all his own teeth – including two capped ones – and his hair was thick and springy. He wore his hair short – only just long enough to part – and washed it every morning when he showered. He had it trimmed every week and the barber whom he always used knew without being told that excess hair on the ears and nostrils and eyebrows must also be trimmed.

His hair was light brown, a shade darker than fair, but because of its cleanliness gave the impression of having gold threads in it. His eyes were pale blue and inclined to be cold; his skin was fair and he had to be careful with it. He used only baby soap, having discovered from experience that as he grew older any other kind would bring small irritating red patches out on his face and hands. He used Cuticura powder after his shower; if he didn't there was a tendency to soreness between the toes and the thighs. After-shave lotions, colognes, and scented talcums were never used by him and he was always slightly prejudiced against other men who did. At the same time, rather irrationally, he was ashamed of having so sensitive a skin; whenever he went away from home, he would conceal the bar of baby soap and the tin of Cuticura as soon as he'd finished with them.

Strictly speaking, he had a shade too much chin and nose to be good-looking; his was the sort of face which looks its best on the stage. He had a deep, resonant voice and at his public school had acquired the kind of accent known as *educated*; if his father had not been a rich man, he might well have drifted into the theatre. For he did have a small talent in that direction: he could sing in tune, he could mimic regional accents without making too big a fool of himself, and before his marriage he'd even taken small parts in amateur productions. That, in fact, had been how he'd met his wife, Robin.

This isn't to say that he was a thwarted actor. Acting had been one of the diversions of youth, no more. Half the pleasure of it had been in waiting backstage for his cue, using theatrical terms offhandedly and expertly, inhabiting temporarily a world cut off from real life. And in that world, jokes and tea and coffee – the limpest of jokes, the weakest of tea and coffee – had a better, stronger taste, and smoking a cigarette, instead of being a commonplace indulgence, was a dramatic gesture, raised to one's lips before the firing squad or the dawn patrol. All this of its nature could not last. But if there had been no other way of advancement and if there had been someone around at the right time to push him, he would quite happily have settled down in the professional theatre.

As it was, he went into the family business, which was the production of fine worsted, with a sideline in mohair and synthetics. He would have gone with equal willingness into steel or soap or building or haulage – in fact, into any business which would give him a decent living. He had a quick intelligence and wasn't without imagination; but his main asset was his ability to get along with people. The production side at Lendrick and Sons was largely taken care of by his younger brother Donald.

Donald, unlike Clive, worried a great deal; Donald, unlike Clive, couldn't handle human relationships very well, even when he most wanted to; Donald, unlike Clive, worked his problems through slowly and painfully. But Clive could come up with the wrong answer; and on more than one occasion those wrong answers could have caused serious damage. The truth is that Donald had a vocation and Clive hadn't. It worked out very well; Clive in general looked after publicity and sales, Donald looked after the thousands of details which make up production. To put it as an over-statement, if Donald had been in sole charge of the mills there wouldn't have been any customers and if Clive had been in sole charge there wouldn't have been any cloth to sell them.

His job didn't claim much of his energy. He could, as they say, do it in his sleep. Perhaps if, like his father, he'd had to build up the business instead of merely inheriting it, his story might have been different. But struggle and ambition had never been any more than words to him. If ever there had been tension at Lendrick and Sons, if ever there had been times when the future hung in the balance, it had been his brother who had pulled things together, not Clive. It wasn't that he couldn't rise to an emergency and, indeed, he had done so on a few occasions. Over a short period he could do spectacularly well. But in the wool trade it's a succession of emergencies which have to be coped with day by day over the years; here he would never have shone. And the long-term planning had all been his brother's. Otherwise, to choose only one example, the mills wouldn't have been equipped with modern machinery but would have made do with the old, that being the least trouble.

So Clive glided through his business life, cheerful and charming and unperturbed. He was well liked by everybody, not least by Donald; in a way he was a walking advertisement for the mills, the flesh-and-blood manifestation of their prosperity. He never wore the same clothes two days running and he virtually never wore any cloth that was not of Lendrick and Sons' weaving.

If lives were cloth, most of us would be wool – durable enough, but needing attention and effort to keep in the proper shape. Clive's material would have been one of the new wash-and-wear synthetics – throw on the bedroom floor at the end of the day and it's still as if newly pressed in the morning, wash it in the washing machine like a nylon shirt and hang it up to dry. As a material it lacks warmth and it wouldn't be the first choice of any tailor wanting to create subtle effects. You might also argue that its appearance is on the stagey side, that it doesn't look like real cloth.

Clive at first sight wasn't quite real. Everything had gone too smoothly for him in the past, everything was going too smoothly for him in the present. At forty-six he could have passed as ten years younger; physically he was luxuriously indolent but could rouse himself to play a hard and savage game of tennis and, every now and then, to tramp, or rather stroll, twenty miles over the moors.

He'd had what is described as a good war, mostly in the Western Desert and Italy, ending up as a Major, with a MC, and a shrapnel wound across his belly which left a foot-long purplish scar but no permanent ill-effects. Enough active service came his way for him to be respected by the troops, but mostly he was attached to HQ. This wasn't the consequence of wangling, but of the fact that senior officers liked having him around; he was unfailingly cheerful, he was clean and smart and incredibly English-looking.

Neither was he, from the point of view of his seniors, over-ambitious. He had enjoyed himself in the ranks, but had no sentimental feelings about staying with his comrades. It was more agreeable to be an officer, to have a better uniform and more pay and perquisites, and the additional responsibility didn't perturb him in the least. He was generous with his money but took care not to flash it around too much; there were too many of his brother-officers who had wives and children and mortgages, who had to make every penny count.

A year after he was demobbed, he married Robina Covington, the eldest daughter of a civil engineer. Robina (or rather Robin, as she was always called) was tall, with large brown eyes and fair hair and a smooth skin, golden rather than olive; she was three years younger than Clive and a secretary at the Charbury BBC studio. In many ways she was Clive's counterpart. Everything had been easy for her too, she'd glided through babyhood and childhood and the very good convent school of St Perpetua's and through the School Certificate and a secretarial college and into the coveted BBC job. The BBC job was coveted because it carried glamour, could entail expense account travel, and above all was interesting; it was the sort of job for which there's intense competition. Robin glided into it; she had the right accent, the right clothes, the right air of cheerful competence and, thanks to St Perpetua's, had at least a nodding acquaintance with the arts. She'd also gone to the trouble to cram into her head a few basic technical facts about broadcasting; no questions were asked her about it, but the possession of this knowledge gave her extra confidence.

She enjoyed herself at the BBC, just as much as she had enjoyed herself at St Perpetua's. The people she worked with sometimes drank too much and were liable to say outrageous things even when sober; married or unmarried, they all made passes with what at first seemed alarming frequency. But they never held it against her when she refused to cooperate, saying generally in a mock-affected voice *I'm afraid you're not wholly serious, sir*, or *For shame! For shame! I'm not that kind of girl*, always keeping a smile on her face.

There were times when she was attracted, but on those occasions she needed only to remind herself of their salary scales, which she knew by heart. Occasionally one of the broadcasters would attract her – these were the last days of radio as a big-name medium – but she also knew how ephemeral the rewards of this kind of entertainer were, and she had no intention of becoming one of the amenities of Broadcasting House, Charbury.

Of all the men she met at the BBC, with only one did she ever come near abandoning her virginity. It was a week after she'd become engaged to Clive, on a wet November night when she'd been working late with the man in question, Stephen Belgard, a young drama producer who was, so he said, serving a sentence in Charbury for rank insubordination. (This wasn't true; he was simply doing a stint there to gain experience in the Regions.)

Stephen was a Charbury boy originally, the son of a railway porter. He was small, with a dark bad-tempered face, and was inclined to be scruffy. He wore his hair long and always seemed to need a shave, and his taste in clothes ran towards coloured shirts, sweaters, and duffel coats. He had been invalided out of the Army after Dunkirk with pleurisy and a perforated ear drum, had been awarded a place at Charbury University, had had a miserable year teaching, and then found his way into the BBC.

She knew that he was regarded with some respect not only in Charbury but in London – he was a wild man, he drank too much, he was exaggeratedly, destructively unpredictable, but he had real talent, he had original ideas; some of the poetry which he had published in the many little reviews of that time had genuine promise. And at some period in his life he seemed to have read everything, to have seen every picture and every play, to have heard all the music.

One couldn't be bored in his presence, she came to discover, though very often one could be shocked. Clive was no fool, nor was he completely uncultured, but compared with Stephen he simply wasn't grown-up. Except in one important way: he was stable, he was predictable, he was even-tempered. Stephen could be depressed for days at a time and when he was depressed it was impossible for everyone around him not to be infected by his depression.

On that wet November night he was just emerging from one of these bouts. He'd never asked her to have a drink with him alone before, any more than he'd ever made a pass at her. Normally they'd have had a drink with the members of the cast, but there were only three members of this particular cast, and they had made their own arrangements.

Broadcasting House, Charbury, stands by itself in Leeds Road near the Town Hall. It is essentially a large concrete box with rather too many windows for the comfort of its occupants; the concrete, as might be expected in a Northern industrial city, is cracked and blotchy.

'Christ, what monstrosities the Bauhaus is responsible for,' Stephen said as he took her arm crossing the road. 'Now look at this.' He pointed to the Jolly Waggoner's black Victorian exterior. 'That *belongs* here. It's rather ridiculous that it should try to look like a church with those funny little spires and those arched windows and stained glass, but at least it suits this bloody awful climate—'

But inside the pub didn't suit him; by some chance that night it was full of students from the University. Or it might have been, she often thought afterwards, that there was some girl there he didn't want to see; from stray gossip at the BBC she'd gathered, feeling unreasonably jealous, that he preferred students for his mistresses because they were birds of passage and could sometimes understand as many as one of his words in six.

'Let's go to my place,' he said in his harsh voice from which he had long ago ferociously scrubbed every vestige of Yorkshire.

She hesitated. 'I shouldn't—' She had never felt so happy in her life, the rain beating into her face, drumming against her hood and raincoat, aware of her body warm and dry underneath. Clive was away in London on business. She'd told her parents she'd be working late, and in any case she could please herself. She only knew that she wanted to keep on being with Stephen, even if it had meant merely standing outside the pub in the rain with him.

'You want to,' he said in that harsh voice. She squeezed his arm but didn't speak. *I'm on the verge of doing something stupid,* she thought. Any of the cars which passed by along Leeds Road could contain someone who knew her and probably who also knew Stephen, who was in his way a local celebrity. Irrespective of whether Stephen wanted to marry her or not, she didn't want to marry him. She was at this moment in a real street in a real city; Stephen was in transit, Leeds Road in Charbury would take its place with other streets in other cities, he was going to move on, and her figure would become smaller and smaller as the train gathered speed.

They didn't speak until they were in her car, a pre-war Wolseley Nine that had spent the war greased and on blocks in her Uncle Tim's garage. Her uncle had given it to her because its original owner, his son, was killed on D-Day. It wasn't very beautiful, but it was a good example of the pre-war quality car, and the little engine ran like a sewing machine, but more quietly. She liked that car better than any she ever owned; she always had the notion that Young Tim would have approved of her owning it. There hadn't been anything sexual between them – they were first cousins, which would have been practically incest – but he'd always been kind to her when she was small, and when he came home on leave had always brought her some little present.

She could have talked about this to Clive, but she couldn't to Stephen. He might even have said something nasty about it being splendid to afford to give away the equivalent of five hundred pounds, and that would have spoilt everything. The smell of leather and Stephen's wet hair, his hand casually on her knee, his harsh voice giving her directions through the narrow cobbled streets off Leeds Road – nothing must be allowed to spoil it, you had to take these moments as they occurred.

His flat was much as she imagined it would be, on the ground floor of an old terrace house with a dingy red-carpeted entrance hall that smelled of cats and gas. In the hall on a marble-topped table was a pile of letters; some of them were discoloured with dust. Stephen ruffled through them and put half a dozen in his pocket; two, she despised herself for noticing, were in female handwriting.

Inside, the same red carpet as in the hall was made to appear even more dingy in contrast with a new white lambswool rug by the gasfire. Stephen put a shilling into the meter and lit the fire. It was an old pattern of black cast-iron with cracked elements and seemed to give out more noise than heat. All the furniture, except the new divan and the bookcase, was cheap and rickety – the fawn covering of the slab-sided three-piece suite was threadbare and soiled, the leatherette seats of the four dining chairs sagged, the top of the dining table and the sideboard were marked with white rings.

The bookcase, to the left of the fireplace, was a solid piece of Victorian mahogany; she inspected the books whilst he went through the door which led to the kitchen.

Though she didn't know it, the contents of the bookcase represented what was pretty well the standard collection for intellectuals of that period. Auden, Day Lewis, MacNeice, Eliot, Barker, Céline, Koestler, Kafka, Rilke, Stevie Smith, Durrell, Hasek, Empson, Isherwood, Mann, Orwell, Henry Miller, complete runs of *Horizon* and *Poetry London* and

New Verse, Herbert Read, Wyndham Lewis, Hemingway, Palinarus and Marx and the orange volumes of the Left Book Club. These were the core of the collection, those which would be part of his library twenty, thirty, forty years from now. The textbooks and BBC handbooks and paperback thrillers would be shed on the way.

She picked up *Autumn Journal*.

> *Who has left a scent upon my life and left my walls*
> *Dancing over and over with her shadow;*
> *Whose hair is twined in all my waterfalls*
> *And all of London littered with remembered kisses ...*

Coming back into the room with a tray, he looked over her shoulder.

'Bloody marvellous,' he said. 'Decadent, of course, but bloody marvellous. He's finished now, of course. The BBC has got him.'

She closed the book, the lines still in her head. This room, of a kind she'd never known – furnished on the cheap for strangers, uncared-for except as the means of making a profit – was becoming familiar, the spluttering little gasfire was the archetypal fire in the clearing in the forest to keep away the wolves and tigers and the night, the rain, driving against the window added to her well-being; she put her raincoat on the armchair nearest the fire, accepted a gin-and-orange, and sat down, taking care to arrange her skirts decorously.

'You do right not to trust those chairs,' he said. 'You'd think the old cow of a landlady'd invest in some loose covers.' He sat down opposite her. There was a tuft of black hair on his cheekbone; she badly wanted to touch it.

'I didn't think you'd care about such things,' she said.

'I do. But this is only temporary. I'll have served out my sentence soon.' He finished his drink at a gulp and poured out another. He looked at her untouched glass. 'You're not drinking, Robin.' He very rarely used her name; when he did, it sounded surprisingly tender to her, a special term of endearment.

She shook her head. How could she explain to him that nothing could be as superfluous as alcohol now?

He rose abruptly, bent over her, and kissed her. Then he pulled her out of the chair and took her over to the divan.

And here comes what is not difficult to explain. It isn't that either of them had any moral inhibitions. She was a virgin, at least technically, but she was in love with him and he'd considerable sexual experience. This was some twenty-five years before the Pill, but he was prepared. If he hadn't been, he'd enough neural control to use the oldest method of all. But they didn't have sexual intercourse. And on the five subsequent occasions she visited his flat before his return to London, they didn't have sexual intercourse.

This was 1946. No one knows exactly what the incidence of extramarital intercourse was then as compared with to-day. (Sex surveys merely tabulate the statements made by the strange people who take part in sex surveys.) What is certain is that Robin and all the girls of her acquaintance, for whatever reason, were prepared to allow men anything except the insertion of the penis into the vagina. How much they allowed, for the majority, would depend upon what they felt for the man. Very occasionally there would be a shotgun wedding; more occasionally still, a girl would have an appendix removed that had been removed already, or leave the district suddenly and sometimes permanently. This was very occasionally: often enough, however, to confirm Robin and her friends in the belief that theirs was the only way to solve the problem of what to do about sex before marriage.

Clive's generation of young men accepted this. That is, all the young men of Clive's acquaintance. A few of them had, so to speak, the shotgun pressed in the middle of their backs, one or two had affairs with married women, one or two went with prostitutes. But overwhelmingly they went to the marriage bed virgins.

Clive himself had just two affairs, one with an ATS in Cairo, one with a nurse in Rome. It's unlikely that he would have been able to get to first base with either girl if he hadn't been an officer and personable into the bargain and, most important of all, attached to Headquarters.

When he returned home, he went back to his old ways as if the affairs hadn't happened. The larger part of the attraction of Robin for him was that the war hadn't really touched her.

He was fair-minded enough; if she hadn't been a virgin, it would have made no difference to the engagement, except that he would have refused to be denied what another man had been granted. But as it was, he was quite happy to accept her values, particularly since they were pre-war values.

If, when she lay down with Stephen on the divan, she'd gone the whole hog, that would have been the end of her engagement. And Clive was exactly what she required as a husband. She had grown up in a solid detached house with central heating, a house of regular and nourishing meals where the fruit bowl was always full, where every item of household equipment was of the best and renewed as soon as it showed any signs of wear, a house in which trouble, whatever form it might take, was never money trouble.

And she lived in Hailton, a pleasant little town north-east of Charbury and wished to keep on living in Hailton. She wasn't neurotic about it; if Clive's job had necessitated him living somewhere else, she'd have made the best of it. But Clive was perfectly happy about living in Hailton for the rest of his life. He was used to the part of Charbury where his parents' home was, but there was no doubt about its having gone downhill since the war. Hailton was one of the coming places to live in and it was within easy commuting distance of Charbury. And if they didn't like the house which his father had bought for them, they could easily get another. What was important was that they had a house in the town in which she wanted to live.

This went through her mind even as Stephen touched her breasts; she thought, with one part of her mind, how generous Clive's father had been, how fortunate she was, whilst another part of her mind was rejoicing at the touch of Stephen's hands, hairy, stubby-fingered, with nails that were none too clean. It was ridiculous to keep on her jacket, she broke off her kiss to wriggle out of it and then, impatiently, took over the unbuttoning of her blouse. Her hand, independently of her wishes – for at this stage she wanted him merely to kiss her, to hold her, to explore very gently – threw off her blouse, unfastened her brassière, pulled down her slip, her voice, which had wanted some assurance of love, asked fiercely: 'Do you like them? *Do you like them?*'

And as she pulled his head down between them, she felt the first stirring of her orgasm; it had never happened so quickly before. She reached for his groin, the poetry now filling her mind – *a scent upon my life* – and heard him grunt with surprise. What he did now seemed unimportant; his hand busied itself expertly, swooping straight down on the trigger of pleasure, but what mattered was the pleasure he was receiving. With Clive what she was doing now was a way of recompensing him; with Stephen her pleasure was felt through him.

Washing her hands in the kitchen, she had to remind herself of who she was and how her life was going to be shaped. This kitchen – small, chilly, the stone floor showing through patches in the brown linoleum – was as alien to her as an African mud hut. It had a faint, earthy, sweet-sour smell – mice, blackbeetles and dirt, probably – and there was a bath with a hinged deal top which did duty as a table. To judge from the accumulation of jars and bottles on the top it wasn't very often used for its proper purpose. And yet there was nothing strange about the notion of cooking a meal here on that grease-stained little gas oven or even of taking a bath. And it was as sugary, as sentimentally silly as the daydreams she'd once had of being married to Clark Gable and living in California – except that for all she knew, Clark Gable might be kind, amiable and home-loving and she knew Stephen wasn't any of these things.

The drink that she had when she returned to the sitting-room was the first one she'd ever had which she really needed. It seemed to pull her together, bring her back to her senses.

'This won't ever have to happen again,' she said.

'Why not?'

'You know why.'

'You're very sweet,' he said.

'No, I'm not,' she snapped. 'And I'm not one of your silly little students, either.'

He pulled the two letters out of his pocket, ripped them open and walked over to her. 'Here.'

'I don't want to look.'

'You do, you know. They're very good value at this age.'

'If I wrote you a letter, would you show it to another woman?'

'No. You're grown-up. Aren't you going to look at them?'

She shook her head.

'All right. I'll burn them.'

She giggled. '*My darling, Thank you for being you. Now at last I see what I was born for* – oh, Stephen, you must answer it. How were you especially *you*?'

'I poked her.'

'Did you enjoy it?'

She'd never had a conversation like this before with any man; there didn't seem to be anything they couldn't say.

'I didn't enjoy it very much,' he said. He poured himself another drink. 'You're going to ask me why, aren't you?'

'I'm glad you didn't enjoy it. I don't really care why.'

'I'll tell you, just the same. I didn't love her. She was always putting on an act. Going on about books and music … Oh hell, it isn't her fault.'

'Does she want to marry you?'

'I'm a great catch for some girls,' he said. 'A BBC *producer*. Though I'm not a great catch for you, am I?'

She read from the other letter. '*My sweetheart, I'm writing this in bed. It's very quiet. Somehow you seem near to me*—'

He snatched both letters from her. 'Yes. I poked her too. It takes them different ways—'

'Have you had a lot of girls?' She'd never felt less conscious of her body, so free and light, nor more conscious of it, more concentrated with every part of it. She didn't want to look ahead or to look behind her; the rain that was lashing the windows, the red velvet curtains moving in the draught from the kitchen door, the spluttering gasfire, the sound of a tap dripping into the sink, told her that, authentically and permanently she'd arrived at adult love. All that it boiled down to with Clive was that she wanted to get married and he wanted to get married.

What became evident as she talked with Stephen was that he didn't want to get married. Yes, he'd had a lot of girls. Yes, he'd never known a girl like Robin. But yes, he wouldn't stay in Charbury all his life. It smothered him. There was too much of his past here. If he was going to write, he'd have to get away from it. He started to pace the room restlessly; and now she could see that she wasn't much more to him than the drink he'd just had or the cigarette he'd just stubbed out half-smoked.

'I must be going,' she said.

'I wish you could stay.'

He kissed her. When his tongue went between her lips she broke away. She'd acquired enough information about male tumescence to recognize the danger signs. She was a healthy and mature girl and what had satisfied them both before might not satisfy them both again.

This was the pattern of their next five encounters which took place over a period of four months and ended when he was transferred to Newcastle two months before her marriage to Clive. They didn't write to each other and made no arrangements to meet. If he'd asked her to marry him, she would have accepted – there was a limit past which good sense became a lunatic abnegation – but she couldn't help hoping that he wouldn't. The sort of life which she'd have had with him would have been nomadic, disorganized, tormented by jealousy and the feeling of inadequacy. Stephen wasn't a marrying man.

She heard about him in the *Charbury Gazette* and occasionally ex-colleagues in the BBC would tell her something about him with, she fancied, a malicious gleam in their eyes. He moved to London eventually, got into TV, published a novel, went over to ITV, got married to an actress, left ITV to freelance, did very well, changed from producing to performing, started collecting young girls, the sillier the better, was divorced, married again, an actress again, and went back into ITV as an executive. He didn't write any more novels, but articles under his name frequently appeared in the posh Sundays; they were high-pitched and controversial and always caused a stir but seemed to tell one nothing about the man himself. One thing she didn't need to be told: as she'd surmised, Stephen wasn't good husband material.

Two

Clive was. The wedding at St Raymond's in Hailton was, naturally, white. There were two hundred guests and at the reception at the Hailton Country Club there was more than enough champagne. Her two younger sisters, Jennifer and Edith, were bridesmaids, and Clive's cousin Myra was matron-of-honour. Her cousin Malcolm, her cousin Tim's brother, was page; their likeness for a moment prickled her eyes with tears.

Donald was Clive's best man and his groomsmen were Walter Fareland and Gerry Sindram. They had first met at school, drawn together by their common background and, defensively, by their Yorkshire accents. They lost the accents, but the friendship remained. It was Gerry who introduced Robin to Clive and on their bachelor night it was Gerry who drank the most. *She's better than you deserve, you rotten bugger*, he kept on saying; in the end it became rather wearisome. Clive paid little attention at the time, but from then on there was a change, gradually he became closer to Walter. Walter became his solicitor and knew things about his affairs which no other human being, not even Robin, knew; but it wasn't this which caused the change. He and Gerry were still friends; but it wouldn't be the same again. It was much later that he worked out the reason.

The honeymoon was in a villa near Biarritz. The villa was lent them as a wedding present by a friend of her father-in-law; there was also a Citroen Fifteen in the garage, a well-stocked wine cellar, and a cook; it was then she discovered that Clive could speak fluent idiomatic French, that he had in fact a gift for languages.

Their first night at the Savoy – where they broke their journey, since they were travelling by ship – wasn't a success. It's possible that she had Stephen in her mind and that Clive instinctively sensed it and resented it. She didn't mind being hurt, or even him entering her without any sort of preliminary; but it was over at one thrust and afterwards, with the bare minimum of endearments, he slept heavily till the morning tea was brought.

'I'm sorry,' he said, when the maid had left the room. 'But I was so damned tired. I'm better now, though.' He drank his tea. 'Oh God, isn't that lovely?'

He looked so healthy, so pleased with himself, that she had to smile. He wasn't complicated, he wasn't moody, he always enjoyed himself; life for him would always be a bowl of cherries and if now she ever had the hankering for stronger, sourer tastes – medlar and Amer Picon, so as to speak – it had to be put firmly away.

'Don't worry, darling,' she said. She slid her hand under the sheets. 'Sebastian will get his chance.'

He put down his tea.

'Not now,' she said.

He lit a cigarette. 'There's plenty of time.'

'Give me a cigarette.'

He lit one for her, an expression of faint surprise wrinkling his face. 'I didn't know you smoked.'

'I like one occasionally.'

That was another new experience: she'd never really needed a cigarette before.

She considered her situation coolly. A wrong word now, a wrong gesture even, any indication that there'd been anyone else, and her marriage wouldn't survive. She had to take Clive as he was, and not as a substitute for someone else; because once she had got into the habit of thinking of Stephen it would grow, one night she'd scream out the wrong name. And that would be something that not even the most easy-going of men would take. She'd spoil everything, she'd never get through to him again. If only she was careful now she would learn to love him. He would be very easy to love; she'd find out about his faults, and there were stresses and strains ahead which would bring out faults which hadn't existed before; but she was positive that he hadn't any cruelty in his make-up at all.

They had intercourse that night at the villa with complete mutual satisfaction. The minor discomforts of the villa – the lack of comfortable chairs, the bathroom in which there was a huge bath and a new bidet but no WC, the outside hole-in-the-floor WC which tended to flood, the bare walls – mattered very little at their age, and in any case they spent very little time indoors. There was the sun which bleached Clive's hair almost white and which gave her the best tan she'd ever had; there was steak and seafood and fresh fruit and, best of all, real crusty bread; they didn't drink very much, but they learned to use wine without any false reverence, to put ice and soda-water in if they felt so inclined, to use it as a drink rather than part of a ritual.

Satisfaction rather than rapture would have been the keyword to describe their honeymoon. There was goodwill between them and no awkwardness about using the word *love*; and certainly neither of them had ever before known so much physical pleasure. But now and again, eating or drinking, moaning with her legs round his waist, waking from sleep after lunch to the sound of birds and children and the smell of seaweed, sampling wine in a cellar in Chablis, walking down a narrow street in Toulouse, she'd feel that there should be something else, that the fifty years or so, barring accidents, ahead of her had a fixed, predetermined weight and density, that she had somehow been cheated.

They returned to the four-bedroomed detached house in Hailton; Robin continued to work at the BBC until she was two months gone with her son, George. There wasn't any need for her to work; but she liked the feeling of having money of her own. Often, looking back, she would remember this as being the best part of her marriage. New events were still ahead of her, she liked her job but wasn't dependent upon it, her life contained virtually no chores, she had a social life, because of her new status as Clive's wife, even fuller than before she married. There were no empty spaces of boredom; there was always something more to do to the house, something more to buy. At that period everything was in short supply; but so was high-grade cloth; Clive, like most of the people they knew, got whatever they needed by barter. And furniture, in any case, was no problem: if you bought secondhand you could not only save money, but acquire pieces of a quality simply not obtainable today. Both she and Clive had a fondness for Victorian furniture long before it became fashionable; this was a great bond between them.

Their taste, incidentally, was not her father-in-law's taste. Jim Lendrick believed in having the best of everything but the best had to be the latest. The son of a weaver, he'd grown up in a house full of old furniture, given or bought for a song, he'd been clothed, being the youngest of six, in handed-down garments, he hated everything secondhand, his measure of success was to be surrounded by the shinily new and modern, bought, of course, cash for a discount.

Part of the reason for his success and, indeed, for the survival of the firm after his death in 1954, was his preference for new machinery, his positive hatred for the Charbury fetish of making do with the old. It's extraordinary that he continued to live in a district of Charbury which was rapidly becoming unfashionable; but human beings are rarely totally consistent, and he liked to be within easy reach of the mills and on a fine day with the aid of binoculars to be able to see from his mansion – it was no less than that – the back-to-back house where he was born.

Every time he visited Clive and Robin he would offer to get rid of all of what he called their 'funeral parlour' stuff and change it for new; and the offer was entirely serious. Robin liked her father-in-law; but there was no mistaking his desire to dominate his eldest son and with him his daughter-in-law.

'If you give in to your father too much now, you'll never get any respect,' she said to Clive one autumn evening in the first year of their marriage, when Clive had accepted his father's offer of a new three-piece suite.

'He loves to give us things,' Clive said.

'He loves to impose his taste on us.'

'I don't see what harm it does. We've room for the suite. We're not filling a museum.'

'Clive darling, if you let him always get his own way you'll just become his shadow. Phone him and say you've changed your mind.'

'It's not worth the trouble.'

It was eight o'clock on a November evening and they were on the verge of leaving the house to go out for dinner; abruptly she unzipped her black cocktail dress and pulled it over her head; her brassière and waist slip followed and she sat down facing him and took off her pants, unfastened her stockings and wriggled out of her girdle.

After a year of marriage they still had a healthy hunger for each other but imperceptibly the gratification of that hunger had become confined to certain times and places; she knew that standing there in the drawing-room her naked body would be suddenly a novelty to him.

'Phone him now,' she said. She walked up to him, the thick plum-red carpet slightly rough in texture, feeling as springy as turf beneath her bare feet. 'Aren't I very nice?' she asked him. 'Aren't I very nice?'

He took hold of her roughly; she pushed him away, and then knelt down before him, her fingers then her lips busy at his groin.

'Oh Christ,' he said. 'Oh, you devil. Yes, yes—'

She had taken her mouth away. 'Phone then.'

She leaned over him as he phoned, stroking his hair; when he put the phone down finally she switched the lights off and lay down on the leopardskin rug by the fire. It was as if they weren't married; the leopardskin, which was real enough, smooth one way and rough the other, made the situation unreal – on a leopardskin in the firelight in a middle-class drawing-room full of dark furniture the naked woman tempts the man to betrayal and betrayal means disaster. She stroked the leopardskin against the direction of the hair then drew in her breath sharply and closed her eyes; she opened them to see Clive kneeling naked beside her. He looked her over for a second with a strangely cold expression on his face, then took her without any preliminaries. But this was a time when she didn't need any.

The house that they were living in then had in effect been chosen by her father-in-law. It was fair enough in a sense, since he had paid the deposit and legal charges and had in some way she didn't quite understand made the mortgage repayments the firm's responsibility. But the house wasn't her choice, or Clive's either. She had settled the business of furniture once and for all. That wasn't difficult; by now she knew how much Clive liked old furniture, how much their trips to salerooms and secondhand shops meant to him, how much he was caught up with her in building a home. This was something – there was a certain sadness in the thought – that would outlast the kind of sex they were having now.

It was a good house, built in 1930, with solid fuel central heating, a large bathroom, WCs upstairs and downstairs, four decent-sized bedrooms, a drawing-room, dining-room, a small study, and a large kitchen. The style was what their architect friends called 1930 Pebbledash Speculative, with a porch, and bay windows on the ground and first floor. There was a third of an acre of garden, mostly at the back, and a rather ramshackle summerhouse. It wasn't very well-planned but it had been built to order at a time of depression and the workmanship and materials hadn't been skimped.

It wasn't her house, though. Neither was it her district. For there her father-in-law had been misled by the estate agent. Prince's Road, at the top end of which the house was situated, had been a good address once. It had been where most of her father's friends in Hailton had once lived. It was a street of large detached houses with large gardens, designed – as far as they could be said to be designed – to be maintained by servants. But what had made it popular among the mill-owners and the professional men, its proximity to the centre of Hailton, was the very reason for it not being popular now. Apart from that, people didn't these days want old houses that size in that situation. Already three of the houses had been converted into flats; and most of the houses had grounds large enough to make it worth any builder's while to buy them simply for the sake of the land. The houses would be demolished, and eventually Prince's Road would be crammed with three-bedroomed semi-detacheds. Their occupants no doubt would be decent enough, but they wouldn't be her choice of neighbours.

It was of no consequence before she had children and most of her time was spent outside the house; but with the birth of George in the second year of their marriage, everything changed. She wasn't lonely; Hailton was her hometown, and she had an abundance of friends and relations there. But none of them lived in the Prince's Road area; when they came to see her, they'd never fail to evince surprise at her living there.

It was some three months after the birth of her second son, Roger, that a visit from her father brought matters to a head. It was a fine afternoon in early July; they were sitting on deckchairs in the garden, and George was running up and down the garden singing a nonsense song to himself and Roger was sleeping in his pram. Her mother was knitting.

It was Wednesday afternoon; on Wednesdays her parents always came to tea and she and Clive would go out in the evening. It was a fixed event, irrespective of how often she saw her parents otherwise, and she'd long since forgotten the reason for the day being a Wednesday rather than any other.

'Not many young couples round here,' her father said.

'Clive and I get about quite a lot.'

'I mean in Prince's Road.' He lit his pipe; out here in the garden it smelled surprisingly fragrant, she could visualize tobacco as a growing plant with flowers instead of the compressed packaged substance bought in shops.

The delphinium near the summerhouse was in full bloom and she lazily wondered if a dress that blue – if ever you could get that marvellous shade with all the summer in it – would suit her. Her father, she could see, wanted to make some suggestions which would lead to change; what she wanted – both the children having given her a sleepless night – was to lie back in the deckchair, her eyes half-closed, and look forward to a bath, an evening at the Hailton Players, and afterwards a meal which she hadn't prepared and didn't have to clear away.

'Oh, I've got used to Prince's Road.'

Her mother looked up from her knitting.

'I hope you haven't, Robin. There are some very *common* people here.'

Judgement had been passed in that unvaryingly quiet and gentle tone.

'They could be worse,' Robin said perversely. She loved her mother; she was always so calm, always carried herself so well, had so fresh and unlined a complexion for her age. But she was inclined to lay down the law a little too frequently.

'They say there's going to be a Council estate at the top end,' her father broke in. Since he'd retired, he'd become more than ever before an authority on Hailton; it was said that if you listened to him for half an hour you didn't need to buy the Hailton Express.

She sat up. 'It's not true!'

'Heard it from the Town Architect.'

'The next thing you know you'll be living next door to Clive's workpeople,' her mother said.

Robin lit a cigarette. Since the birth of her first child the occasional cigarette had gradually become fifteen a day.

'The Council estate won't be built in five minutes,' she said.

'Neither will any other new houses on the road,' her father said. 'But ten years from now you won't know the district. And you'll be lucky to get what you paid for this house. Yes, lucky.'

His tone had become more and more portentous and he had deepened his naturally deep voice. He had broken into her mood of contentment, and he had reminded her of something she should have been taking steps about herself. Whatever she did now would appear to have been done on her father's advice; he wouldn't neglect the opportunity to tell her father-in-law that it was information received from him that had spurred her and Clive into action.

There was no feud between her father and Clive's; but there was a rivalry. They were of an age and had begun from roughly the same point in the social scale; but her father had been an only child and his father had been one of a family of six. They were even physically alike, tall and heavily built, with straight backs and faces of the kind generally described as commanding, with large noses and firmly held mouths and chins on the protruding side. Her father, though, was dark in colouring with brown eyes and a leathery skin; Clive's father had blue eyes and in his sixties had the pink-and-white complexion of a much younger man.

They had never quarrelled; but Clive's father was a very rich man and her own father was no more than moderately well-off. She knew that her own father resented this, though he never let it show. There would be unpleasantness – not very serious, but enough to disrupt her life uncomfortably, enough even to make Clive mulish about leaving this house.

She was non-committal with her father that afternoon, and when he brought up the subject of the Council estate with Clive, deliberately played it down.

But when she and Clive were in their four-poster bed that night, she said, 'We really ought to think of moving, Clive.'

They were drinking tea and smoking; when they had finished the tea and their cigarettes they would brush their teeth and switch out the light. This was an invariable ritual, no matter how late they'd gone to bed; there were days when it seemed almost the only time when they could talk together.

'I don't see anything wrong with this house,' Clive said.

'It isn't so much the house, it's the district.'

'You've been listening to your father.'

'I *haven't* been listening to my father. Or yours either. This isn't their business.'

'Where do you want to live, then?'

'We could look around, couldn't we? And not tell anyone? Wouldn't you like to choose a house *by* yourself, *for* yourself, not have someone else choose it for you?'

'There aren't many decent new houses round here.'

'It doesn't have to be a new house, does it? Or even round here?'

'You sure you weren't thinking of Deeton?'

Deeton was the suburb of Hailton where her parents lived, four miles south-west of Prince's Road.

'God forbid. I wouldn't live too near my mother, she'd be popping in every day.'

'We seem to know a lot of people at Throstlehill.'

Throstlehill was a small village some four miles north of the Hailton town centre; it was on the edge of the moors, but the large pinewoods on three sides of it acted as a natural windbreak. The village green had a fourteenth-century stone cross and four of the houses round it were seventeenth century and scheduled as ancient monuments. The church, St Keith's, was eighteenth century, very plain, very bare, in sharp contradiction to the nineteenth-century Methodist chapel with its tall spire and profusion of carved stonework. The village pub, the Heckley Arms, was named after the village's only inhabitant of note, a farm labourer's son who had risen from the ranks to general and who had died in Cheltenham in 1920. It was a medium-sized Victorian pub with the usual profusion of bars; at weekends in particular it had more and more taken on the character of a roadhouse.

The village still retained its character, more through the

accident of the best building land being around the green than through design. The houses which had been built there just before the war were none of them beautiful but didn't quarrel too outrageously with the older houses. And, as a result of the Hailton Civic Society's efforts, trees had been planted on all the new roads.

There weren't any medium-priced houses in Throstlehill. There were a few old farmworkers' cottages; but as soon as they became vacant they were snapped up at extortionate prices, gutted, and modernized. Throstlehill became a good address, was even eventually to gain a reputation for snobbery. This wasn't deserved; there were a few extremely rich residents but most were middle-middle class and newly-arrived in that status.

Clive and Robin did know a lot of people at Throstlehill; it was this in fact which made her determined to live there. But Clive, easy-going though he was, liked to feel in charge; like most easy-going people he had a streak of obstinacy, and if she pushed her preference for Throstlehill too hard, he'd be liable to choose somewhere else to live, somewhere even that he didn't like half as much.

So for the next two months they spent most of their time in viewing houses, not only in Hailton, but in Burley-in-Wharfedale, Ilkley, Harrogate, Skipton, Nab Wood in Shipley, Bingley, Baildon, Guiseley and finally came to Throstlehill.

It was a fine evening in August. It had been savagely, oppressively hot down in the valley but as they drove into Throstlehill a cool breeze sprang up. Clive ran a two-and-a-half litre Jaguar drophead coupé then; approaching Throstlehill from Hailton they had a panoramic view of the whole village and the woods beyond it. There was the smell of grass, the darker, more aromatic smell of trees, of flowers and fresh paint and cooking from the houses they passed, taking Boggart Road off the north-west corner of the village green, the sunlight was predominantly lemon-coloured now instead of orange and, if it had had a taste would have tasted like lemon too, sharp and refreshing.

Neither of them ever thought very much about death. Clive, because of his wartime experiences, had seen more of it than Robin, but then it had been a professional and technical matter, it had never seemed very real. If his luck hadn't been so good, if he'd ever reached the point where constant demands on his stock of courage had, so as to speak, brought him to the verge of bankruptcy he would have been forced into thinking about it. But only occasionally, on the rare occasions when he awoke in the small hours, would it ever occur to him that one day he wouldn't exist. And Robin had only started thinking about death when she'd had her first child; now and again, irresistibly, there'd be a picture in her mind of a small body broken and still. And often, looking at the baby asleep, she'd touch his chest gently to make sure he was actually breathing. She didn't, however, believe that she herself could die.

And yet, as they drove slowly along Boggart Road, they both were thinking about death. Their thoughts weren't clearly defined but if they had a form it was this: here in Throstlehill they could live for the rest of their lives, here the pattern, which now they could perceive was a good one, the pattern which is the same for us all, wouldn't be wasted on poor material.

So it was decided, without either of them saying a word, before they saw Tower House. It was a large house of biscuit-coloured stone at the end of Chipfield Close, a short cul-de-sac off Boggart Road. At the right was a double garage in the same stone as the house, at the left a conservatory. The porch was glass-sided. The windows were plain, the general style severe; but at the left was a square tower, obviously meant for occupation because of the curtains in the windows.

The front lawn was newly mown and the front drive was freshly laid tarmac; the white paintwork was new and some of the tiles on the roof had, to judge from their lighter red, only recently been replaced.

Clive stopped the car outside the entrance.

'Are you sure this is the place?'

She nodded.

'Strange for them to have all this work done when they're going to leave it. After all, they're not asking a very high price ...'

'Don't you want it, then?' With an effort she kept the impatience out of her voice.

'I didn't say that, darling. But it's even bigger than I thought it would be. Cost the hell of a lot to keep up ...'

'If you honestly think we can't afford it, we may as well turn round and go home.'

Her heart was beating so fast that she was surprised he didn't hear it. She wanted to see inside the house so badly that it was all that she could do not to jump out of the car and run down the drive. But she knew by now how exactly to handle her husband.

He was silent for a moment. 'Oh, hell, it does no harm to look.' He turned the engine off.

She put her hand on his arm. 'I don't want you to look at it just to please me,' she said. 'We mustn't buy it unless we both want it.'

'We're having a look inside,' he said firmly. 'And that settles it.' It was as if he'd won a fierce argument; she kept the look of triumph off her face with a real effort.

The owner, Major Tomkins, was a tall spare old man with a clipped grey moustache, sharply pressed grey flannels and a white linen jacket yellow with laundering. His wife was some twenty years younger, with a low soft voice and a heavy gold bracelet and a diamond ring which would at that time have been worth, Robin estimated, a total of at least five hundred. She was amused to notice Mrs Tomkins' large dark eyes pricing her own engagement ring and her watch and – with one quick glance – her dress and shoes and stockings.

Six bedrooms, two bathrooms, one *en suite* with what the Major, wincing slightly, said these estate agent chaps called the master bedroom. Downstairs cloakroom and WC, drawing-room, dining-room, morning-room, huge kitchen, laundry. Two huge attics; one could be kept as a lumber room, another would make a marvellous playroom when the children were older. The tower? The Major's den; a workbench with lathe, tools, solder, a gas-ring, pieces of model ships, cars, locomotives. A spare bedroom perhaps, but she wasn't going to run a hotel. An old-fashioned solid fuel central heating system; that would have to be changed. Decorations in good order; good enough to live with for a year or so. Fitted carpets everywhere, even in the bathrooms. But I have to try to see it absolutely bare, echoing, empty. And in the winter. Then there's the garden. One and a half acres; I don't see Clive looking after that by himself. But most of it's at the back, and there's a high fence at both sides; the boys will be quite safe there. They'll be delighted with the Wendy house, though they won't want to call it a Wendy house. If I had a little girl . . . I'd buy her pretty dresses and there'd always be someone on my side . . .

She heard the Major's voice from a distance. 'Going to Portugal . . . All the children grown-up . . . Nothing to keep us here . . . Sudden decision, always act on sudden decisions . . .'

Yes, he would, she thought, as she accepted a sherry from him in the drawing-room. She glanced at Clive, who hadn't spoken very much as they were being shown round. He was still a little suspicious, still a little undecided.

'You have little ones, Mrs Lendrick?' Mrs Tomkins asked.

'Two boys, George and Roger. Two, and six months.'

'Splendid house for children, this,' the Major said. 'We have four boys. Nothing like boys, though my wife always hankered after a girl . . .'

'This is a real family house,' Mrs Tomkins said. 'I only wish we could have spent all our married life in a house like it.'

'Birds of passage,' the Major said. 'That's what we've always been.' He glanced at Clive. 'You've been in the Army, Lendrick?'

'Tank Corps. Middle East mostly.'

'I can always tell by the way a chap carries himself. I remember now, you were a Major, weren't you?'

Clive nodded, looking faintly surprised.

'I keep in touch,' the Major said. 'Besides, I'm interested in your firm. Very sound. Some of them are done for, you

34

know. Naturally, they make money now – can't help it – but once real competition begins again, they'll go down the drain. Not your firm. By God, no.'

'I'm happy to hear it,' Clive said, laughing. He took a Sullivan from the box the Major offered him. 'This is a very pleasant room.'

There won't be the marble-topped table here when they go, Robin reminded herself, or the gold brocade suite, or the glass-topped occasional tables, or that marvellous leather-topped Regency writing-desk or the collection of china in what was certainly an eighteenth-century glass-fronted cupboard, or those very nice old hunting prints or all those new books or the cream Persian rug – but the ceiling would still be as lofty, the proportions still as good; it was twice the size of the drawing-room at Prince's Road.

'We love this room,' Mrs Tomkins said. 'In fact, we love this house, but what can you do?'

'Can't stay here to be ruined,' the Major said. 'And to see the country ruined by a pack of bloody – excuse me – traitors. Different for you younger people. You're young enough to do something about it ...' He paused. 'You won't have any difficulty with a mortgage,' he said. 'But we've had some real idiots round here. They just want to look around, you know. Sent one of them packing the other day. I know what her husband's job is, and they couldn't afford to buy the front door knocker ...'

'I might just manage that,' Clive said. 'How about carpets and curtains? Are you taking them all with you?'

He'd made up his mind; and he'd never be able to say that he hadn't chosen the house himself. She decided to make certain.

'Darling,' she said, 'are you quite sure that you don't want to think it over?'

'Why?' The rather soft mouth was set firm, the forehead ready to scowl. 'You like the house, don't you? Then there's no point in wasting time. I'll see Walter first thing, and he'll arrange the survey. You can give me an early completion date, can't you, sir?'

The Major did give him an early completion date, there

was no difficulty with the mortgage, and Robin spent what was in retrospect the happiest time of her life haggling with the Major about the furniture and fittings, ordering new furniture and fittings, planning not only new decorations for the house but the whole shape of her new life in Throstlehill.

The Major enjoyed himself too. He was fond of presenting himself as the simple soldier, lost and bemused in the hard acquisitive civilian world, but in actuality he had a hard business head. 'I really don't know very much about prices,' he would say, then would name a figure that wasn't a very large reduction on what the article cost new. She would beat him down when the article was carpeting or curtains or modern furniture, but with the more valuable pieces the struggle was to find a price which would be above the dealers but below the shop price. It cost him some effort to decide what to sell; he was moving, she gathered, to a much smaller house, and had to be ruthless, but for every piece of furniture he had a genuine affection.

In the two months before completion she came to know the Tomkinses very well; better, in some ways, than she knew her own father and mother. The Major had never risen as high as his talents could have taken him because of ill-health and the wrong postings; ill-health had kept him on home service for most of the war, and the wrong postings had always seemed to take him away from trouble spots just before they became trouble spots. And it was in the trouble spots that you got promotion or were ear-marked for future promotion. But he had a lively mind – not in the least like the collection of stereotyped reactions she'd always been led to believe professional soldiers possessed – and a genuine passion for beautiful things.

His wife was quieter, calmer, having in all the years of moving from foreign country to foreign country developed the ability to be an intensely private person behind a social mask. But with Robin for some reason the social mask was dropped; a friendship rapidly grew between the two women. And Robin became aware of how much she'd always lacked a confidante, how much ever since childhood she'd been withdrawn from others. She even told Mrs Tomkins about Stephen one evening when the Major was away on business and Clive – it was a period of reorganization at the mill – had brought some work home.

Mrs Tomkins was a great reader; Stephen's name had come up as an example of how talent can be extinguished by the corporate job; to her astonishment Robin discovered that he'd been a visitor to this very house.

'He never told me,' she said.

It was a rainy September evening, they were sitting over tea in the drawing-room and Mrs Tomkins had just turned on the gasfire, there being a faint chill in the air. The sound of the rain against the windows, the faint muttering of the gasfire took her back to the first time she'd been alone with Stephen in Charbury; as soon as she spoke she found herself blushing, aware in a shamefaced way of her naked body beneath her clothes.

'I dare say it wouldn't seem very important to him.' Mrs Tomkins had a smooth unlined face; for a moment it seemed to relapse into harsh lines.

'It was before I married,' Robin said. 'Not a great undying love by any means.'

'They never are,' Mrs Tomkins said. 'He's very selfish, you know. I can see the attraction, though. It's just because he is selfish and demanding.'

'I don't think of him. My life's so full. I used to think it was too full before I had the children, but now there doesn't seem to be a spare moment.'

'It's the best time,' Mrs Tomkins said. 'Then suddenly the children aren't babies any longer; they grow up and move away. And if you're not careful you make a baby of your husband, and that's all you've left – one baby. And nothing else.'

'Were you careful?'

'Oh yes.' She nodded towards the books. 'I've always had those. And music. And I see to it that I go to the theatre and the cinema. Otherwise one stays at home waiting for people to come. And they won't, you know. And if you've got the right sort of house, you won't care. Not until it's too late. Watch out with this house, Robin. If it isn't the house itself, it'll be the garden. Or both. That's why we're leaving. Of course Graham doesn't do very much in the garden. Otherwise he'd really be caught. But I've seen the signs.'

'I thought you were leaving because of the Government?'

Mrs Tomkins laughed. 'That's always a sound reason, but it wasn't Graham's idea to leave at all. He thinks it was. Your husband thinks it was his idea to buy this house.'

'I love this house, though.'

'I know you do. I can say it now, because it's all settled. I'm glad you're living here. It's a family house and you'll make it into a real home. And you'll look after it too. But don't love it too much. A lot of women in Throstlehill – and some men too – love their houses too much. And then the day comes when they've enough furniture and they can't redecorate again, and they're miserable. Just love human beings.'

'Even the wrong ones?'

'Even the wrong ones.'

Those conversations with Mrs Tomkins were part of Robin's growing up. She'd never before, with the possible exception of Stephen, met anyone who actually applied their intelligence to the business of living. The men she knew used their intelligence and powers of expression only in their jobs, the women only in household matters; living was, so to speak, left to the servants, one's notions about it were borrowed from newspaper columns, from TV person-alities, from the sort of preacher who spoke in words which everyone could understand; one thought deeply about what machine to install, what soap powder to use, but any old cliché would serve for the heart's concerns.

Three

On their second year at Tower House her daughter Petronella was born. She had to fight hard to get her way about the name; she chose it because it was Mrs Tomkins'. Finally Clive gave in because, as she pointed out, no one in either of their families had used the name, so at least there wouldn't be any jealousy.

She'd had easy births with George and Roger – as easy, she would say, as any births ever are – but she had a miscarriage before she became pregnant with Petronella and then came near to having another one. Finally, the birth had to be induced. When she first saw Petronella – skinny, with stick-like legs and large feet with a literally bluish tinge – she compared her with the boys, who'd been plump and rosy as baby-food advertisements, and for the first time in her life knew the salty choking taste of fear. When she'd been home for two days she had a haemorrhage one morning. Her mother was staying with her; as she lay on the bed she put towel after towel between her legs, her face calm but as white as Robin's. Robin could hear Petronella screaming from the nursery and hoped to God that Clive would keep George and Roger away from the bedroom; there was no pain, only a feeling of being carried away. She opened her eyes once and then seeing the pile of red towels on the floor and the pool of blood on the bed and her mother's red hands, closed them again.

She was given blood transfusions at the Victoria Nursing Home in Charbury and after five days was fully recovered. But that part of her body which had always been the almost affectionately regarded source of pleasure or simply a reliable uncomplaining functional organ had now let her down; it was nearly two months before she could bear to think about sex again.

Clive was very good and uncomplaining and that was another worry. Was he getting what she couldn't give him, what she hadn't been able to give him for some five months, elsewhere?

She asked him one night when they were lying in bed drinking tea. Though it was summer, she had on a bed-jacket and there was a hot water bottle in the bed; since the haemorrhage, she seemed very often to feel unaccountably cold.

'Clive,' she said, 'do you mind if I ask you something?'

He put down *The House of Moreys*. 'I expect I shall mind,' he said. 'But you'll ask me anyway.'

'You're not going with someone else?'

'Yes,' he said. 'One for each day in the week. From sixteen to thirty. I just go up to them and take John Thomas out and put it in their hand. It never fails.'

'Be serious. Tell me the truth. I won't even ask who it is.'

'Not much you wouldn't. But there isn't. You nearly dying put me off. It wouldn't have been fair somehow.'

It wouldn't have been fair somehow; he was telling the truth, and the tears came to her eyes. She hadn't thought of his needs, and he'd put them aside. She still couldn't bear the idea of sex, of the hot column of flesh inside her; but she switched the light off, unfastened his pyjamas, and moved her head downwards, touching his body very lightly with her lips. He gasped; her lips searched, found, held, her fingers stroked the throbbing vein, moved downwards to lift heaviness; she thought fleetingly what a shame it was that there were no pretty words for this variation of love, no Sunday best, so as to speak, but only a choice of battered dungarees. She had never been nearer to him; her pleasure was all from him, then during his deep moaning and afterwards walking downstairs into the kitchen, filling the kettle, making fresh tea, putting chocolate biscuits on a plate, going upstairs with the words still in her head: *it wouldn't have been fair somehow.*

And yet, when they made love again, it wasn't the same as it had been before. Before she hadn't cared whether she became pregnant or not, had even thought of a large family, at least six; now fear overshadowed the act, not acknowledged, in time hardly thought of, but manifesting itself in a determination to have no more children. And Petronella, during the first six months of her life, claimed her time in a way that the boys never had, eating badly, yelling night and day, seeming to go through every ailment peculiar to babies in rapid succession. Even when bathed and newly changed, she wasn't endearing as her brothers had been; she had a strangely oily, not quite healthy smell which nothing could mask, and they never caught her smiling. And, unlike her brothers, who had fair hair and blue eyes, she had brown hair and dark brown eyes; Robin had had the picture in her mind of three fair-haired and blue-eyed children matching each other, and felt somehow cheated.

She seemed to know when Clive and Robin were about to make love; it was impossible to disregard that shrill screaming. Clive would either finish quickly or not begin, and for at least an hour the small screaming bundle would be fed, winded, walked up and down; more than once they prevented themselves in the nick of time from falling asleep with her in the bed between them.

And then, gradually, she changed. She began to smile, to feed more greedily, sometimes to sleep the whole night through. Her smell changed, became dry and clean and very faintly aromatic; she became affectionate, lying still in Robin's arms, her face suffused with an animal content: she gave Robin a keener happiness than either of her other children, perhaps because of the contrast with what she was like earlier.

But making love had lost its sharp edge, at least for Robin; the Dutch cap and the rest of the apparatus on the highest shelf in the bathroom played too large a part in it. And she then felt happy to have her periods not only because they were the evidence that she wasn't pregnant but because for a while the risk wouldn't be present.

They became more and more prosperous as Throstlehill became more and more prosperous; the house acquired a sun-room, was eventually redecorated and re-carpeted and re-curtained from top to bottom, the garden was reconstructed, the whole house was repainted inside and outside regularly, whatever she had come to realize was inferior was quietly got rid of and replaced; she developed an interest in cooking and silver and flower arrangement and especially in wine. The house became visibly sleeker, almost self-satisfied, seeming on a fine day to be grooming itself like a cat.

It was the prototype for the district, which now had become a place only for the rich or those on the way to being rich. A handful of new houses had been built in assorted styles and mostly to order – Californian split-level, Regency, glass-and-concrete modern, and styles which reflected God knows what private fantasy of the builders. But they were all expensive, all meticulously maintained, the car which stood outside the double and sometimes triple or quadruple garages was more often than not a Rolls or a Jensen or a Mercedes or in more than one instance a huge American car.

Prices were almost London level; the Residents' Association had scotched proposals of Council estates, medium-priced developments and, most recently, a remand home. There had been an outcry in the national Press about this, the adjectives snobbish and opulent and stand-offish and heartless and exclusive being freely used but, as Clive had said, it would have taken hundreds of pounds off the value of their houses. Who wants to live near a remand home? The bus service had now diminished to two a day, but this wasn't a serious problem to the residents. It kept the village secluded and those with daily helps who lived in Hailton could always fetch them by car.

The national Press wasn't quite accurate about Throstle-hill. It wasn't snobbish in the sense that anyone cared about how a resident's money was made or who his father was. Nor was there any sort of local aristocracy, even of long-term residents. It was, if anything, almost excessively friendly; most people in Throstlehill had visited most houses in Throstlehill and, apart from more formal entertaining, there were coffee parties almost every morning in the week. In fact, Robin was invited to one on her first day at Tower House and given along with the invitation, the potted biographies of most of her neighbours. Her caller, Mary Hardrup, was one of the few in Throstlehill who'd been born there and had lived there most of her life; she was a great talker and, without appearing to be, a great listener. Her rather pale face was always still and without expression but her large grey eyes were never at rest; Robin was aware at that first meeting that she'd taken in not only every detail of Robin's appearance but every item in the room where they were sitting. She was, no doubt, a gossip, but the village wouldn't have been the same without her. If you got to know her, you got to know everybody else; and if she told them your secrets she told you theirs.

And there was a thriving Arts Society and Women's Institute and, in 1954, a new Village Hall. There was no need to be lonely or bored in Throstlehill. It was in the Council estates and medium-priced developments in Hailton that there were the sufferers from housewife's *cafard*.

The children grew up in Throstlehill, or rather Petronella did. For at the age of nine George and Roger went as boarders to their father's old school. It was the cause of one of the few quarrels between Clive and Robin. Or rather it was the excuse. The real cause was that Robin had married Clive for other reasons than love or even simple physical desire. She was angry with Clive for not being the man she was in love with; and he was angry with her because he was for once able to sense this. Neither of them brought their thoughts out into the open; to have done so would have been to put at risk all that they were building together. It was this repression – imposed upon themselves by a mutual unspoken agreement – which gave the quarrel its savage intensity.

'What's the use of having children if you don't ever see them?' she asked furiously. 'If you want to get rid of them, why did we have them?'

'We're not getting rid of them,' he said calmly. They were sitting in the drawing-room one June evening after

43

dinner; from where she was sitting she could see the roses, yellow and bronze and red and pink; her pleasure in them and in having a quiet evening and a simple meal after having guests to dinner three days in a row was quite spoilt.

'They'll be strangers to us. They'll think more of the bloody matron than they will of their own mother. And what about the cost? All this talk about economy and me changing to a smaller car – and then you propose spending over a thousand a year. What's wrong with the Grammar School?'

She was screaming now; there was almost a sexual pleasure in it. 'Is it that my father went to the Grammar School? Is that it?'

'They're not going away for a year yet,' he said. 'And they're not going both at once. And the money's taken care of.'

'By your bloody father. I don't want to be beholden to your bloody father, interfering old bastard!'

He frowned. 'Sometimes you sound very common.'

'Who the hell are you, then? Who the hell are you? Your father was born in a back-to-back in the slummiest slum in Charbury. He worked half-time in the mills. Then he sent you to public school to get you out of the way so he'd be free to plot and cheat and swindle to get ahead. And have his whores in. You were brought up by whores after your mother died. Only he called them housekeepers.'

'*Your* father wouldn't have the guts. He's the great philosopher smoking his bloody pipe and moaning about lost chances. He'd like a change, poor sod, but he's too frightened of your bloody mother. Jesus Christ, you grow more like her every day—'

'She's a decent woman, and you wouldn't understand that. And my father's a decent man. He's never been nearly in jail like your father—'

He stood up. 'You're pleased to spend his money, aren't you? Chucking it away like a drunken sailor. I expressly asked you to economize for a while and what the hell do you do? Buy a bloody dishwasher, you fucking idle slut.

44

What the fucking hell's the fucking au pair for? And talking about whores, where the hell's she off to tonight?'

The present au pair, a French girl with enormous breasts, was one of a succession they'd had since the birth of Petronella. On the whole they were fortunate with them as with everything else; the present one, Monique, was the exception, and was asked to leave after she'd been with them only three months.

'Fancy her, do you?' She was being totally unfair but she was enjoying herself. 'Fancy a nice little eighteen-year-old with big tits? Tits. That's what you call them, isn't it? I saw your business friend looking at them the other night—'

'Oh God,' he said, 'what crap you do talk. What the devil has old Brown got to do with me? Her tits are there to be looked at, aren't they?'

She started crying. 'You don't love me. You don't love your sons. I'll go away and I'll take them with me and you won't ever find me. I won't let them be taken from me, I won't, I won't!'

They were finally reconciled in bed: she was so avid that in the small hours, lying back exhausted and sweating, he said, grinning: 'Maybe we should have a row more often.'

They didn't; she'd been rather frightened by the strength of her very real hatred and no less by the recklessness of her sexual passion. The hatred would pass, and Clive wasn't the sort to brood over what she'd said or indeed to brood over anything even remotely unpleasant. But the sexual passion could lead to carelessness, even to wanting another child – she had found herself wishing at the moment of climax, that she hadn't taken her usual precautions, it had seemed that flesh wasn't totally meeting flesh, that there was a barrier that she wanted to break regardless of consequences – that in fact absolute satisfaction was only to be had if she were regardless of consequences.

So they didn't quarrel again about the question of boarding-school; in due course the boys went away and, seeing how other women were bound down by having their children at home all the time, she wasn't sorry. And, after all, she had Petronella, who grew up dark-haired and quiet – perhaps too quiet – and who was affectionate in a way that the boys had never been. Every face has its period; Petronella's was pure 1940, a forage cap would have sat easily on the dark hair, mysteriously making it not less but more feminine, her habitual expression was serious and determined – and over and above this, the large brown eyes were ready to suffer without complaining. When she was ill, she was pathetically still and docile, taking her medicine without a murmur, submitting to injections without a cry; the boys, on the other hand, resented illness fiercely, spitting out medicine or throwing the bottle down, screaming in rage at the prick of the needle. Robin loved them, but they were exhausting in a way Petronella, after the first six months, never was; their chief virtues were that they were good-looking and cheerful. George at twenty was reading economics at Oxford, Roger at eighteen had rather surprisingly announced that he wanted to be a doctor.

'Do you want to help people?' she asked him once. She was rather touched when she'd dragged his ambition out of him.

He looked a little startled. 'Hadn't thought of that much. It's just that people's insides are jolly interesting. Of course, being a doctor isn't frightfully remunerative at first. But you never starve.' He grinned, showing big white strong teeth. 'I shall probably do very well. Charm all the rich ladies and have a huge practice in Harley Street.'

She felt a twinge of loss; he'd spent most of his life from the age of nine away from home, and now the first thing he thought of, however jestingly, was to make that absence permanent.

George too, talked of going away when he'd graduated, in his case to the USA. As he explained to her one evening, England was on the way out. 'Everyone's so damned tired, there's all these insane taxes and rules and regulations, everything's geared to the deadbeats and the dopes ... Ambition's a dirty word, no one seems to want to get rich. Well, *I* do ...'

46

His sunburn made his fairness still more accentuated; like his brother he was two inches above six feet, with broad shoulders and narrow hips. Like his brother, he spoke well, was almost annoyingly self-assured, and had impeccable manners. There wasn't anything left for her to do; the school had certainly given Clive – or, to be more accurate, his father – value for money. It didn't seem as if they'd ever been adolescents, ever suffered from any doubts or stresses or fears; if they had, neither of them had ever come to her. If they'd plunged headfirst into real trouble she'd almost have been glad, because it would have brought them nearer to her; but unlike Petronella, they never confided in her. She knew that they had girlfriends; sometimes they brought them home. And in these days of the Pill they probably slept with the girlfriends. But they didn't talk about them.

Her sons were strangers. She loved them but they were strangers. When they were home, they were guests in a good hotel; they had as much, and as little, affection for Tower House as for a hotel. Nor did they have much affection for their home county; they had grown up used to a softer, tamer, landscape, grown up nearer the centre of power. Whether Roger got to Harley Street or not, whether George got to the USA or not, the North wouldn't be the place where they settled down.

It had been different when she was young: people were more fixed, you lived where you were born, and expected to keep on living there. Her sons and their friends seemed not to be attached, to travel light and fast, and if they had any family affection they certainly didn't show it. Sometimes she felt that Tower House was too big, that it had become a huge showcase rather than a home.

But these moments were rare. She was proud of her sons, and if they didn't confide in her, at least they never gave her cause for worry. They didn't wear their hair long, they bathed every day, they dressed normally and if ever they misbehaved, misbehaved normally. There were many women of her acquaintance who envied her, no matter how bravely they might talk of rebellion being a temporary phase and showing at least generous instincts and outward appearance being unimportant and pot no worse than cigarettes. She and Clive had been standing outside in the drive with George one day in late July looking over George's new Mini-Cooper when Harold Thomas, whose father lived at the Grange four houses away, walked by, his hair shoulder-length, wearing tight faded jeans, sandals and a pink Nehru shirt.

The Mini was mustard yellow with magnesium alloy wheels and wide-section tyres; Harold saw it, stopped and then walked slowly down the drive towards them as if dragged against his will.

'Hello, Mrs Lendrick. Hello, Mr Lendrick. Hello, George.' He seemed to be looking at the Mini, but Robin knew he was looking at her; she was wearing a sleeveless linen summer dress with a square-cut neck that showed the beginning of her breasts; he came close to her to look inside the car and she caught a whiff of stale sweat, which she should have disliked but didn't.

'Cool, George, cool,' he said. 'But what about the insurance?'

'Costs a packet,' George said. His fair hair was, if anything, shorter than usual; his dark grey trousers were sharply creased, his shirt was white, there was a white handkerchief in the pocket of his navy blue blazer, and his dark brown, almost black, shoes were gleaming.

'Fundamentally such vehicles are decadent, of course,' Harold said.

George grinned, showing big white teeth. 'That's the best possible argument you could put forward,' he said. 'Now I feel absolutely happy about owning it.'

'Possessions are death to the spirit,' Harold said. 'Possessions kill love.' He looked very pasty beside George, and his eyes, a paler blue than George's, were red-rimmed.

'Oh, *love*,' George said, with a sidelong glance at his parents. 'You'd be surprised what a difference a nice shiny possession like this makes with the birds, Harold. Of course, I'm not saying that your old van mayn't have certain advantages ...'

'Love isn't just sex, man,' Harold snapped. 'Love is for everybody. Love should be the *raison d'être* for society.'

Clive laughed. 'Not in the wool business it isn't,' he said. 'You ask your father, Harold.'

'My father belongs to the past,' Harold said. 'The future will overtake him and eat him up bones and all. You too, Mr Lendrick.' He fished in his pocket and put on a pair of dark glasses; the pasty immature face seemed suddenly sinister and prophetic.

'I'll be indigestible,' Clive said. He had on a pair of old flannels and a faded blue sports shirt and battered and scuffed old shoes; today was his day for pottering about doing odd jobs in the garden. In an odd way he looked as young as George and George looked as mature as his father.

'The Revolution has an iron belly,' Harold said.

Stephen had talked rather like that once, she thought; and the gleaming car, the colours of the rhododendrons and roses, the sound of water from the garden sprayer in the house across the road, were seen and heard not through her eyes and ears but in her loins.

George whistled. 'Dig that metaphor,' he said. 'Oh, Harold, you do talk lovely.'

'You laugh now,' Harold said. 'But you won't laugh when it comes.' He looked at his watch. 'I must be off. Ciao.' He waved, and slouched off down the drive, taking one quick backward glance at Robin's breasts and the Mini.

'I must be off too,' George said. 'Don't wait up for me.' He jerked his finger in the direction of Harold. 'Notice his eyes? He's on pot. Roger told me.'

'I noticed his smell,' Clive said. 'Is he giving up washing for the Revolution?'

'He's only a silly boy,' Robin said. *Possessions kill love*: but weren't they rather part of love? The house, the garden, Clive, her children, the furniture, the silver, the ornaments, her jewellery – wasn't all this part and parcel of her life, hadn't she put love into it all, and got love back?

'I can't think what girl would have him with all that hair,' she said.

George, climbing into the Mini and sliding back the sunshine roof, pulled a face.

'He picks them up in Charbury dance halls, Mama,' he said. 'Dead common little girls from Council houses. His old dad would kill him if he knew. And he goes to all the demos. Lots of spare there. Don't worry, Harold's not repressed.' He put on his sunglasses, threw his jacket in the back of the car and let in the clutch. He lit a cigar; the smell drifted to Robin's nostrils, faintly festive. 'Ciao, my darlings'; and he was off before she could caution him not to go too fast, which she could never help doing, futile though she knew it was.

'Don't worry,' Clive said, reading her thoughts. 'He can just as easily kill himself in an ordinary Mini.'

'I wish you hadn't bought him the damned thing just the same.'

He shrugged. 'What can you do? He's a good boy, and he's worked damned hard. God, you look at other men's sons, like Harold, and you realize how lucky you are. Mind you, Harold's at least normal.'

'I saw him looking at me.'

He grinned. 'You're worth looking at.' He moved closer to her. 'Let's go inside.'

'Petronella's in her room working.'

'What the hell difference does that make? The house is big enough.'

She didn't want to; the voluptuous warmth that was settling down over her was satisfied by being outside in the sunshine; she wanted to go into the back garden and sit there with a book and, half-asleep, smell the flowers and the grass and remember not just what had happened a long time ago, but what had not happened; sex now wasn't part of her plans. But if you didn't give a man what he wanted when he wanted it he always had an excuse to go somewhere else, and quite a few women in Throstlehill had indicated an interest in Clive. It was all in jest – 'If ever you grow tired of him, send him to me' or 'What have you done to deserve such a gorgeous man?' or 'If she doesn't treat you right, Clive, you know my address' but from instinct and observation she knew that no women ever said these things if they didn't mean them. Men did; women didn't; she'd seen more than one affair begin from such remarks.

She didn't think that Clive had ever strayed or that if he ever had done it had been very serious; but there were women in the neighbourhood who wouldn't mind changing their husbands for one as rich and good-looking as Clive. It was as well to take no risks; although he seemed contented enough, she hadn't forgotten what his father had been like. And again from her instincts and observations most men were in the end their father's sons. And Clive's father was of a generation to whom divorce was unthinkable. Perhaps that was the reason that so many women one knew needed tranquillizers and sleeping-pills.

She followed Clive to the house. It was pleasantly cool inside; all the curtains were half-drawn to protect the carpets from the sunlight. She paused to straighten an ashtray on the hall table and noticed with annoyance that Joan, the daily help, had put magazines in the bottom of the bookcase instead of the magazine rack in the drawing-room. She never had been able to find out why she did this; but if she hadn't happened to have noticed it, then the magazines would have been lost or, as they put it. Joaned. But Joan was a good worker and clean and honest and this habit of hers of putting things away in any place but the right one had to be endured. She was fifty now and not likely to change her ways; and she herself was over forty and suddenly for no good reason couldn't get out of her head the name of a man she hadn't, except on television, seen for nearly twenty years.

And when she looked back a year later she remembered this, just as she remembered straightening the ashtray and noticing the misplaced magazines. And as she followed Clive up the stairs, walking, like him very quietly, she saw that the grey carpeting had worn badly on two steps; it would have to be replaced because it wasn't only unsightly but in time would be dangerous.

There was no sound from Petronella's room at the end

of the landing; Robin knew that she was asleep. She'd been to the Tennis Club dance the night before and hadn't come in until three in the morning; but she'd risen at eight to punish herself, since she was, like Robin at that age, going through a religious phase.

She bolted the bedroom door. The curtains were already drawn; the fitted carpet was of a very delicate pink with which you couldn't take any risks. Clive came behind her and unzipped her dress; she saw herself in the dressing-table mirror, her eyes very bright, her face flushed.

Lying naked on top of the Maltese lace coverlet she closed her eyes. The tongue which probed her mouth, moved to her stiffening nipples, moved downwards over her belly, was Stephen's; but this Stephen wasn't the man she'd seen on television six months ago, but a younger man, twenty years younger; the man on television was not the one she knew.

She opened her eyes, keeping them on the plum-coloured canopy above her; if it had been Stephen, her Stephen, she'd have kept her eyes open. Danger, danger; but she didn't care; the mouth left her, it always left her there, when the pleasure was just beginning, and she reached her hand down automatically to guide inside her what she should have guided inside her twenty years ago; she closed her eyes again and repeated the name under her breath: danger, danger, but this summer afternoon for no good reason she didn't care.

Afterwards, when they'd showered and dressed, they did what she'd wanted to do in the first place, and sat out in the back garden drinking tea.

Petronella came down just as the tea was made, yawning and rubbing her eyes.

'How did you know we'd made tea?' Robin asked.

'Instinct.' She yawned without covering her mouth; showing neat little white teeth like her mother's.

'I don't think you've done much French somehow,' Clive said.

'I was tired, Daddy.' But even as she stretched herself, the fatigue was leaving the smooth, just a little too plump face; a cup of tea to wash the sleep from her mouth, and she'd be ready to stay out until the small hours again. They'd returned from a fortnight in Malta only last week and Petronella was an even golden brown; next week she was going to France with two other girls for a fortnight's camping tour, longer if the money held out.

The eldest, Olive Villendam, was nineteen and was doing the driving; she was a sensible girl and the car, a Renault shooting brake, was only six months old; but from time to time Robin would be visited by an extraordinarily vivid mental picture of the car squashed flat by one of those huge French lorries or of Petronella's dead body naked and bloody in a clearing in the Ardennes. Why the Ardennes she didn't know; but it sounded like the sort of place in which a young girl was most likely to be raped and murdered. But if anything happened to any of the three it was certain that it wouldn't be either Olive or Olive's sister Elizabeth – Petronella had always been accident-prone and it was a miracle that she'd reached the age of sixteen unscarred and uncrippled.

Looking at Petronella now, tall and only just beginning to get rid of her puppy-fat, she felt a great rush of protective love.

'I keep thinking about this camping holiday,' she said. 'I must be mad to let you.'

Petronella sat up in her deckchair suddenly, managing in the process to spill half her tea.

'Oh Mummy, you wouldn't stop us now!' The brown face was puckered, the dark brown eyes with their slightly bemused look were beginning to moisten.

'No, you silly. Just be careful, that's all. I hope Olive's father is having the car specially serviced.'

'It's been done already, Mummy. Olive took it in herself.'

'And be careful about strange men.'

Petronella giggled. 'You mean *rape*,' she said.

'Just remember not to show too much. Men can misunderstand you—'

'Oh Mummy, don't. You're spoiling it all.' Petronella's eyes moistened again.

Clive, who had been listening with an expression of amusement on his face, cut in. 'Don't upset yourself, honey. I'm sure you'll be careful. But maybe I'd better come with you to keep an eye on the Villendam girls. I'm very good at keeping an eye on young girls.'

Petronella fluttered her eyelashes at him. They were long and dark, darker than her hair, and all her own, 'But who'd keep an eye on you, Daddy?'

Robin laughed along with Clive; she was as she grew older increasingly grateful that one at least of her children was at home and seemed actually to like living at home. But she found herself thinking hard about Olive Villendam who was small and thin, almost painfully so, but who had a flawless skin and apparently unlimited energy and who, more than once, she'd caught looking at Clive coolly and speculatively. There was something else; Olive had been in and out of their house all summer, planning the trip to France; and never had she encountered Clive without making some complimentary remark about his personal appearance, even if it were only to compliment him on a new tie or shirt.

She shaded her eyes against the sun, looking past the evenly mowed lawn with its pattern of regular stripes towards the darker green of the woods, shimmering in the heat. There were more houses between them and the woods than when first they came; but each had trees around it, each stood in grounds of at least three-quarters of an acre. They'd kept the garden simple, almost austere – one big lawn with flowerbeds round it, mostly roses, and a few bushes; mostly lilac and rhododendron; there was a tennis court at one end, and room enough for a decent game of croquet and, for that matter, a garden party. They had thought once of having a swimming pool, but that would have meant eventually holding open house to all the children in the neighbourhood and their parents too. (And the opportunity for the elder Miss Villendam to show off her small but very firm breasts and to have her back rubbed with suntan lotion.)

'When I was your age, Petronella,' she said, 'we only liked young men. Now all the girls go for older men. Why is that?'

'Father substitutes,' Petronella said.

'But Olive has a father. A big fat one.'

Clive pulled a face. 'It's too hot to be serious.'

'But I want to know,' Robin said. 'Why this great change? Look at Jeannie Hepple. Her husband's fifteen years older than her and no one thinks anything of it. When we were young, it'd have been a nine days' wonder, if not a scandal.'

'It's the Bomb,' Clive said. 'Nothing certain any more. As for Jeannie Hepple, her husband's loaded. Perhaps that's it. Girls are keener on money. It's simple.' He stretched out in his deckchair, and his eyes closed.

But it wasn't simple, Robin thought. Just lately Clive had changed. For weeks he'd just go to bed to sleep, then, as this afternoon, he'd be as eager as when they first married. He was nearly asleep now, and she knew why. If Olive did call that afternoon, he would have no more than a theoretical interest in her. Was he keeping a mistress? Would he, like other husbands she'd heard of, come home one day and announce that he was going off with another woman? At forty-two she'd kept her figure and, despite three pregnancies and a miscarriage, her teeth; she knew that men still looked twice at her, although she'd only ever in the real sense of the word, slept with one man, she was, as they say, good in bed. Which only meant that she liked it; there were a lot of women who didn't or who said that they didn't.

After a while Petronella went into the house to phone; and now Clive was asleep. He kept his hand under his chin as if to keep his mouth from falling open. She didn't go to sleep herself but watched him through half-closed eyes. She should have been content, but she wasn't. To breathe in the smells of summer, to feel the sun hot on her face, which after Malta could come to no harm, except that she'd better put something on it in an hour or so, to relax and think only of a drive over the moors in the cool of the evening and dinner at the Oakwood Hall Club with the Sindrams and her new dress which she would be wearing for the first time that evening – one added all this up more than once and the answer was always if not ecstasy, contentment.

No, happiness. For she liked the Sindrams. Gerry was an old school friend of Clive's and he was not only a nice person but a good dancer. For some reason the better the dancer the more horrible the man, but he was the exception which proved the rule. And she could talk to Fiona, who had a marvellous sense of humour; and, what was equally important, Clive liked her too. She was attractive enough to interest him; with red hair which now she helped along a little, but not so damned attractive that she, Robin, felt outshone.

When you were young you hoped every time you went out that you'd meet someone who'd change your whole life; but when you were over forty and married twenty years you hoped only that everything would go according to plan, that your life wouldn't be changed. The house was exactly as she wanted it, her children were the sort of children other women envied. She could have wished that Petronella was less easily hurt, more practical in outlook, she could have wished to see more of George and Roger. George would be off to Greece soon. Roger had already gone youth hostelling in Scotland. They'd be home for about a fortnight during the summer if she was lucky. But Petronella, like her, loved Hailton and all her friends were there; and for all the boys' talk, they might well settle near home. They weren't fools, and they'd eventually realize the solid advantages of doing so: Clive could help them a lot, but not in the USA and not in London.

Her life was full, but not too full: from Clive she'd learned to avoid good works and public life in general. She was a member of the local Conservative branch and very occasionally would help to serve tea and sandwiches or assist at a stall at a garden party, but she steadfastly refused to serve on any committees or help with canvassing or addressing election notices or in fact with any chore large or small. She attended no charity function except the occasional charity ball, and every appeal for charity went straight into the wastepaper basket. There was a handful of local charities which published subscription lists; Clive gave to these because his father had always done, but his total expenditure was no more than £50 a year.

Both of them had nevertheless been approached as candidates for the Hailton Urban District Council; both had firmly refused. 'I've only got one life,' Clive said to Robin, 'I won't spend one moment of it being bored stiff and not even getting paid for it.'

'My sentiments exactly,' she said.

For all this, as a couple they didn't have a reputation either for meanness or for being anti-social. Clive's name was on the few subscription lists which were taken any notice of in Hailton and he contributed well over the minimum subscription to the Conservative Party. Lendrick and Sons always paid above trade union rates and had good labour relations; the profit-sharing scheme they introduced in 1952 helped, but so also did the fact that he and his brother Donald were the only Lendricks in the firm. You didn't have to be related to the boss to get ahead at Lendricks; in fact, he and Donald steadfastly refused to employ any relations. It wasn't difficult to refuse them: none of their father's brothers or sisters had particularly distinguished themselves, nor had their children.

The Lendricks weren't, in fact, like the usual West Riding textile family – Nonconformist, employing in senior positions only its own members, or members by marriage, mixing socially with very few outside its own ranks, up to its eyeballs in public life, and in a surprising number of instances giving the statutory tenth of its income to charity.

They no doubt led a satisfying enough life in their own way; but Robin was only grateful that the Lendricks weren't like that, because even to think of the sort of life she might have led if she hadn't met Clive depressed her. The life she led now was as if made to order for her: there was the house, always the house, and her growing love for it, there

57

was a fair amount of business entertaining but far more private entertaining, there was the theatre and the cinema, there was for her occasionally small parts at the Hailton Players, there were the children – which after the boys went away to school, meant in effect Petronella; and there was Clive.

For she'd always known that her chief job was to look after him. She wasn't likely to get anyone better, and if she did Tower House wouldn't be part of the deal; and when the children grew up and left home, he would be all she'd got.

So his comfort and well-being became her chief preoccupation. He always had a clean shirt and underwear every day, his clothes were always pressed, he was never given anything to wear with buttons missing, he had nothing in his wardrobe that was torn or patched. He liked a cooked breakfast, so he was always given one; and when he came home to dinner, as he did most evenings, he was always given a proper meal, never sandwiches or anything prepacked. At the very least he got an omelet; and she always ate with him. She spared him details of household worries just as he spared her all financial worries: all their married life, with brief intervals when he had economy campaigns, whatever she asked for she got.

Some of her friends thought that she spoiled him; but she noticed that these were the very ones whose husbands gave them the most cause for worry about money. There were times when, perversely, she wished that there'd been for them some period of early struggle, so that her abilities and energies could have been used to the absolute maximum, so they would be able to look back and see how far they'd come.

She consoled herself for this by reminding herself that there were firms in the wool trade as apparently well-established as Lendricks which nevertheless had gone to the wall and that as far as she could help Clive she was helping him. To keep him immaculately turned out, healthy and cheerful, never to grumble about entertaining the most boring and obnoxious people no matter how short the notice, and always to be a credit to him herself, mightn't help him but it certainly wouldn't hinder him.

She looked at Clive, his body absolutely relaxed in sleep, his face peaceful. She'd let him sleep another half-hour then she'd give him a drink of lemonade and ask him to do something, or to go for a short walk with her. If he had any more than an hour's sleep in the afternoon he'd wake up lethargic and complaining of a headache; an hour refreshed him, recharged the batteries.

She'd earned her keep as a wife, she'd done a good job. If Clive could be taken for five, if not ten years younger, he had her to thank. If they saw enough people and went out often enough to prevent them from becoming dull, he had her to thank. If they didn't see too many people, didn't go out too often, could enjoy regularly the quiet evening at home, he had her to thank. She had planned their life so that there wouldn't be any fatigue – aching feet, the fixed social smile – or boredom – another night slumped in front of the television, the clock ticking loud in the quiet house.

There was nothing wrong; everything was going according to plan. And yet there was something wrong somewhere. She looked at Clive's scarcely noticeable belly, the taut, smooth face, brick red – the nearest he approached to a suntan – with few lines for his age. Even his hair was a younger man's hair – thick and lustrous and springy. It was she who'd got him into the habit of washing it every day so that now he couldn't remember a time when he didn't. And it was she who had got him into the habit of having it trimmed every week. But for her he might well have been like most of his generation, overweight, with wrinkles and broken veins on his face, hair thinning and dandruff laden, a little twitchy, a little wheezy, hands inclined to tremble, another middle-aged man doing himself rather too well, another middle-aged man who'd be in and out of hospital in his fifties if he didn't suddenly drop dead before. Her own father was still alive and looking ten years younger than his seventy-two years of age; Clive's father had died of a coronary thrombosis at sixty-six on his way to the motor showrooms to buy his latest mistress, a twenty-year-old typist, a Mini for her birthday. It had perhaps been his bad luck that his prostate had held out as long as it did.

Clive was his son, no matter how outwardly contented he might appear. If she was careful now, if she looked after him properly, these could be the best years of their lives; the business was now on an even keel, and soon she'd be able to persuade Clive to take a decent holiday of at least six weeks and to take more long weekends and days off during the week. She couldn't imagine herself living anywhere but Tower House, but when they retired, they'd travel a lot – when that time came, she wanted him to be able to enjoy it all, not to be a husk of a man waiting for death.

It was all planned; she had now the sort of husband, the sort of children, and the sort of house she'd always wanted and there was no reason, barring illness or accident, why the rest of her life shouldn't go according to plan. Barring illness or accident; but in her experience no one was seriously ill or had a bad accident unless something inside them – discernible at a glance from the way their faces moved when talking, the way they walked, the sort of clothes they wore – hankered after misfortune.

She sat there until her big red Old England wristwatch with the waterproof cover – she had three watches and this was the one she wore when pottering about outdoors – told her the hour had nearly passed. Then she took the tea-tray through the french windows into the morning-room and into the kitchen. The morning-room was a large room with plain cream walls; the colour came from the matching orange carpet and curtains and the pictures, which she'd chosen for their brightness rather than for their subject. There was a large deal table here with a Formica top and an Ercol suite covered in red and a floor-to-ceiling cupboard in a red which matched the suite. She kept her sewing-machine here and clothes to be repaired; in effect it was a general catch-all where everything went for which no place could instantly be found. On an old oak trolley stood a Murphy portable TV and next to it on a whitewood table painted in a red matching the cupboard, a Sanyo portable stereoradiogram. In a small oak bookcase was a collection of cookery and gardening books.

She spent most of the day in the morning-room; there was a footstool which made any one of the chairs into a chaise-longue and every day after lunch she had an hour's rest there. It had served as the nursery once and still was the room to which the children seemed to gravitate; but as she glanced around her on her way to the kitchen she knew that something would have to be done to it. The table had been admirable for painting and drawing and plasticine modelling, but it was really kitchen furniture. The trolley and the occasional tables were battered and undistinguished and she was tired of looking at the prints of uniforms of the British Army and the two Blue Girls. And the red cupboard, orginally a toy-cupboard, was altogether too much of a catch-all; most of the stuff in it should have been thrown out long ago.

She was already beginning to visualize a decoration scheme for the morning-room as she emptied the teapot and tea cups, put them in the dishwasher, and put the sugar-bowl in the pantry. The pantry was ten feet by five with stone shelves and grey lino over the stone floor, lit by a tiny window at the far end. It was always cool, even today. It wasn't really a room, but a store cupboard; nothing had been done to it except to whitewash it occasionally, but she always spent a minute longer than she needed to whenever she went in there; from the neat rows of tins and packets and neatly labelled jars and canisters she was always able to extract the assurance that her life was going in the direction it ought to go.

She loved her parents and they'd given her a good home. Her mother had kept a clean and tidy house; there was nothing of the slut about her. But in her mother's pantry there were no labels, biscuits and cakes were kept in toffee tins, and there wasn't much attempt at any kind of classification. Because of this, her mother would often think she'd run out of things when in fact she hadn't. And her mother had never kept a reserve of tinned food so that there'd always be some sort of meal available for unexpected guests; but then her mother had had few unexpected guests.

She went to the huge refrigerator – taller than she was – put away the milk, and took out the jug of lemonade. When she went to the freezer compartment for ice, one of the ice-trays was empty. That would be George; for fifteen years now she'd been asking him to refill the ice-tray after emptying it, and evidently he'd never heard her once. She emptied the ice-tray into the jug; Clive liked the sound of ice clinking against glass. As always she resolved to leave both ice-trays empty to teach George a lesson; and as always she refilled them.

Suddenly she felt a little dizzy and sat down on one of the large rush-bottomed chairs at each end of the big pine table. She'd bought the table fifteen years ago very cheaply; it was very plain, very solid, very strong, and she'd always imagined it in some farmhouse kitchen. Years of scrubbing had brought out the grain of the wood and given it a warm smoothness; it went together quite happily with the white refrigerator and the big electric cooker, but wouldn't have been out of place in a more old-fashioned kitchen. She looked at the rows of pans in the open shelves above the kitchen bench; they would need replacing soon. The dizziness came over her in waves; she put her hands on the table for support as the room blurred – grey linoleum, pale wood, copper, white enamel, chrome, lemon-yellow walls, all blending, shapes, doubling, trebling, then jolting back to normal. It might be too much sun but it was more likely the Pill. She went to one of the drawers in the bench and took out a packet of cigarettes. If it was the Pill, she'd better give it up; but that would mean going back to the old method, to the sordid apparatus in the locked cupboard, to having to make a big production of what might sometimes, if Clive was tired, last only a few minutes. At her age she should be able to forget about birth control; but she'd known women who'd had babies at fifty. A baby now, and the whole structure of her future came crashing down.

The dizziness had gone. Outside in the sunshine it was as if it had never been. She shook Clive gently by the shoulder; he awoke smiling at her. That was one of the characteristics which after twenty years she still found endearing; he had handed it down to George and Roger, but not to Petronella who, like her, dragged herself back to consciousness slowly and painfully.

'That did me the world of good,' he said. He drank a glass of lemonade thirstily, then poured himself another.

She heard the swish of tyres and a car engine outside, and then the front doorbell. 'Damn,' she said. 'Who can that be?' There were footsteps and voices and then Petronella appeared at the french windows with Olive Villendam. Robin saw Clive, who had been lying back in his chair, sit up and turn eagerly.

'Mummy, where's the Michelin?' Petronella asked. 'I can't find it *anywhere*.'

'I noticed it in George's room,' Robin said.

'George always takes the very book I want,' Petronella said. 'I say, is there any lemonade going?'

'Get yourself two glasses,' Robin said.

Olive Villendam sat on the grass facing Clive. She'd had her hair cut very short, but it didn't make her look less feminine. She had no stockings on, and as she sat down there was a glimpse of blue flowered pants; Robin knew that Clive had noticed too. 'This is a heavenly garden,' Olive said. 'Ours is all rockeries and rare blooms you mustn't go near. I think you planned it very well, Mr Lendrick.' Olive had the sort of skin which didn't so much darken with the sun as become a dusky gold; her light brown hair was bleached with the sun.

'It's a children's garden really, Olive,' Robin said. 'We wanted a place where children could play.'

Olive's eyes narrowed.

'But I'm just a child really, Mrs Lendrick.'

'Don't say that,' Petronella said, putting two glasses on the table. 'Or Daddy won't let us go to France.'

Olive rose in one movement. To show her pants again, Robin thought viciously, and to prove how lissom she is. She put her arm round Clive's shoulder. 'Oh, Mr Lendrick, you wouldn't be so mean!'

And that, thought Robin, is not only so that he can feel her hot little paw, but so that he can smell her youth; if ever he's alone with her, how long will it be before he succumbs?

'I've told you,' Clive said. 'I'll come with you. Foreign parts are full of sex maniacs.' Olive's hand didn't move; she merely giggled.

'You can't have my old man, Olive,' Robin said. She kept a smile on her face which she hoped wasn't too fixed. 'He's taking me to the Canaries.' She handed Olive a drink and then a cigarette from the packet on the table.

'Super,' Olive said, and bent down to take a light from Clive, managing to display the shape of her breasts; the only angle, Robin thought, at which they'd be discernible.

'Our first holiday alone together for eighteen years,' Clive said. 'A second honeymoon.'

He smiled at Robin and she smiled back at him; but Petronella for an instant seemed as if deserted, as if the main party were going too fast for her. Olive's green eyes behind the black eyelashes, so obviously false as to be pathetic to anyone else but a man of forty-six, looked faintly derisive and then, Robin saw to her delight, envious.

Four

But Robin's early warning system had misled her; or rather gone into operation too early. Clive was in no danger from Olive Villendam; even if Robin had not been watching her closely, the opportunities for a nineteen-year-old girl and a forty-six-year-old married man are, in the circle Robin and Clive lived in, almost non-existent. This isn't to say that Clive never thought about Olive Villendam, didn't sometimes positively lust after her; but he was too comfortable, too settled in his ways, to take any active steps about it. And Olive, whilst reckless enough to have welcomed an affair with a married man without thought of consequence, wasn't experienced enough nor in the position to arrange the right combination of time and place.

But sometimes when she'd brush past him or lean over his shoulder to see what he was reading and he'd feel the warmth of her body and catch the clean, childish, faintly peppery smell of her hair, he'd be visited by an emotion more dangerous than lust. Disquiet, discontent, an urge to be free, a picture in his mind of a small window opening instead of a door – there were simple ways of dispelling lust, but no simple way of dispelling this feeling, and no name that he could find for it.

Up to his forty-seventh birthday his life continued on its accustomed course. He went to the mill most days at nine and left at about half past five, and made several business trips to London and Paris and West Berlin and Milan and New York, travelling to New York and back on the *France* to give himself a break. He gave customers lunch and dinner, entertained them at Tower House, gave parties for the more important ones, visited them at their offices to smooth over difficulties. He smoothed over difficulties at the mill too; when he was away in New York there was very nearly a strike, ostensibly over a new overlooker's bad language but in actuality because the overlooker, Donald's choice, wasn't the workers' choice. Clive talked to the weavers one by one, beginning with the trade union representative, taking as much trouble to persuade them as he did with his customers. Unlike Donald, he had a good memory for faces and Christian names and family histories; and he could keep the irritation out of his voice when confronted with impregnable stupidity, which Donald never could.

He saw the overlooker last. 'Charlie,' he said, 'you've given me a lot of trouble. I know you got your job because you're a bloody good man, because I know my brother only promotes good men. But you've got to learn how to handle people. Smile at them though they make you sick. And don't ever swear at the buggers.'

'They're not bothered about bad language,' Charlie said.

'I know, Charlie, I know. But any excuse is better than none. Between you and me – and if you ever let this go any further, I'll have your guts for garters – they're jealous of you. You can't alter that, but you can throw your weight about a bit less. And be polite to them. You don't have to lick their arses, but be polite to them. And don't swear, fuck it.'

Charlie smiled for the first time. 'I'll be like a mother to the rotten bastards,' he said. 'Don't worry, Mr Clive.'

Donald came into the office as Charlie went out.

'He looks cheerful,' he said.

'So should you,' Clive said. 'There won't be any more trouble in that direction.'

Donald frowned. His face wrinkled and for the moment he looked fully four years older than Clive instead of four years younger. 'You've spent a lot of time over this business.' He smoothed his fair hair with a nervous gesture which was becoming more and more frequent as the hair became thinner.

'You'd have had plenty of time on your hands if there'd been a strike,' Clive said.

'Don't think I'm not grateful,' Donald said.

'Prove it, then.' Clive looked around the office with its shabby red carpet, its incongruous gimcrack Thirties cocktail cabinet, its far too large and heavy mahogany desk, its green filing cabinet, its four creaking leather-backed chairs, its oak panelling with its over-fussy carving. 'Redecorate this mausoleum and chuck out all the old furniture.'

'It's a big room,' Donald said. 'You're not in it all that much.'

'It's beginning to depress me,' Clive said. 'And I'm sure it depresses customers.

Clive had had his way; the furniture had been thrown out, the oak panelling been stripped down, and now he had an office which seemed twice as big, twice as light, and immeasurably more cheerful – oranges and scarlets and a gunmetal grey carpet and a teak desk and cocktail cabinet and a huge sofa and armchairs and on one wall a mural specially commissioned from the Charbury College of Art

– the history of textiles in Charbury, told by pop-art figures with balloons of dialogue issuing from their mouths. It was very young and high-spirited and gaudy, and no other mill in Charbury had anything like it. Donald from the beginning would have preferred water-colours of the Yorkshire countryside, but Clive overruled him.

There's a time in everyone's life when everything goes right, and it was so now with Clive. It wasn't that things had ever gone badly with him before; but he'd had his set-backs, he'd made a few mistakes, he'd not always been able to get exactly what he wanted. It may be said that he didn't want much – to bring in the orders he went out for, to keep the mill running smoothly, to have a tranquil domestic life, and to suffer no discomfort of any kind. But what he wanted few humans ever get; when they do it's instantly recognizable. People had always liked Clive; now they began positively to love him. There was no taint of failure or bitterness or envy about him; he exuded cheerfulness, after talking with him for a few moments you couldn't help feeling that the world was a better place than you'd thought it was before.

And, more unmistakably than ever before, women would signal to him that they were available. He was sensitive enough to read the signals, but didn't feel any necessity to respond. It was pleasant to be admired; but he knew, or thought that he knew, that the women who would hold his hand a second too long or straighten his tie or touch his knee, didn't have anything under their skirts that Robin didn't have.

Robin discovered a new interest in the Hailton Players. She had before occasionally taken small parts; now she worked backstage in charge of costumes or as prompt or assistant stage manager, was elected to the Reading Committee, and attended virtually every Club Night. He was not any less well looked after, except that he spent more evenings alone; he didn't mind this, having seen enough people in the course of his daily work. In fact, these evenings alone reading or listening to gramophone records in the big quiet house seemed to replenish something which had been taken from him in the day. Sometimes Robin would bring people from the Players home for coffee or a drink, and that too replenished him: here were people with whom there was no sort of cash nexus, who wanted nothing from him and from whom he wanted nothing.

The Players set tended in Hailton to be young and varied in their occupations; he rather enjoyed that too, because since his Army days his circle of friends seemed gradually to have restricted itself to people of his own age and income and position in life. But the Players set were mostly people with their way in life to make; it was all still ahead of them, nothing was cut-and-dried. Some even had the ambition to write or to act or to produce; their dreams gave everything they said panache, filled the house with vitality. And some had settled for a steady job in the day and the Players in the evening: they didn't have any dreams of fame in the West End but they were contented. He hadn't met many people like this before, either: in the wool business no one can afford to relax, to assume that the profits will continue to pour in. He was a relaxed sort of person himself, but only because Donald did the worrying for both of them.

At this period of his life he never stopped to ask himself whether he was happy. But he had actually never been happier except perhaps on leave during the war and immediately after the war, savouring civilian life with a pocketful of money and more where that came from, young and free and genuinely grateful to be alive. Even then, there had been a snag; much though he loved his father, the old devil had been very much in charge, and not only at the mill.

And now he had Petronella. She was a normal girl, she liked to go out; but at least once a week they'd have an evening together. He felt himself becoming very close to her; as long as one knew how to listen, there wasn't much she wouldn't confide in him. She'd been through the stage of wanting to be a nun, a nurse, and an actress; now to his delight she was becoming more and more interested in cloth, in colour and texture and weave, and he thought it possible that she might end up as a textile designer. He'd never tried to force either of the boys into the mill; he didn't want them to end up hating both him and the way they made their living. But the thought of Petronella being in the business pleased him.

George and Roger were good boys, kept their hair and fingernails clean, and were properly contemptuous of the students in revolt. George dropped a condom from his wallet one weekend when he was home; both he and Robin pretended they hadn't noticed it. He was, actually, rather glad that the boy should be so sensible; even if a girl were on the Pill, it didn't prevent her from having the pox.

He was proud of his sons; they worked hard, played hard, and kept their noses clean. And, yes, he loved them; but he'd never be as close to them as he was to Petronella. They didn't really seem to need him; and that was as it should be. Petronella needed him; and this relationship was one of the best he'd ever had, because he didn't want anything from her. He would worry about her sometimes, as he never worried about the boys; she was pretty and gentle and trusting and easily hurt. The permissive society was marvellous for men, but not so hot for girls; they, after all, had the anxiety and the babies and the abortions. He didn't brood over this, however: most girls managed to battle their way through to marriage without any disasters on the way, and he had a notion that Petronella, like her mother, would hang on to her virginity until the honeymoon.

Sometimes he worried about her obvious interest in some of the younger men in the Players set. Tom Charvis, for example, was eighteen and good-looking with a reverberating voice which he used to talk very well with for his age; he was studying English Literature at Leeds, but what he really wanted to be was an actor. What he was more likely to end up as was a teacher or at best a university lecturer; and even if he did become an actor, it was a precarious sort of existence. He liked Tom, though in his opinion he needed a haircut and a sulphur bath, but he wasn't the sort of young man he'd welcome as a son-in-law. This too Clive didn't brood about; though everybody was as good as everybody else now, in his experience girls in a position to marry rich men married rich men.

And there was plenty of time. Up to his forty-seventh birthday there always seemed plenty of time. When he looked back afterwards he'd find it hard to credit, just as during the war one couldn't credit that once there'd been no rationing and that death came to people in bed at threescore and ten. Time during that period seemed as limitless as in childhood. It had stopped running, it had come up to him and put its nose in his hand, he had stroked it and patted it, and still it hadn't run away.

That was the year that he – or rather Lendrick and Sons – bought the Mercedes, a white 250 SE saloon with automatic gearbox and reclining seats and an electric sunroof and a radio and tape-recorder. Donald had first of all objected that the Rover was good enough and then that some customers might object to a German car, but Clive had in the end worn him down. The argument that clinched it was that it was good for the firm's credit; for some reason people always thought that a Mercedes cost more than it actually did. No one worried about it being German any longer, least of all the Jews. He had had a car since he was eighteen, beginning with one of the old Ford Populars, and had always regarded them simply as transportation. The Mercedes was a bit more than that; it was beautifully balanced and you could chuck it round like a sports car. And in it you got respect from hotel doormen and head waiters and car park attendants and other drivers (probably because they thought that damaging a Merc would lead to hefty insurance claims) and that respect translated itself into more personal comfort, into there always being a good table at a restaurant, a space in the car park, customers always having time to see him, a long line of cars stopping to let him turn to the right.

He bought a new camera, a twin-lens Bolex. He'd never wasted much film before and could edit with a fair degree of competence. But now he just didn't seem able to take a bad shot; he scarcely needed to cut at all, but simply to join up the reels. It might of course have been the camera; but the only way of proving this would have been to take the same shots with the old camera. No doubt the Bolex helped; it was twice as easy to operate as the old one and, like the Mercedes, got him respect. But most of all it was a question of his eye being in, of everything being always on his side. It was at this time that his golf improved and, though he never achieved tournament standard, more than one member of the Hailton Golf Club commented on the change in his game.

It was at this time that he rediscovered the cinema after a long period during which he scarcely went at all, Robin's taste not being his. He didn't go regularly but followed what the reviewers most warmly recommended: he wasn't often at variance with them but, apart from that, it offered an especial refreshment. Going by oneself one could escape completely, one didn't have to give out to others after giving out all day at work.

The greatest pleasure was his discovery of reading. He wasn't exactly a non-reader, as many of the people he knew seemed to be, but his reading had always been confined to bestsellers and the occasional novel with a Yorkshire setting. Most of the books in the house were textbooks, coffee-table books, or cookery books. He occasionally used the Charbury public library for reference, but had never borrowed a book from any public library. There was a good bookshop in Hailton run by two partners, Ruth Inglewood and Norman Radstock. Ruth Inglewood was in her early thirties, brisk and cheerful in manner. She had never on any occasion been seen in a skirt. But she wasn't at all masculine: though her hips were narrow and her belly flat, she had very full breasts, and her always glossy chestnut hair, though short, was not excessively so. And her slacks and suits and shoes and accessories were women's; she was in no way butch. In any case, she was known to share a flat in Charbury with Norman Radstock, and outside the shop was more often seen with him than not. Their relationship was evidently one of long standing; the reason for their not being married wasn't known, since neither of them were local people and neither were in the least communicative about personal matters. Norman Radstock was a small neat man who might have been any age between thirty and forty; he had sparse, wispy brown hair, a snub nose and a curiously wizened complexion. You couldn't have said he was effeminate, but neither did he have the gamecock masculinity so often affected by small men.

Most of their social life seemed to be lived outside Hailton; but when they were invited to any function there they were always treated as a married couple. They were on the fringes of the Players set; Ruth very occasionally took small parts there and Norman designed sets and costumes. He was extremely accomplished at this, being one of those people to whom all materials are obedient and for whom no materials have any secret; he could make effective and original sets and costumes out of coloured tissue paper, cardboard, and sackcloth.

Both he and Ruth were well liked in Hailton and the bookshop, in a good position at the busiest end of the High Street, had about it in its third year the unmistakable air of a going concern.

Clive called in there one Saturday afternoon in late August to collect a book on flower arrangement for Robin. It was raining heavily; there was no one except him and Ruth in the shop, and the rows of brightly jacketed books, the glaring orange and red and green wallpaper muted in the half-light, the grey buildings, grey sky, grey pavements through the big picture-window, gave him the sensation of being cast in a play and not having learned his lines.

Ruth was wrapping up the book. She had an interesting face, less angular than her body, the face of a mischievous choirboy, the kind who would let a mouse loose at a wedding. She saw him looking at her and he turned away and picked up the first book that came to hand. Trollope's *The Warden*. After two pages he became lost in the story. He looked up with a start when Ruth touched his sleeve.

'Would you like a cup of tea, Mr Lendrick? I'm just making some.'

'Please,' he said. He glanced at his watch. Half an hour

had passed. It was an experience of a kind he'd never had before: it was a book he wanted to take slowly so that the pleasure wouldn't be over too quickly, the characters and the background were real and solid, and yet what they offered was absolute escape. He'd often wondered about Harold Macmillan's liking for Trollope and now he could understand it.

He felt Ruth's hand on his sleeve again.

'Here you are. Sugar?'

'No, thanks.' He closed the book reluctantly.

'Haven't you read Trollope before?'

'I'm ashamed to say I haven't.'

'Oh, but that's marvellous.' She smiled. 'I envy you, I really do.'

'Isn't this the first of a series?'

'Oh yes. You know, some people hardly read anything else. It's a cult.'

'I'll take this. And the others.'

'Hadn't you better make sure you like *The Warden* first?'

'I am sure. You mustn't turn business away, love.' He offered her a cigarette. That afternoon their friendship began. She had a deep love for books and an urge to share that love; he couldn't have chosen a better guide, since she never recommended any book to him which she hadn't herself enjoyed. He didn't always share her enthusiasms: with most contemporary women novelists, for instance, he couldn't get on at all. Nor was he ever able to finish a book by Jean Genet or James Baldwin or Iris Murdoch, though he tried hard.

It would be inaccurate to say that she educated him; she wasn't the type who has the urge to improve other persons' minds. But gradually he discovered that he could hold his own with people whom he'd always considered as being well-read. He could even impress them with scraps of gossip about authors; Ruth had once worked for a publisher and had met a great many authors and knew the facts that the papers didn't print.

She was the first woman he'd ever had as a friend, and the first woman he'd ever met with whom he didn't contemplate even the possibility of a sexual relationship. He liked talking to her, and not only about books, she had a lively and well-stocked mind, her responses were never tired or banal. He acquired no information about her personal life beyond what she let slip out; she came from London, her father was a senior Civil Servant, she had an Oxford Honours degree in English, she'd worked in a publisher's and as a PRO for a department store and as a teacher in a private school, and had finally drifted into bookselling on the strength of a legacy from her grandmother. Of her relationship with Norman she spoke not at all; if his name entered the conversation, it was as a husband's name would enter the conversation, not a lover's.

It was this friendship with Ruth which helped him to surmount what otherwise might have been a difficult period in his marriage. Robin had had to give up the Pill and for three months or so seemed almost always to be fast asleep or petulant with a headache or stomach-ache whenever he turned to her in the night. On the three occasions that she was awake and not unwell, she endured the act of love rather than participated in it.

He would have been hurt and frustrated by this once, but now he found himself able to accept it as something which would pass. In a strange way his friendship with Ruth provided him with a substitute for female sexuality. Whenever Robin rejected him he would think of something Ruth had said or that he was going to say to her; or sometimes he would simply visualize that face of a mischievous choirboy and her sudden grin when he came into the shop. He never talked to anyone else about Ruth, he knew no one who would have understood.

Walter Fareland, his lawyer and his oldest friend, certainly didn't understand. Walter and he had been to school together, kept in touch all throughout the war, met each other always at least once a week, knew each other as well as two men can know each other. He'd do anything for Walter, and Walter would do anything for him; and each was the custodian of secrets of the other which not even their wives had any inkling of. He'd never told anyone about Walter's girlfriend, and Walter had never told any-one about the time when, Donald being ill and there being no one to turn to, he'd pledged the credit of the mills far beyond their assets. It wasn't like him to worry, but for once he'd nearly gone mad with worry, seeing at one point prison lying ahead of him. He had had to share the burden, and it hadn't seemed fair to share it with Robin. He had a feeling, rightly or wrongly, that she'd have made too big a fuss over it, played the tragedy queen; she could have coped with any emergency except a money emergency. He wanted to tell someone who wasn't involved, who wouldn't take it personally. Walter had understood that in the position he was in, he couldn't do otherwise; he had helped simply by understanding. And he had understood about Walter's girl-friend, a silly grasping little bitch if ever there was one, and had talked Walter out of running away with her; and no one seeing Walter at the Methodist Chapel now, stiff-faced and dark-suited, passing round the collection plate, would ever realize what a close call it had been.

That Saturday morning in November Walter had come into the bookshop whilst Clive was talking to Ruth. Clive waved to him casually and went on talking. He was aware of Walter's eyes upon them, but deliberately shut them out of his consciousness. When the shop began to be crowded, Clive paid for his books and turned away from her; the shop was, after all, her bread-and-butter and he didn't want to get in the way of her serving other customers. Walter bought a paperback hurriedly and they went out together. It was a raw morning with an unpleasantly grey sky; Clive shivered despite his thornproof tweed and heavy Jaeger car-digan and sheepskin coat. 'They keep it warm in that shop,' he said. 'Let's have a drink.'

Over a whisky in the White Rose, a small pub next to the bookshop, Walter stroked his moustache – a sure sign with him that he was nervous – and said, 'I hope you don't mind me telling you something personal, Clive.'

'That means that I will mind.'

Walter's rather pale, thin face reddened.

'You're getting yourself talked about.'

'What, for buying books?'

'Anyone can see it's that girl you go for.'

'Didn't you know she lives with her partner?'

'And a funny-looking little sod he is. She looks as if she prefers you.'

'We're friends.'

'All right, you're friends. But why advertise it? I know all about needing friends. It happens to a lot of men when they're forty.'

'But that's the whole point! There isn't anything to be secret about. Godammit, I've never been on my own with that girl, not once ...'

'It only needs once,' Walter said.

'It wouldn't happen. Really, Walter. I've never thought of her like that.'

'The point is, has she thought of you *like that*?'

'Go to hell,' Clive said. But Walter had, in that rather shabby little bar parlour five minutes after opening-time, taken a little of the bloom off things. His friendship with Ruth continued and, when Robin began to mix with the Players set, she and Norman were occasional visitors to Tower House. But it wasn't quite the same as it had been. Soon after that Saturday morning his sex relations with Robin returned to normal; they didn't talk about it, and he would have been hard put to it to say exactly when the return to normal took place, but by Christmas it was once or twice regularly each week and he ceased to think about Ruth. Sometimes he wondered if Robin hadn't been told that he was on friendly terms with her; there was more than one woman of his acquaintance who would rush to inform her of her husband's new-found interest in literature.

But she never mentioned it and, until his forty-seventh birthday, his life continued to glide along into greater and greater contentment. His only problem on his forty-seventh birthday was that he had everything he wanted or needed. If anyone had asked him, he'd sometimes think to himself, he would have had to confess that he was perfectly happy, that he hadn't a care in the world.

Five

The day before Clive's forty-seventh birthday party Stephen
Belgard was lost in Charbury. He was working at the BBC
again, but his office had been furnished as a schoolroom
with a blackboard and rows of little desks; his programme
was due on the air in five minutes, but he could neither
find a script nor could anyone tell him from which studio it
was being transmitted. He ran from studio to studio very
lightly, his feet scarcely touching the ground; every face he
saw was blank and hostile, and then there were no faces,
and the walls of the corridors were no longer cream and
pale yellow with Lowry reproductions and the floor was no
longer buff composition; they were black greasy stone, they
grew narrower and narrower, and then he was out in Leeds
Road, but in a part of it he'd never seen before; the trams
which hadn't run there since he was a child were back again
but they wouldn't stop for him; there was a manuscript in
beautiful italic handwriting in which he was reading about
himself being no longer in Leeds Road but in a long tunnel
and then in a street where half the houses were demolished.
He ran faster and faster, past a row of empty shops, past
Lendricks' Mills, where the tall chimney, the tallest in
Charbury, was very slowly falling; and then he was in a
courtyard with a blackened leafless tree in the centre and
all the windows in the buildings bricked up, and he was
lost.

His face against the tree he saw his wife Jean; she was
holding a mug of tea in his big Zodiac mug.

'You asked to be called,' she said.

He yawned. 'So I did.' He drank a mouthful of tea.
'Christ, what a night it was last night ...'

She sat on the bed and took a cigarette from the packet
on the bedside table. 'Was Crispin very tiresome?'

'If it weren't for his ratings, I wouldn't put up with the bastard for one minute. It was the usual caper. Nobody loves him, nobody understands him, for two pins he'd leave the country ... One of these days I'm going to give the sod two pins. And then there was one of his *bon vivant* performances about the bloody plaice. Sent it back twice. Christ, I knew him when he'd have been grateful for frozen fish fingers.' He drank some more tea, feeling it astringent in the mouth and hotly comforting in the stomach, and stroked her long blonde hair gently. In the morning sunlight it was a genuine gold, with a faint red overtone. It was genuine too; there were times when he wondered how long he was going to hold on to her. They had each married on the rebound from previous marriages; after three years she might well be speculating about what chances she'd missed. When she married him she'd appeared in three flops in a row and was beginning to smell of bad luck; now the play she was leading in, after a shaky start in the provinces, had been playing to packed houses for eighteen months. At thirty-four she had made it; she was on the verge of making it internationally, depending upon the play going to Broadway, depending upon Broadway liking it, depending upon a certain film company having a certain amount of money available and upon their not having under contract any other actress capable of playing the part.

His hand left her hair and went to the small of her back. She stood up suddenly. 'Honey. I must leave you. I've some shopping to do before lunch.'

She always had some shopping to do; that was why the house was crammed with expensive furniture and her wardrobe with expensive clothes, and every available inch of wallspace with expensive originals and every available inch of flat surface with expensive ornaments. Only the ornaments, being mostly good china figures, would hold their value; a long time ago he'd recognized that she had no taste at all.

'Who are you having lunch with?' he asked.

'Marcus and a creepy producer and a creepy author. You know – I told you about it.'

Marcus was her agent: the producer and the author, young men going up but not yet up to the stage where backing was easily available, hoped to talk her into appearing in their film. If they did they'd get the backing. They weren't aware, however, that Marcus was coming along. When he did the producer would either have to revise his budget or give up the idea of having her in the film.

'Enjoy yourself,' he said. 'They'll enjoy themselves looking at you in that dress.' It was of red jersey worn with black fishnet stockings and only just cleared her buttocks; it would have been whorish but for her clear blue eyes and fresh complexion and general air of youthfulness.

She bent down and kissed him. 'You enjoy yourself in the North,' she said. 'Give my love to your parents and don't go with any of those great fat Northern women. Phone me tonight. Promise?'

'Promise.' He leaned his head back on the padded headboard as the bedroom door closed behind her. For a while he was by himself in this stage set of a bedroom with the purple carpet and the bright blue and silver wallpaper and the white and red and green and gold psychedelic pattern on the fitted wardrobe, specially painted at an enormous cost by a set-designing friend of Jean's about whom even before their marriage he had always had suspicions: his name cropped up too often in the conversation, when they were together they were just a little too casual, just a little too much the colleagues who admired each other's work. The set designer's Christian name was Seamus and in his experience Englishmen with Gaelicized Christian names were always at bottom bogus because, if you worked it out, their parents were bound to be bogus. Seamus was the same age as Jean and over six foot, which was another good reason for disliking and mistrusting him.

He lit a cigarette. He was old enough to remember when this had been an unalloyed pleasure, but now every time he lit one he made a vow to give them up at some time in the future. Seamus didn't smoke; and that was the best reason of all for disliking him.

He thought of the writer who was his ostensible reason

for going North. He disliked him too, but for different reasons. The writer had the sort of talent which once he himself thought that he had: he was a novelist, and a genuine one, though operating within a very narrow range. What he didn't realize yet was that he was a far better TV writer than he was a novelist, that TV would open him out, turn his shorthand to plain language, use his facility for dialogue and incident to the fullest. The Board had taken a great deal of persuasion to see this: the company's policy was either to approach successful novelists and playwrights with the old crap about TV being a challenging new medium and a great creative adventure, or else to rely upon contracting the old faithfuls, the established TV writers, who weren't growing any younger or perceptibly more numerous.

There was more to it than that. In the long run professionals were best. They had to produce the stuff when you wanted it, because if they didn't, they didn't eat, or rather didn't eat in the way they very rapidly became accustomed to. And it was best to have them in London where not only was the cost of living higher but one had them close to hand. In fact, it was essential: writing for TV was a co-operative activity.

So he had to persuade Jack Byrock to give up his job as lecturer in English at Charbury University, to exchange his house in Charbury for a smaller one in London at twice the price, and to exchange the security of an academic job for a two-year contract with a TV company. It wasn't going to be easy.

He looked at his watch and went into the tiny bathroom and had a cold shower, deliberately not thinking of anything but the pleasure of the shock of cold water and the warmth rubbing himself dry with a huge towel afterwards.

Back in the bedroom he shaved and then opened his wardrobe and took out clean underwear and a clean cream nylon shirt and dressed quickly, selecting a dark-grey lightweight suit and a maroon tie and matching silk handkerchief. The shirt had double cuffs; he hesitated for a moment, then selected a pair of large gold cufflinks and went over to the box on the dressing-table which held his gold watch. He generally wore a steel one, but it was as well to emphasize to Byrock the fact that there was money in TV.

Automatically he emptied his briefcase into the bottom of the wardrobe and put in the electric shaver, toothbrush and toothpaste, a lightweight silk dressing-gown, a blue silk handkerchief and two white silk handkerchiefs, a tube of Alka-Seltzer, two pairs of Y pants, a blue-and-red tie, a vest, two pairs of dark-grey nylon socks, and a suède brush. From the dressing-table he took carkeys, doorkey, change, a small packet of Kleenex, an American Express card, Barclaycard, cheque book, AA and RAC cards, two Parker Airflyte pens, a nailfile, a comb and a pocket diary, and half a dozen visiting cards, and evenly disposed them in his pockets. His money was carried in a gold noteclip. Once he had crammed a great deal into his pockets, but as he had grown older he'd developed a phobia about his five foot six inches, which bulges in his clothes could only have the effect of emphasizing. He also had a fixation about travelling light; however far he travelled, he virtually never took any luggage apart from his briefcase.

He put his cigarettes and a book of matches into his right-hand trouser pocket. He could smoke anything providing it were filter-tipped and Virginia, but he always bought Peter Stuyvesant because of the shape of the packet. Sometimes he worried about whether these little foibles of his – to which he kept adding – weren't building up into a serious neurosis, but he only had to look at his colleagues in the company to be reassured. At least he didn't believe in astrology like Hunslett, or literally wash his hands a dozen times a day like Tremayne, or fiddle incessantly with Greek worry beads like Jenkins, or not make decisions on a Friday like Carver; and those, he'd heard over the office grapevine, weren't the least of it. He'd got through life so far without recourse to any sexual divergency or drug – even sleeping pills – and he'd never consulted a psychiatrist or felt the need to.

All in all, he thought, walking through to the kitchen to put the kettle on, he'd survived pretty well. He hadn't done any of the things he'd set out to do when he was young, beyond publishing a handful of poems in little magazines and a first novel which was best forgotten, but at forty-six he was in good health and earned six thousand a year plus expenses and up to two thousand from journalism. His first wife had married again and cost him nothing apart from the education of his son Hilary. He didn't mind that: it confirmed his right to see Hilary regularly, so that he wouldn't forget who his father was. He'd missed seeing Hilary grow up; but he'd also missed a lot of trouble and responsibility.

The kettle boiled: he made himself a cup of instant coffee and took a Bath Oliver biscuit from a tin in the cupboard above his head, a segment of La Vache Qui Rit cheese from the refrigerator, and an apple from the fruit bowl on the yellow Formica-topped kitchen table. He drank the coffee black and unsweetened.

The kitchen was, as usual, spotlessly clean and tidy, without the faintest trace of cooking smells. There were always a couple of chickens and some vegetables and packets of frozen foods in the big deep-freeze which ran along one wall, just as there were always tins of soup and packets of biscuits and coffee and tea in the wall-cupboards, and milk and orange juice and yoghurt and butter in the large pink refrigerator. But few meals were prepared there: mostly they ate out. The pale-pink walls, the cream and yellow lino, the pale-yellow curtains, the big Moffat cooker inside and out were as if new. There was a refuse disposer and a dishwasher, but they were almost superfluous; there were weeks when the whole of the washing-up amounted to only a few knives, cups, saucers, glasses, and tea plates, and the whole of the rubbish to a few apple cores, orange skins, and yoghurt cartons.

As he lit a cigarette he momentarily felt cold and lonely and found himself remembering Hilary sitting at the other end of that very table last summer eating apple strudel from the delicatessen in Kensington High Street, followed by a homemade Knickerbocker Glory, all on top of about a pound of beef and pork at the Carvery in the Strand and Coca-Cola and candy floss at the Battersea Pleasure Gardens. The kitchen had seemed very different then; it was wonderful seeing the amount of mess a nine-year-old boy could create. He hadn't taken Hilary to the house again, because after he'd gone he'd been too upset, the child's high piping voice had seemed to hang about the kitchen, he could see the large dark eyes intent upon spooning out the layers of fruit and cream and ice cream, see the long thin fingers – he had his mother's hands – round the glass. It didn't matter about taking the child to the Carvery and the Battersea Pleasure Gardens; he would only go to these places in his company. But he had to live in this house.

He suppressed a sudden aching desire for a drink: eleven o'clock was too early and he had in any case to drive over two hundred miles. Instead he made himself another cup of coffee and took it into the studio. The previous owner had actually been an artist; it was a very large room with a parquet floor lit by a picture window at one end. The wallpaper was dark-red flock. Only Jean could have managed to make it seem over-full; there was a profusion of little tables, cabinets, big armchairs, two big sofas, four big chests-of-drawers, a big dining table, six dining chairs, two carvers, a long sideboard, far too many rugs and far too many pictures on the walls. The furniture was predominantly dark; but for the sunlight pouring in through the picture window, the effect would have been depressing. One of these days, he thought as he settled down in the shabbiest and most comfortable armchair, she'd realize it, and down would come the dark-red wallpaper, out would go all the dark furniture, and in would come the trendy wallpaper in pastel colours, in would come steel and beech and leather and inflatable plastic. There, or in another house, or, more likely, a flat. She didn't seem likely to have any children, unless she had one just to show that she could do it.

He recognized the onset of depression; if he stayed in the house any longer he'd have a drink and then he'd be forced to go by train and he'd have more drinks on the train and, though he wouldn't be drunk when he met Jack Byrock his brain wouldn't exactly be razor-edged.

At the wheel of the Jaguar on the M1 the depression began to lift. The Jaguar was provided by the company; it was the 2·5 model, the next step up in the scale being the XJ6 or a Rover 3½ litre. Taxes being what they were, some extra incentives had to be provided; his promotion was recent enough to make driving the Jaguar extremely agreeable. It was a visible status symbol at the studios and, when he came to think of it, a way of being one up over the Government. And it was a nice car; a little old-fashioned, but fast enough for him, with an interior opulent with walnut and leather. This in the end was what counted – the tangible rewards, the tangible pleasures and, above all, moving, always moving, moving away from himself at a steady eighty, moving away from the not very palatable suspicions of Jean having an affair with Seamus, and the even more unpalatable suspicion that he didn't care if she did, moving away from the memory of his son at the other end of the kitchen table, moving away at a steady eighty, his mind emptying itself of thought.

Six

'No, not the Danish,' Robin said. 'The garlic sausage. *The garlic sausage*. To your left.' She shifted her weight from one foot to the other, but her feet still hurt. She liked this little delicatessen shop by the Charbury Market; it smelled sharp and spicy and stocked cooked meats and sausages and relishes you couldn't get anywhere else. But today, after a frustrating afternoon when nothing she wanted seemed available, she was beginning to wonder if in future it wouldn't be better to hand over all the catering for Clive's next birthday party to a catering firm. She felt hot and sweaty; it was more like June than March. The weight of her shopping bag felt as if it were dragging her arm out of its socket; and when she put it down it wouldn't stay upright, a fact which evidently caused the girl behind the counter some amusement because for the first time since Robin had entered the shop her dark face broke into a smile.

And what have you to smile about with that big nose and greasy skin and all those gold fillings? Robin thought viciously. The girl cut off a piece of garlic sausage, weighed it, and began to wrap it up.

'Sliced, please,' Robin said. The smile left the girl's face. It returned when a middle-aged woman, another Pole, entered; the girl said something in Polish, and began to laugh.

It wasn't any use saying anything; as Clive often remarked, whenever it suited them they simply said *Me no understand*, though they understood quickly enough when it was to their advantage. The garlic sausage was added to the little pile of purchases and Robin mentally totted up the bill, rather to her disappointment found it correct, and rammed the packages into her shopping bag impatiently, remembering too late that there were two boxes of meringue cases on top.

Outside the street was crowded and, to judge by the number of people who bumped into her, she seemed to have become invisible. There were no taxis available in this part of Charbury and it was a good half-mile walk to the car park; the street was full of the smell of meat and fish and rotting vegetables and she felt momentarily sick. Her tweed suit and sheepskin jacket, which she'd needed when she set out, were now too warm for her, and the straps of the shopping bag were cutting into her hand.

She didn't come very often to Charbury and bought most of her ordinary requirements in Hailton. But she'd had a fitting at Tarlton's in Charbury that afternoon, Tarlton's being the only dress shop in the district where there was a decent choice, and there had been a coffee morning she couldn't put off, and it had seemed best to do the shopping for the party in Charbury, so she could have the day clear tomorrow. Besides, there were some things, like the garlic sausage and the ham sausage and the mortadella and the blood sausage, which just weren't available in Hailton. And she'd fancied a trip to Charbury; it made a change, and lately she'd been getting into a rut. But she hadn't enjoyed herself; today for some reason it seemed too dirty, too crowded, too smelly; she'd had a bath that morning, but she'd need another when she returned home.

She stopped to shift the bag to the other hand and then found that a package was slipping out. A man had stopped too and was staring at her. He had a black nylon fur coat and short dark hair and though he wasn't very tall – no taller than her – wasn't bad-looking if you liked the dark saturnine type.

'Robin,' he said, and put out his hand. 'It is Robin, isn't it?'

The hand was square, hairy, with stubby fingers; it had been over twenty years since she'd touched it or it, rather, had touched her.

'Stephen Belgard,' he said. 'The BBC. You haven't changed, Robin.'

'You've changed,' she said. 'You're much smarter than you used to be.'

He picked up her shopping bag. 'Was I very scruffy?'

'Hairy tweeds and coloured shirts.' Seeing him on TV – and the last time was over two years ago – hadn't prepared her for the shock: you couldn't feel anything for a mono-chrome image, couldn't connect it with a flesh-and-blood man who'd once made love to you. To her consternation she found herself beginning to be overcome by an ab-solutely explicit need to touch and be touched by him. It was absurd: order and calm and tidiness were suddenly broken into, the bull was snorting and bellowing in the china-shop.

'That was before nylon,' he said. 'And wash-and-wear—' He broke off, and took hold of her hand, and they stood silent for a moment. 'There's a lot we don't need to say, isn't there?'

She nodded, squeezing his hand.

'We'll have a drink,' he said.

She laughed. 'I was wrong. You haven't changed. You don't say *Would you like a drink*? You say *We'll have a drink.*'

'I've got very bossy,' he said. 'Drunk with power.'

He steered her down an alleyway at the top of the street and into a pub.

'This is quite respectable,' he said. Inside the pub it was very quiet. The room was low-ceilinged with blackened oak rafters and plain white walls with prints of old Charbury. There wasn't very much light let in through the four small lace-curtained windows let into the thick walls; she was grateful for this and for the hop-scented coolness of the place. She leaned back on the red upholstered bench that ran the length of the wall and eased her feet half out of her shoes.

Stephen came back from the bar with a gin-and-orange and a pint of bitter and sat down opposite her.

'You see, I remember.'

'I might have changed my tastes.'

'If there's something else—' He looked anxious and she didn't like him to look anxious. Self-assurance, down to the most minor matters, was part of him.

'No, that's fine.'

'You married Clive?' he asked as she took off her gloves. She nodded. 'We have three children. Two boys and a girl. The eldest's twenty.'

'Christ, that makes me feel old … But you don't look any older. You've still that marvellous skin.'

'It's the water,' she said. 'The soft water … You're married too.'

'Twice. An actress each time.' He put on a Yorkshire accent. 'Some fowk nivver learn … I had a son by my first. He's nine now. Lives with his mother.'

'You don't write these days. Or did I miss something?'

He grimaced. 'You missed nothing. I'm an executive now, honey. I corrupt writers. I'm here specially to corrupt one, in fact.'

'Are you really?' The question was serious; she wanted to know, as she wanted to know everything about him.

'I'm going to persuade him to stop writing not very successful novels and to write successful TV plays instead. And to leave Charbury University for London. You don't really care, do you?'

'Not really,' she said. 'As long as you're doing what you want to do.'

He put his hand on hers; it was very warm and dry. His nails were gleamingly manicured now; she wasn't sure that she liked the change.

'You're as calm as ever,' he said. She didn't draw her hand away; the worst of it was, she thought dazedly, that she wouldn't have drawn it away wherever they'd been.

'Not really,' she said. 'Perhaps I'm growing tired of it. Of being calm and well-balanced. Of being surrounded by calm and well-balanced people. Do you ever feel like that?'

'I'm never surrounded by calm and well-balanced people,' he said. 'In fact, I don't think I know any.' He took out a packet of cigarettes from his trouser pocket, put two in his mouth, lit them, and handed one to her.

'Tyrone Power used to do that,' she said. 'Will you give me those cigarettes? I'll buy you some more.'

He handed her over the packet. She put it away in her handbag. He watched her intently, and she knew that he realized why she wanted them. She gave him a ten-shilling note and he put it in his breast pocket, then went over to the bar and returned with a packet of the same kind and some change, which he handed to her.

'It's nice to have beautiful women buy me cigarettes,' he said. 'I'm not used to it. Every time I as much as look at a woman it costs me money.'

'I never cost you much,' she said.

'No, you didn't. You didn't seem to want anything at all.' He spoke in so low a voice that she had to strain to hear him.

'Are you here for long?'

'I'm going back on Sunday.' He looked at a wafer-thin

watch on a heavy gold bracelet. 'I have to meet this *bâtard incroyable* of a writer at seven.'

'I was going to invite you home with me. To meet my husband. And my children. It's my husband's birthday tomorrow. He's forty-seven.'

'Has he worn as well as me?'

'Oh yes. Clive's a very handsome man. I take good care of him.'

'I know you will.' He had taken off his topcoat; she could see that his suit was of a lightweight material she'd not seen before, with a high sheen on it. It was very smart, but she hoped that he wouldn't catch cold; it was like summer today but it could snow tomorrow.

'You'll come to the party tomorrow?' She caught his left leg between her calves under the table; the pub was filling up now with people mostly in grubby white coats and obviously from the market. She opened her handbag and took out a visiting card. He took it from her; his hand was trembling.

'What time, Robin?'

'Eight.'

'I want to stay here.'

'You've nice time to get back to your hotel and freshen up before you meet the *bâtard incroyable*. Are you at the Grand?'

He nodded.

'I'll phone you in the morning.'

'Why didn't we meet before?'

She stood up and began to put on her gloves.

'That's a silly question,' she said, her voice not very steady. 'It is a silly question, isn't it?'

Seven

Clive was wearing a new fawn suit with a blue pinhead pattern, a pale-blue polo-necked cambric shirt and a handkerchief and socks to match, and sealskin shoes. On his right wrist, rather selfconsciously, he had a gold identity bracelet. The shirt and the handkerchief and the socks were Petronella's present, the identity bracelet, Robin's. He had had his doubts about the matching of shirt, socks and handkerchief but Petronella had put so much thought into the gift that he hadn't the heart to leave one item out as he felt that he should have done. It was at least a present he could use: already he'd been given three bottles of cologne all expensive and exotic, and guaranteed to give him dermatitis for the rest of his life. And there would no doubt be more to come when the guests began to arrive. And bottles of liquor of a kind he didn't drink and cigar-cutters for the cigars he virtually never smoked and pen-stands and electric backscratchers and ties he wouldn't wear – but he still had a childish delight in being given presents, always found his birthday exciting.

Robin and Petronella and Joan had been busy since early morning; they hadn't let him do anything to help but every time he'd sat down with a book they'd moved him out of his chair. The house now was almost unnaturally tidy with every visible inch dusted and polished, not to mention what wasn't visible. Lunch had been cold ham and tongue, eaten in a desperate hurry, tea had been merely a cup of tea. He wondered as he always wondered on the eve of parties, whether it was really worth it, whether the party was to celebrate his birthday or to show their friends what a splendid house they had and what a splendid housewife Robin was.

Now at a quarter to eight she and Petronella were upstairs still dressing and he was walking aimlessly round the house, coming to a stop in the entrance hall. He sat down on the sofa there and lit a cigarette. Half-guiltily he tapped the ash into an ashtray on the coffee table beside the sofa. The ashtray had been washed that morning together with every other ashtray in the house; the blackened match was a jarring note.

Robin came downstairs in a red dress which revealed a great deal of her legs and breasts.

'What are you sitting there for looking so gloomy?' she asked. 'Come in the study and have a drink.'

He whistled. 'I haven't seen that before.'

'You weren't supposed to.' She looked at him anxiously. 'Do you think it's too young for me?'

He poured her a large gin and then added ice and a spoonful of tonic. 'You look about twenty,' he said. 'Just old enough to be interesting.' He took the drink over to her and leaned over and kissed her. 'Let's cancel the party and go to bed.'

'Nobody would see the dress then, silly.' She moved her face away. 'Be careful, or you'll mess up my hair.'

'You're dressing up for someone else,' he said. 'Is it Gerry?'

'I've known him too long,' she said. 'Besides, I don't fancy him. A two-minute wonder, he is. In and out.'

'Good God,' Clive said, pouring himself a whisky. 'How did you know that?'

'Fiona, of course. She told me the other night.'

'Christ, when women let their hair down they really let their hair down. What do you say about me?' With her new dress her mood had changed, she was no longer the harassed housewife but, and he wasn't being sentimental, the girl he'd married.

'I make them all envious,' she said. She held out her glass. 'Give me another before the thirsty horde arrives. At it night and day, I tell them. Always ready and more than ready.'

'If I see any of the women looking at me curiously, I'll know, won't I?'

'Oh, you look very smart too; thirty-five at the most.'

'I don't know about this bracelet,' he said. 'They'll think I've turned queer.'

'You keep it on, or I won't sleep with you again. Think yourself lucky I didn't give you a medallion. That's what's really trendy now.'

'Not in Hailton it isn't. They've only just caught up with wristwatches and collar-attached shirts.'

'You're very difficult to buy presents for,' she said. 'You seem to have everything.'

It was then that his discontent began. He didn't mind her saying it, but it wasn't true. There was something that his life lacked, just as there was something this big tidy room lacked, that, in fact, the whole house lacked. It had been there when the Major and his wife lived there, but it wasn't there now. There wasn't the feeling that there was a world outside. There wasn't the feeling of limitless possibilities existing. He didn't want to change his life; but he wanted to feel that he could if the mood took him. He wanted some excitement, but more than mere titillation; he wanted the real thing, the throat-constricting battlefield excitement. If he didn't change now, he'd never change, time would move faster and faster, he'd awake one morning to find his hands knotted and useless, his limbs wasted, waiting for death with a querulous impatience.

Half an hour and two more whiskies later he felt more cheerful. The study was nearly full and more people were arriving; the atmosphere of the whole house had changed. Some houses don't welcome crowds and noise; Tower House wasn't one of them.

Most of the guests came from Hailton and had left their cars behind. These were already perceptibly drinking more than those who had come from a greater distance. The event was far from being an orgy, but the cost of the drink alone wasn't far short of a hundred pounds, which, considering that several of the guests were teetotal, meant that some heavy drinking was being done. But so far, over the sixteen years they'd been having these parties, there hadn't been any disasters. Someone was always sick – and astoundingly enough tonight it was going to be his own brother Donald – but so far they'd always managed to make it to the bathroom. And even before the breathalyser neither he nor Robin had ever allowed anyone to drive home who was in no condition to do so.

And someone always made a pass at someone which they'd been saving up all year; but so far he'd not heard of anything resulting from these passes. He had himself made the odd pass but it had never amounted to much more than a quick kiss. He didn't know about Robin but, despite what she'd said, he was sure she'd somehow manage to be alone with Gerry Sindram for a few minutes; tomorrow it would be forgotten.

Though most of the guests were neighbours it was extra-ordinary how many didn't know each other and how many married couples stuck grimly together, which could be death to a party; he and Robin for an hour kept on the move, breaking up married couples, introducing people to each other, watching out for guests standing apart, until at last the party had an impetus of its own, became a kind of cere-mony.

He struggled with the thought, then found Ruth beside him in a gold lamé trouser suit. Her cheeks were flushed and her eyes bright; suddenly he wanted to run his hand over the glossy chestnut hair, touch the full breasts. It was strange that he hadn't noticed it before, but her eyes were blue-green, sea-green, drowning green.

'You've not being a very good host,' she said. 'Standing looking Byronic in that rather camp polo shirt. Entertain me.'

'I was thinking,' he said.

She smiled.

'It hurts a bit at first, but then becomes quite pleasurable.'

'I was thinking that if a lot of people bath and shave and scent themselves and put on their nicest clothes and then get together, you have a ceremony. People, that is, not androids.'

Androids were robots constructed to look and behave exactly like human beings, with every human function except reproduction. Android-spotting had started as a joke between them; it was fast becoming a bond.

'You have the *makings* of a ceremony,' she said. 'If after that all you do is eat and drink and talk about trivialities and flirt, you just have a party. Perhaps that's what is wrong with Western civilization.'

'You think we should have a hymn? Or a sacrifice?' He was still fascinated by her eyes: they seemed to change colour as she moved.

'You're an odd man,' she said.

'Why am I odd?'

'You're growing, aren't you? You keep on understanding a bit more. I wonder what you'd have been if your father hadn't left you the mill?'

'A commercial traveller. Or a layabout. Or an Army officer. I rather enjoyed that, actually.'

'You're trying to shock me.'

'Why do I shock you?'

'Saying you wouldn't mind being a professional killer.'

He laughed. 'I enjoyed the war. It's a question of luck.'

'My father always said that.' It was the first time she'd ever referred to her family. 'Get me a big whisky, Clive.'

He went to the table where Joan's sister Enid was serving the drinks. Standing nearby talking to Walter Fareland was a tall woman in a low-cut white dress, which made the most of her rather small breasts. She had an attractively husky voice and a big mouth which she didn't make the mistake of trying to disguise. It was big, but it was firmly held, and her teeth were good; but what held him, held him staring beyond the bounds of politeness, was the intelligence in her eyes. They were a startling blue, almost too big for her rather narrow face. It wasn't a conventionally pretty face, and half the women in the room had the same light brown hair, but it wasn't a face, he thought with surprise, that you'd grow tired of looking at, or a voice you'd grow tired of listening to. She smiled at him and he returned the smile. It was, he recollected, his neighbour, Vicky Kelvedon, from one of the new houses at the bottom of the road. Robin had invited her.

'What pretty eyes you have,' he said. 'You're Vicky Kelvedon, aren't you? I'm your host, Clive Lendrick.' He held out his hand. Her hand was very thin with long fingers. It was very cool: for a moment he felt large and clumsy and sweaty.

'Your wife's very kind,' she said. 'In fact, everyone here's been very friendly.'

'A pleasure,' he said. 'Excuse me for the moment.' He slapped Walter's shoulder. 'See you look after her, Walter.'

When he gave Ruth the whisky, she took half of it at one gulp.

'I needed that,' she said. 'Who were you talking to?'

'A new neighbour. Vicky Kelvedon.'

She looked over at Vicky Kelvedon, her eyes cold and appraising.

'Don't, Clive.'

'Don't what?'

'Are you my friend?'

'I hope so,' he said, rather touched.

'Do you listen to your friends?'

'Sometimes.'

'Clive, I've had a great deal more experience than you, even though you're nearly old enough to be my father. Don't. You know what's in your mind. Don't.'

'Have you met her before?'

She shook her head. 'I've got eyes and I've got ears.'

'You needn't worry,' he said, 'I'm all for a quiet life.'

'Do you believe you have any choice in the matter?'

Robin was introducing Donald to the small dark man with a blue chin, Stephen Belgard, whom Robin had introduced to him as being high up in TV. He'd been on TV quite a lot once; it was curious how people like that always seemed smaller and dimmer in the flesh. Donald caught sight of Ruth and came over to them. He was walking a fraction unsteadily. With a malicious pleasure Clive noted that his hair was definitely thinning and that he had wrinkles on his face which he, Clive, hadn't.

Donald kissed Ruth on the mouth.

'You're smashing,' he said. 'Why should my big brother monopolize you?' Keeping his arm round Ruth's waist, he glared accusingly at Clive. 'Where's the big eats, Clive? My belly thinks its throat is cut.'

'Robin will give the signal,' Clive said. He felt a rush of affection for Donald. Whatever manner he was affecting – cool efficiency at work, which always appeared as a grumpy fussiness, or breezy bonhomie as now – it never quite succeeded. It wouldn't be like that with that little TV chap, who, Robin having now left the room, was chatting up Fiona Sindram with some degree of success to judge from her peals of laughter.

'I've seen that bugger somewhere before,' Donald said.

'He was almost a TV personality. Robin was his secretary once when he worked for the BBC.'

'You'd better watch out,' Donald said. 'The women seem to like him.'

'He's going back to London tomorrow. Robin ran across him in Charbury yesterday.'

'That's a wash-n'-wear suit he has on. It's the coming material but do you think the bloody Board'll listen?'

'Stop worrying, Don, and have another drink.'

His son Roger joined Fiona and Stephen Belgard; Clive felt proud of the way that the boy carried himself. He was fair like his brother but, despite his apparent nonchalance, felt more deeply; Clive was afraid that he was beginning to fall in love with Fiona who, in a backless green cocktail dress, with her red hair newly tinted, looking more like thirty than forty, was exactly the sort of woman a boy of eighteen would choose to dream over. Not that he'd get much further than dreaming; Fiona was a bit of a teaser.

Gerry Sindram was talking to Robin. Bulky and cheerful, with a nose broken from Army boxing, Gerry was always at his most cheerful when with Robin. It wouldn't be long before Fiona would notice it and, without being obvious about it would break up the tête-à-tête. And now she was going over to them and Roger was joining his brother at the drinks table. George, now, wouldn't waste any time over teasers: from what he'd been able to observe, George only bothered with those women who would deliver.

'Nice place you've got here.' He recognized the speaker, a thin, sandy-haired man in his early forties, as Bruce Kelvedon, the husband of Vicky.

'Thank you. We're very fond of it.'

'Vicky and I really would prefer something like this, but the firm shifts us from pillar to post. A bit more salary each time, but still ...'

He had a suit in the same material as Belgard, but in a dark blue: another travelling man. Clive found that he didn't like him; there was something rather inhuman about him. He was obviously an android; he wondered if Ruth had spotted him too.

He played too many games with Ruth, he thought, with an effort turning his attention to Kelvedon, who was after all his guest and a new neighbour. The games led to nothing and he was content that they should lead to nothing, but it was wrong that he should be content.

'You're in computers, aren't you?' Donald asked. 'Someone mentioned your firm the other day. Bloody good thing for Charbury. We need new industries. Too many eggs in one basket.'

'I suppose I am in computers in a sense,' Kelvedon said, his tone indicating that this was a crude and illiterate way to put it. 'Let's say that I look into production problems right at the beginning. Some of the problems can appear terribly complex, but they aren't really.' His manner indicated that the problems would only appear complex to people like Donald or, for that matter, like Clive.

'Oh, all our problems are simple, aren't they, Don?' he said to his brother. 'In fact, there's only one. Will people buy what we make?'

Kelvedon's smile was cold. 'We could give you the answer to that question soon enough, if we had all the data.'

'I bet you could.' Clive remembered something he had read in an American book which Ruth had lent him. 'Here's a question for your computer. Epimondas the Cretan says all Cretans are liars. True or false?'

'Ah, I was talking about production problems.' The smile this time was a trifle warmer. Clive was no longer to be written off as an uneducated woolman.

Robin struck the gong in the hall – only used for parties – and Donald instantly left the room. Kelvedon looked startled.

'Supper,' Clive explained. 'Excuse me, old man, I must have a word with my wife.'

Robin was already busy separating husbands from wives, so that every woman had an escort.

'The next party,' she said, 'we'll have cards and then no one will have any excuse to be with their spouse all evening. You'd think they'd welcome a change ... I hope you don't imagine you're going to be with me for supper, Clive. I've already chosen.' She put her arm around Belgard's waist. 'Have you got yourself someone, then? I can guess who.' She looked over at Ruth.

'Then you'd guess wrong,' Clive said. He went over to Vicky Kelvedon, for a moment feeling a nervous seventeen. Ruth's face was expressionless, but Bruce Kelvedon went over to her and she gave him a social smile.

'Let me get you some supper,' he said to Vicky Kelvedon, and took her arm.

'I thought no one would ask me,' she said.

'I made my mind up as soon as I saw you.'

'I thought you were keen on that girl in the trouser suit.'

He found her a place on the window seat in the dining-room. 'She's merely a friend.'

She put her handbag down on the window seat and took a plate from him. The long mahogany dining table had all four leaves in and extended nearly the full length of the dining-room.

'That's what you say.'

The table was full of serving-dishes of cold chicken, ham, garlic sausage, mortadella, brisket, ham-and-veal pies, pork pies, cold roast pork, hard-boiled eggs, pickled onions, pickled cucumbers, beetroot salad, corn salad, mushroom salad, hot sausages, mushroom patties, shrimp patties, Cheshire cheese, gorgonzola cheese, Danish Blue, crocks of butter, French loaves, bowls of fruit, and jugs of cream.

On a side table stood enough bottles of hock and Beaujolais and orange juice and lemonade and tomato juice and pineapple juice to quench the thirst of twice the number of guests.

'I'll tell you about her some other time.' He noticed that her plate was piled high with meat only. 'Don't you like salad?'

'It's my diet. Just protein.'

'Very nice too.'

'It works,' she said, and began eating with an elegant wolfishness using her fingers for the chicken leg. Her body felt very warm beside him on the window seat.

'This is a marvellous room,' she said.

The dining-room was very large, larger than the study, half oak panelled with a magnificent tiled fireplace in which now roared a huge fire; the weather had turned cold and there might even be frost tonight. Even with the card-tables which they'd borrowed the proportions of the room could be seen to be good; on the plate shelf where the original picture-rail had run stood rows of old plates and crockery and china figures chosen by Robin for no other reason that that she liked the look of them. The four small pictures on the wall nearest the door were original Flax-mans; the room wasn't austere, or gloomy, it had spaciousness and dignity, but it had comfort too.

'We generally eat in the kitchen,' he said. 'But it's nice to have a decent room which you don't use every day.'

'I know,' she said. 'We've just the kitchen and one big room and a tiny tiny study. Not that we entertain at home very much. I'm a lousy cook.'

'Robin said you had two boys.'

'Angus and Keith, fourteen and sixteen. They're both away at school. So I haven't much to do most of the time. I could work, but it really isn't worth it because of the tax. That's a good way of telling you that Bruce earns a lot of money, isn't it?'

'I expect it is,' he said, amused.

'He's enormously clever. He was a lecturer when I met

him. Mathematics. Very pure mathematics. Did you know what the basis of computers is?'

'You tell me.'

'They're stupid. We think in tens and they think in twos. That's all there is to it, Bruce says. It's just as well, because it's all I know.'

'It's all I know too.'

'He's rather a sod, is Bruce at times. He's not very pleased with me tonight. He thinks I've been drinking too much.'

'I hadn't noticed it.'

'I don't think you would. You're rather obtuse in a nice way. Most men don't notice things. Now Bruce does.'

'You'll be sorry tomorrow.'

'Oh no I won't. I make it a rule never to be sorry for anything. Do what you want to do, say what you want to say, and don't even feel guilty.'

'It's an attractive idea.'

'Yes, it is, isn't it? I bet you never thought of it before.'

Her dress had a deep slit behind; he saw running down her back the faintest fuzz of fair hair, visible only when she turned half towards him.

He wanted her and he knew already that she would be bad for him. It was like his passion for seafood: he'd learned to resist it, but every now and again he'd decide that a bowlful of *moules marinière* followed by lobster or crab was worth feeling like death for a day afterwards. He put the thought out of his head: he was merely going to flirt with her, to sniff the seafood – subtly sweet, subtly salty, subtly aromatic like some marine rose. He wouldn't taste, he was too sensible not to realize what that would lead to. But from that moment onwards she was never long out of his mind.

'I'm too respectable to be in that position,' he said. 'The question has never come up.'

'Not with a good-looking man like you? Surely you've had offers?'

'I'll bring you some wine,' he said.

'Red, please. But surely you have?'

'I'll tell you some other time,' he said when he returned with the Burgundy.

'All for us?'

'All for us.'

'Your girlfriend in the trouser suit keeps on looking at us,' she said happily.

'She's my friend, not my girlfriend.'

'Pull the other leg, it's got bells on.'

She had very good legs, strong and straight with slim ankles and through her sheer stockings no hair was visible. She might have been sent expressly to match his mood of dissatisfaction, to allay it with no harm done; she was too free-spoken to be serious. Those who do, he thought, don't talk about it, those who talk about it, don't do.

But soon the party would enter its final phase and he'd put on the record-player and turn the lights down in the hall and he'd dance with her and perhaps if the chance presented itself make love, very gently, and tomorrow there'd be nothing to remember except that husky voice and the smell of her hair and the feel of that line of down on her back. That would be quite enough. He listened to her chattering on, a faint indulgent smile on his face, a handsome well-dressed healthy man in the prime of life enjoying a mild flirtation, the calm surface of his life unbroken and apparently impregnable.

Eight

When Stephen woke up in the hotel room the morning after it was with a feeling of extraordinary elation. He felt the elation before he remembered its cause; the plain buff walls of his room, the black Gideon Bible, the plain cream fitted wardrobe and the dull-red carpet didn't, as normally they would have done, depress him, but instead provided as it were a neutral background for him to see his state of mind to better advantage.

When he remembered Robin's signal at the party, pre-arranged over the telephone, the elation persisted. In some ways it had been no different from twenty years ago. In these situations one was supposed to feel nothing or feel distaste, like Arthur Clennam and Flora; but Robin after twenty years was better-looking, not worse-looking, wiser not sillier, entirely grown-up.

He had felt her breasts and put his hand under her skirt. She swore and pulled him on top of her on the bed. 'Don't mess about,' she had whispered. 'Quick, quick.' And it had been quick; in his nervousness he'd come almost immediately upon penetration, but then so had she, biting her hand so that she wouldn't cry out.

He'd left her then and had gone into the loo across the passage from the bedroom and, with the door bolted, had rested his head against the tiled wall, overwhelmed by a sensation of complete fulfilment in which there was no tinge of regret or shame or satiety. He had done this sort of thing at parties and not so long ago, but then there had been some attempt at embellishment, some word, some gesture that was the equivalent of the frill round the lamb chop, the lemon and the parsley on the fish. He hadn't ever encountered sex in so terribly prosaic and unadorned a form before; words like *excitement, pleasure, ecstasy* didn't even begin to describe it. It was more like getting a bullet in the belly than making love and yet in that one quick thrust he'd been closer to her than he'd ever been to anyone. And that was a trouble in store. He wouldn't be content with substitutes again. After fresh salmon with its clean taste of rivers and the sea, its delicate richness, you could never stomach even the smell of tinned salmon again. But it was a question, wasn't it, of what was available?

As she put down the tray of tea and the *Observer* and *The Sunday Times* and *The Sunday Telegraph* by his bed-side the chambermaid, a middle-aged woman with harlequin spectacles and a grim mouth, stared at him for a moment.

'I've seen you on t'telly,' she said.

'I hope I don't disappoint you,' he said, giving her an automatic social smile.

'You look younger on t'telly,' she said accusingly.

'It's make-up,' he said. 'They can do wonders with make-up.'

'Nay, you don't look all that bad. Just a bit older, that's all.'

It didn't seem to occur to her that no one likes to be told at eight o'clock on a Sunday morning with the church bells chiming that he looks older than they'd thought: she was living up to her character as a plain-spoken Yorkshire woman, never afraid to speak her mind. If he'd told her that those spectacles and that pale-pink lipstick didn't really suit her, what would have been her reaction?

'I *have* disappointed you,' he said. 'I'm sorry.'

'You're not on much these days though, are you?'

'I work behind the scenes now,' he said.

She snorted, whether to indicate disgust or approval he couldn't tell.

'That's where the money is,' she said. 'Well, I must get on.'

He poured himself a cup of tea and took two plain biscuits from a packet in the drawer of the bedside table. This was part of a ritual; he liked to have a cigarette with his morning tea, but had a horror of smoking on an empty stomach. He ate the biscuits with the tea then lit a cigarette and poured himself a second cup and opened the *Observer*.

The phone rang.

'Stephen? Sorry if I disturb your slumber, sweetie, but on the other hand you might be setting off early. Or you might have to see the *bâtard incroyable* again.'

'No, that's all fixed.'

'I'm overjoyed for you, honey, honestly I am. So are you coming back today?'

The room was full of sunlight; he could see the motes of dust dancing in the draught from the partly open window.

'I expect so.'

103

Her voice held a note of asperity. 'You don't seem very keen. Found a bird up there? An old flame?'

'They've all burned themselves out, darling. I'm still a bit sleepy, that's all. Where are you?'

'Moira's place, of course. Why don't you come down and pick me up? They'd love to see you.'

He wondered who else had been at Moira's place. Moira, some thirty years ago, had been a blonde *ingénue* in steady, work because her good looks were of the kind which instantly and obviously appealed. She married a man thirty years older than herself, a stockbroker, and left the theatre. He had died ten years ago and left Moira a rich woman. She'd always kept up an interest in the theatre and had even backed two plays, both investments paying off. But what she was really interested in was getting people into bed together who, strictly speaking, had no business to be in bed together. And Moira was the natural confidant when complications resulted, as they generally did. There were some who thought her a very evil woman, but he himself inclined to the view that she acted as an unpaid madam simply to fend off boredom and loneliness.

'I'll be there soon after lunch,' he said.

'All righty, honey. Love you.'

'Love you,' he said, and hung up.

'Fuck that for a tale,' he said under his breath, and returned to the papers. He read quickly, saving *The Sunday Telegraph* for his breakfast. He erased Robin from his mind, but with some difficulty, telling himself that it wasn't a man who'd poked her, but an image from the magic box, that he'd probably been a figure in her daydreams for some twenty years, that above all, she'd simply wanted a little adventure, a last fling before the menopause. Or perhaps the first of many last flings. If he was going to go through the business of a divorce again, he'd at least find himself a nice little dolly girl with no encumbrances; London was full of them and by a merciful dispensation of providence as a man grew older he became more attractive to them. No one, unless they were extremely perspicacious – would envy him the possession of Robin. The majority of men would envy him his possession of a twenty-year-old, envy him fiercely and flatteringly. And he wasn't yet quite old enough to run the risk of appearing comically besotted – or rich enough either.

He was drying himself after his bath when the phone rang.

'Stephen. I'm phoning from a call box. When are you coming again?'

'I told you. A month.'

He found his voice trembling.

'I've just thought – I can come to London next week. Will you be there?'

'I'll be there.'

'I'll phone you. I do love you, Stephen. I must go now.'

'I love you,' he said, and she hung up.

He put the phone down as if relinquishing a great weight.

'Oh Christ,' he said loudly and savagely. 'I do. I really am afraid I do.'

Nine

'But you promised,' Vicky said.

'My dear girl, I said I would if I could.' Bruce drained his coffee cup and then dabbed at his mouth with his napkin. The napkin was always dry afterwards; it was a habit of his which never failed to annoy her.

'I wanted to see it. It's too bad of you.'

'I've already explained to you that Head Office has instructed that every courtesy' – he snickered – 'be shown to this customer. He has expressed his desire for night life. What night life there is in the West Riding I propose to show to him. Think yourself lucky that I don't bring him home to dinner at five minutes' notice.'

'It's always the same,' she said. 'Anything I want, I can't have, no matter how small.'

'On the contrary, you get everything you want. Clothes, things for the house, trips to London, cigarettes, vodka – you name it, you've got it.' He folded his napkin. 'You get everything you want because I work like an African slave. No one, but no one, has ever given me a damned thing. So, my dear little dunderhead, work comes first. Or do you propose that I should tell Head Office I can't do as they ask because my wife wants to go to the pictures?'

She lit a cigarette. 'You could have someone else show him some night life.'

'He's perfectly well aware of the grades of seniority within the firm. He'll take it as a personal insult if I send an underling.'

She put the spent match in her saucer; without a word he got up, took the cup and saucer away, and gave her an ashtray.

'Oh, do as you like. But you could have told me last night. In fact, you could have taken me last night.'

He stood up abruptly, glanced round the kitchen with a faint air of disapproval and glanced at his watch. 'Last night I wanted a quiet night at home. I was tired. I do get tired sometimes. One thing you seem quite unable to understand is that I have needs.' He folded the *Yorkshire Post* neatly and put it in his briefcase. She followed him to the door.

'Might I ask when you'll be back?'

'That depends upon Mr Cyril Gibson of Chicago. He may weaken early – he's not as young as he was – and on the other hand he may carry on into the small hours.'

'You should just get him a tart and a bottle of whisky and leave him to it.'

'I would gladly but that doesn't seem to be quite what he wants. Expect me when you see me then.' He pecked her cheek; she went back into the kitchen and saw him drive off out of the corner of her eye.

A breeze rattled the window; she looked outside idly and saw Clive Lendrick's Mercedes come out of the drive of

Tower House opposite. He looked pink and healthy and cheerful, the sort of man who always kept his promises. They'd had him and his wife in for drinks a fortnight after the party and the one thing she'd noticed about him was his unfailing kindness.

She emptied the teapot into the sink. She knew that Bruce hated to see it, because in time it choked up the kitchen sink outlet. It was a little act of rebellion to cheer herself up, because without her car it was going to be a lousy day. It was her own fault that the garage was keeping the car for so long, as Bruce had hastened to point out; she never could remember to take it in for servicing at the proper time, so as a result all sorts of complicated things went wrong with it.

She cleared the table of the breakfast dishes and cutlery and washed them up and put them away. It didn't take her very long; neither she nor Bruce ever had any more than orange juice, one slice of toast, coffee for him, and tea for her. But when the boys were home she cooked them a proper breakfast every morning and Bruce ate it too.

Her father, progressive though he was, was paying for the boys' education. If he hadn't, Bruce mightn't have gone so far so fast; she knew, for instance, that he wouldn't have got this last promotion but for the fact that the man originally in line for the job had been too firmly and happily entrenched in Surrey with all his children going to good day schools.

She sat down at the kitchen table and lit a cigarette. Then she rose and switched on the little transistor radio that stood on the kitchen bench. She would smoke the cigarette and half-listen to the radio whilst she planned what to do with the day. But it wasn't much use planning anything now that the car wouldn't be ready until tomorrow. And the plans which she had made all centred upon getting to see *The Secret Life of an American Wife* tonight which now she wouldn't see because tomorrow was Saturday and she and Bruce were giving yet another visiting American dinner. From the sound of him he'd be about a hundred years old and teetotal into the bargain. Bruce never seemed to have to do business with any of these thrusting dynamic Power Game types or if he did he went out on the town with them, stag.

It was an odd thing, she thought, stubbing out the cigarette, then taking the radio, still playing, upstairs with her, but ever since she'd had that bit of hanky-panky with Chuck, suddenly Bruce had ceased to do business with any man whom she might find even remotely sexually attractive. And yet he couldn't possibly have found out about her and Chuck; they had been much too careful.

She took off her dressing-gown and nightdress and stepped into the shower. As she adjusted the taps she noticed a small crack in the ceiling. New defects seemed to manifest themselves in the house almost daily; Bruce had withheld some of the deposit to cover the more glaring ones, but at the rate they were going it wouldn't be enough to cover it. She thought with envy of the Lendricks' house, built solidly of good materials, maintained meticulously; but the Lendricks had been in the district all their lives and when they wanted a job doing would simply pick up the phone. They belonged here; she was just passing through. In all her married life three years was the longest she'd stayed in any one place.

She dried herself with one of the huge towels she'd bought at a Harrods' sale. People said Harrods was pricey, but she'd had plenty of bargains there. If you were careful you paid no more than at anywhere else and got the Harrods' atmosphere into the bargain. That was one of the things she was going to miss.

She sprayed her body with Kiku and walked naked to the airing cupboard on the landing. As she took out a pair of clean white pants and a brassière she noticed for the first time that the slats which ran across the cupboard hadn't been fastened down. She was overcome momentarily by a sensation of absolute despair and rage; there had been no such skimping in her father's house nor in any house that she knew in her childhood. The more you paid these days, the less you got.

The sun streamed through the window at the end of the

landing showing up the joins in the dark-blue fitted carpet. It had come from their previous house and this was the third time it had been altered. She wouldn't bother having it altered again.

From where she was standing she could see the road; the curtains were undrawn and she'd miscalculated the amount of net curtaining she'd need for upstairs. Let them see her, she thought; and if it's a man I hope he feels thoroughly frustrated. But the road was empty; she returned to the bedroom and dressed quickly in a white sweater and red skirt. It was more of a struggle than usual to get into her girdle but she had no trouble with her brassière. As her belly grew bigger her breasts seemed to become smaller, though at least they were still firm. But it didn't seem so long ago – when she was having the affair with Chuck, in fact – that she hadn't really needed a girdle.

She applied lipstick and powder and a little eye-shadow with no great thoroughness or enjoyment; she wasn't going anywhere, not even to the cinema. The radio continued playing, but most of the songs this morning seemed to be pure pop, there wasn't a tune, the words were hard to catch, it was the equivalent of the unattached slats in the airing cupboard.

And then, as she'd gone downstairs and was making herself a cup of coffee, a woman's voice came out sweet and clear. No, not sweet and clear, that sounded like Tate and Lyle's Golden Syrup. Just a woman's voice, every word distinct, holding the melody surely and firmly. *The pleasures of love last only for a day ...* The tears came to her eyes. This was the note she wanted her life to be pitched on, this was how she wanted things to be. A day was generally the most you got, because even when Bruce was away all night the man's wife wasn't and in any case even when the man wasn't married, she couldn't herself stay out all night. Bruce wasn't a jealous man – perhaps he didn't care enough, perhaps he had fish of his own to fry – but he wasn't a trusting man either, he'd always check up.

She thought of Clive Lendrick again. He was much the same physical type as Chuck, big and fair and clean. 'I'm not really good-looking,' Chuck always used to say, 'but I'm so clean you could eat your dinner off me.'

When she'd danced with Clive at his birthday party she'd noticed that especially. Even his hair – crisp and short – was clean. And he smelled clean, simply clean and masculine. His gold identity bracelet was a bit camp, even if it was a present from his wife, but he was masculine enough to get away with it. But he and his wife were still in business; you could always tell. And apart from that he seemed very thick with that bitch in the trouser suit. But with men like that it was only to be expected; if she were the only one who fancied him, he wouldn't be worth fancying.

The coffee drunk, she took out the Hoover from the cupboard under the staircase. A whole day was ahead of her: the housework could be stretched out to one and a half hours at the most, lunch and a rest after it maybe to two, shopping maybe to three since it would have to be done in the village, which meant a good twenty minutes' walk. She didn't feel like embroidering or knitting, and even if she'd felt like reading, there wasn't anything in the house that she wanted to read. There wasn't even a meal to prepare for Bruce. She'd have to begin her usual drill for getting to know people in a new place, but it was awkward without the car. Besides, she wasn't in the mood for it today; it was something that had to be worked out very carefully or you made entirely the wrong friends and in doing so put off the people who would have been the right friends.

In the end, she thought, pushing the Hoover slowly across the parquet floor of the lounge, you could only be friends with people in the same income group. You spoke the same language as people with a lot more money than you, because Bruce, with all his faults, was so obviously a man who was climbing fast. But if they had a lot less and were always going to have a lot less then, no matter how bright and agreeable they seemed, envy always crept in in the form of grumbling, really grumbling, about money.

There wasn't anything so depressing as listening to other people's money troubles. She and Bruce had enough of their own, even taking into account the help they got from

Daddy with the school fees; the higher up in the company you went, the more was expected of you, and the worse your tax position got. If ever she and Bruce did need money, it couldn't even be solved by her going to work; with his salary being what it was, she'd be working in effect for about two pounds a week. But if, after listening for hours to some people's complaints about money, you told them about your own, you didn't get any sympathy, but only nonsense about wishing they earned enough money to pay that amount of tax on, and how they'd swop their problems for yours.

She switched off the Hoover and went over to the telephone. Robin's voice answered.

'This is Vicky Kelvedon,' Vicky said. She glanced at her watch: ten-thirty. 'I was wondering if you'd care to come over for a cup of coffee.'

'Super.' Over the phone Robin's voice always sounded very breathless and young. 'I'll see you.'

Vicky disconnected the Hoover and put it back in the cupboard. Then she went into the kitchen to put the milk on, and laid out two cups and spoons and a sugar bowl. Then she sat down contentedly with a cigarette. At least another hour of the day would pass, which was something; but, apart from that, if you fancied a man you had to get to know him. And if you met his wife you stood a greater chance of meeting him. You had to push it a bit; you got nowhere by dreaming.

She lit a cigarette, her sixth that day. She knew she was smoking too much, but as she grew older she found cigarettes not so much a painful compulsion as a positively enjoyable indulgence. This particular cigarette now abolished the period of waiting for Robin; she had scarcely finished it when the doorbell rang.

Robin, despite a tweed suit with a skirt of what Vicky called WVS length, looked extraordinarily handsome, her cheeks glowing with health and her fair hair shining.

'You look marvellous,' Vicky said with genuine admiration.

'It was such a wonderful morning that I went for a walk

after breakfast. Not that I'm much of an open-air girl generally.'

'A little of it goes a long way with me.' Vicky put on the electric kettle. 'I thought we'd have real coffee.'

'Super. I'm terribly lazy about it myself.' She looked around the kitchen. 'What a lovely bright kitchen this is.'

'I'd rather have an old-fashioned kitchen. In fact, I'd rather have an old-fashioned house. I find something else wrong with this damned place every day.'

Robin laughed, displaying neat white teeth. 'You ought to live in our house, it's falling to pieces.'

'But you don't expect a *brand new* house to be falling to pieces.' She warmed the coffee pot then put in five heaped teaspoonfuls of Blue Mountain from a new packet. There was enough for a pot in a packet she'd only opened yesterday, but it seemed important that Robin should have the best.

When they took their coffee through into the lounge and Robin had accepted a cigarette, Vicky took another look at her under the pretext of admiring her cameo brooch. 'I love your brooch,' she said. 'May I look at it?'

Robin handed it over. 'I picked it up in London,' she said. 'At a little jewellers off the Charing Cross Road.'

'I never see anything like that in London. Or if I do it costs the earth.'

'This was quite – reasonable,' Robin said.

It was a Victorian piece in silver and ivory, a pastoral scene very delicately executed. For a moment Vicky was tempted to press the question of cost further; something in Robin's voice told her that she didn't know how much it had cost because it was a gift.

It was probably expensive, simply because it was a nice piece, quite apart from it being Victorian. But that wasn't why Robin liked it.

'When were you in London?' she asked.

'Last week. I have an old aunt down there. I just went down for the day to see a show.'

'You'll have to tell me when next you go. I'm homesick for the place already.'

She couldn't resist it, even at the danger of antagonizing Robin.

'That would be lovely,' Robin said in a flat voice which made it plain that lovely was the last word she was thinking of.

Vicky laughed. 'It's just a dream, forget it. Bruce and I are having an economy campaign. The vultures have descended upon us.'

'Vultures?' Robin looked puzzled.

'The Inland Revenue. Surtax.'

'Oh. How horrid. I leave it all to Clive and Clive leaves it all to the accountant at the mill.'

'Well, Bruce is supposed to leave it all to his accountant, but he's so clever about figures that he thinks he knows better than the accountant. So he worries.'

'Clive doesn't. He doesn't even *open* anything from the Inland Revenue.'

'Oh, my dear, I'll swap you husbands. Bruce is absolutely bloody. First moans about bankruptcy then lectures about the evils of socialism.'

'Clive does that too from time to time.'

'He doesn't talk about emigrating, though, does he? Bruce is always threatening to join the brain drain, as if we'd not moved enough during the last few years.'

'Emigrating?' Robin laughed comfortably. 'Not Clive. He's as snug as a bug in a rug.'

But are *you*? Vicky thought. There's something going on in London; you're not the kind to be able to disguise it. Except to Clive. That's a nice thing about him; I don't think he's the kind to keep tabs on anybody.

'You wouldn't like to come to the pictures tonight?' she asked. 'I'm longing to see it, and that bastard of a husband of mine has let me down.'

'I'd love to,' Robin said. 'But I'm rehearsing for a play. Not a very big part really, but I'm on in each act. Do you do anything in that direction?'

Vicky shook her head. 'I've no talent at all.'

Robin took a gold cigarette-case from her handbag. 'Oh, you don't have to possess any talent. There's a lot of things you can do. Props, scenery, prompting. It's great fun really. They're a nice crowd.'

Vicky accepted a cigarette. They were filter tipped, half an inch longer than king size, with the initials CJL on them.

'They make them in Charbury,' Robin said. 'All the woolmen smoke them. I pinch them from Clive. I always smoke like a chimney when I'm doing a play.'

Vicky wondered if the man weren't someone in the Players; in the last amateur dramatic society she'd known, in Surrey, there was always something of that nature going on. But a woman speaks of the background of her affair in an especial way, sometimes a little defiantly, sometimes a little shamefacedly. One couldn't quite describe the tone of voice, but it was unmistakable; it wasn't there when Robin spoke about the Hailton Players.

'Is Clive a member?' she asked.

'He used to be before we were married. But he doesn't do anything now – he's tied up too often in the evenings.'

That was useful to know too. She was, as the burglar's phrase put it, casing the joint.

'Doesn't he mind being left on his own when he's not tied up in the evenings?' Careful, she thought: you mustn't be seen lurking about the house too obviously, you mustn't be too interested in their habits.

But Robin had noticed nothing. 'Clive?' She smiled indulgently. 'My dear Vicky, he likes nothing better than an evening on his own. Sometimes he looks at TV, but more often he reads. He spends a small fortune on books. There's a very good bookshop in the town, and he goes there every week. Ruth Inglewood runs it. She was the girl in the gold lamé trouser suit. She and Clive are great chums.'

'Don't you mind?'

'She's not one of those women you mind about, I don't know why. Something *boyish* about her ...'

'Don't you be too sure of it,' Vicky said. 'No man is to be trusted with any woman until the coffin lid's actually screwed down ... They're all rotten lying bastards. I'm a bit off men, to tell you the truth. Particularly Bruce after letting me down this evening.'

'Clive does the same. Their damned work, it's always the same excuse. And moaning and groaning about it, but really they love it ...'

The conversation went along on predictable lines, eventually covering their children, schools, their weight problem, and the characters of some of the neighbours. When Robin had gone at a quarter to twelve Vicky went over to the cocktail cabinet, took out the bottle of Smirnoff Vodka and the bottle of Rose's lime and a glass and three coasters, and put them on a coffee table by the sofa. She added an ashtray, cigarettes and matches, and lay down on the sofa with a sigh of relief. It was her rule never to drink before noon; before noon was morning, and only alcoholics drink in the morning. But lately it had become harder not to break the rule. A quarter of an hour was just the right time to wait, to build up a pleasurable anticipation. Longer would have meant a mountingly painful craving.

On the stroke of twelve she poured herself a stiff drink. Relaxation and warmth and reassurance came immediately; if it was like anything it was like the moment after an orgasm. She took the drink slowly. It had been a good morning, against all expectations: she was getting to know people, she had some useful information about whom she would like and whom she wouldn't like in Throstlehill and, above all, she knew more about Clive. It might come to nothing; sometimes with those big apparently sexy men the nerve was dead. On the strength of his attitude at the party it would appear not, but that might have been simply the effect of alcohol.

She finished her drink and was about to put the bottle away, when she remembered that she didn't have the car, that she didn't have to be careful.

She poured herself another, not so stiff this time. This was a bonus; now instead of being warmly contented she'd be positively happy. But it made her feel a little tearful and suddenly she remembered her sons. Andrew was sixteen, Keith fourteen; they had Bruce's face and colouring but they were tall and broad-shouldered like her side of the family. Already they were growing away from her, they'd been growing away from her ever since they went to school. But not growing away from Bruce; they always had plenty to say to him. She wiped her eyes and put away the bottles and took her glass into the kitchen.

After lunching on an omelet and coffee, reading the *Daily Express* as she ate, she walked into the village. Robin had offered to lend her her car but that would have been pushing the acquaintanceship a bit too much. When people feel that they're being pursued they feel either harried or suspicious or both.

She enjoyed the walk and the village shops were remarkably clean and tidy and well-stocked. The prices at the greengrocer's were well above those in Hailton, but that was only to be expected. It was cold for April – ten degrees below what it would be in Surrey now – but the sun was bright and the wind dry and stimulating. On the hills on the horizon there were still patches of snow. There was something rather romantic about that. When the boys came home they'd take sandwiches and walk over the moors to those hills. And even as she formulated the thought she knew that she wouldn't; the boys were past the age when they wanted her with them. But it was pleasant to think about it.

When she returned she finished her housework quickly and lay on the sofa for a while. She kept the transistor on, because without it the silence would take over again. The village was very quiet too; she didn't even seem to hear any children's voices. She didn't intend to go to sleep, merely to relax, to let go a little, but before she knew it she was stumbling along a rocky shore running from something out at sea which was coming closer and closer towards her, and she woke up in a darkening room with a headache and a raging thirst.

She switched the lights on and drew the blinds and went into the kitchen to mix herself a glass of Alka-Seltzer. Then she went to the cloakroom and held her hands under the cold tap and combed her hair. She went into the kitchen, dragging her shoeless feet: it seemed not only bare but gim-crack, the floor out of plumb, the taps dripping, the two cupboard doors warped.

After a slice of bread and salt – an idiosyncratic taste dating from childhood – and a pot of strong tea the head-ache and the dryness in her mouth disappeared. But the whole lonely evening stretched before her. She went over to the cocktail cabinet, opened the door, then closed it again. Then she counted the money in her handbag and then went to the telephone.

Four hours later, coming out of the Charbury Odeon she felt more cheerful. She had broken a rule, a not very im-portant one but a rule nevertheless: women didn't go to the cinema by themselves. And that was a gain, and one in the eye for Bruce. And it had been a good picture; even the bang-bang Frank Sinatra vehicle with it had been bearable. Cosy and warm in the darkness, she'd escaped into some-one else's life, a life enough like her own to be real and credible, but shimmeringly exotic, smoothly finished, wryly high-spirited. You could remember scenes from a film like that for a long time, putting them inside dull or blank moments like a vase of roses.

It was cold now and the blue-green fluorescent street lights made it seem colder; she shivered, and drew her sheepskin coat more tightly round her.

There was a tall man walking ahead of her, wearing a fawn tweed coat which made him appear enormously broad; he stopped at the zebra crossing at the far corner of the cinema and she saw that it was Clive Lendrick. When he smiled at her she felt for a moment literally dizzy; at the beginning of the day she couldn't have envisaged the possi-bility of the meeting.

But, she reflected as she took her place beside him in the Mercedes, it only bore out what she strongly believed: what-ever it is that you want, that you will get it, if only you want it badly enough. There'd been no one since Chuck, and that was nearly a year ago.

'I thought you'd be at home with a good book,' she said

lightly, as the car moved silently through the after-cinema traffic. She didn't know much about cars, but felt about this one an air of great solidity coupled with glamour; the faces of other drivers appeared unmistakably envious.

'I fancied this picture. I like going to the pictures actually: you don't have to make a ceremony of it and reserve seats and so forth ... Did you enjoy it?'

He had large square hands with square, well-kept nails and a fuzz of golden hair on the backs; they were much more to her taste than Chuck's, which were a little too small and tapering-fingered.

'It was marvellous,' she said, 'though I didn't care for the husband turning all brave and independent. People don't.'

'Don't they?'

'No one ever changes. Even if they get religion or something they don't change.'

They had left the centre and were going along Hurley Lane now, climbing towards the Beckfield Woods road, which by-passed Hailton and led through a complex of narrow country roads to Throstlehill.

'That's a poor lookout for some of us,' he said. 'I'd rather like to change myself a bit, after forty-seven years.'

'You may want to, darling' – this was the right moment for the word – 'but you won't. And why should you? You've got everything.'

She felt rather proud of herself; she'd hit upon the right note as soon as she'd got into the car. The conversation had never been allowed to become impersonal or formal; it was now becoming more and more intimate, and if he didn't see that she was attracted to him, he was more stupid than she'd thought he was.

'I haven't got as much as you think,' he said. There was a straight stretch of road ahead; the car surged up to seventy. 'And I still wouldn't mind changing myself ... I like your scent.'

'Kiku,' she said. 'Fabergé.'

'I thought they made golden Easter eggs for the Czar.'

'What a lot you know,' she said. Cultured conversations with Miss Trouser Suit, she thought. A little of that goes a long way with me; I've no intention of becoming your great *chum*. As they went into the woods she put her hand on his knee; she heard his faint gasp of surprise, then his hand pressed down on hers. She began to stroke his thigh; his hand left hers and he steered into a cart track at a point where the road widened and stopped the car.

He kissed her, then his hand went inside the top of her dress. She unfastened her brassière, taking her mouth away from his for a moment. His hand was warm and smooth. He put it between her legs; she let it rest there for a second then very gently took it away and kissed it.

'We'd better go soon,' she said.

'Don't you want me?'

'Of course I do, you fool. But what if they've come back—' She bit her lip as his hand, disregarding hers, found its way to the part of her which Chuck, for one, hardly knew to exist, the certain source of pleasure; gasping, she drew herself away from him and smoothed down her skirt and fastened her brassière.

'I didn't think you were a prick-teaser,' he said, sulkily.

'Another moment and you'd have found out how much I'm not. And then we'd have found ourselves going back home an hour late with a lot of explaining to do. I don't know whether Bruce'll be back yet or not, but I bet Robin is. And I don't think she's stupid.'

'I expect you're right,' he said, his voice still sulky.

'If you phone me tomorrow morning, we'll work something out. About ten.'

This was the part she hated; it seemed so cold, it could be so drearily complicated. And the cleverest of men seemed to assume that the mere act of phoning would provide a place to meet. But Clive said to her surprise: 'I'll phone you. But don't worry about a place to go to. I'll get a flat tomorrow.'

He could afford it, of course; but it wasn't just that. It was the way in which he was already taking charge of all the details. It had always been she who looked after these matters for her lovers, just as she looked after the mortgage and selling and buying of houses and all the bills for Bruce, despite his cleverness with figures. There was a lot to learn about Clive, he was a type she hadn't encountered before. The outward amiability was deceptive. In the end she'd established ascendancy even over Chuck, he had begun to talk quite seriously about marrying her; but Clive was a grown man. She wouldn't have things all her own way with him; he wasn't cold, but there was some part of him which she already sensed she could never get at.

She finished making up her face and took the cigarette Clive lit for her. She was out of limbo now, or rather, back on the same old drug – excitement, fear, danger, walking the tightrope. So far she'd never been found out, there'd never been any real trouble, she'd been the one who grew tired first.

She'd said that people never changed, that she would never change. It could even be that she was wrong, that the man sitting beside her at the wheel would be the one who'd change her, make her better, make her worse, make her happier, break her heart, but change her.

'Say something nice to me,' she said to him.

'You're the most disturbing woman I've ever met.'

'Have you ever done this sort of thing before?'

'No.'

'I don't believe you.'

'It's true, though. So I couldn't say anything nicer, could I?'

'You'll make me feel guilty.'

He grinned. 'No, I won't. Rather proud of yourself, that's all.'

She stared at him, a little shaken. He knew too much; the grin was masculine, the tone of the remark feminine.

He put his hand on her knee and very gently stroked her thigh; then his hand went under her dress and touched her, still very lightly, between her legs. It moved away and he started the car; but all the way back to Throstlehill it was as if the hand were still there.

Ten

For some fifteen years Stephen had been making the foyer of the Arts Theatre Club his place of assignation. It was central, it was near a Tube station, it was respectable, and a woman could sit there by herself without any sort of embarrassment. Those at least were the reasons he gave for using the place; the truth of it was that it had grown into a habit.

When he arrived Robin was already there; she was reading *The Daily Telegraph* and didn't look up as he came in. He sat down beside her without speaking, noticing that in the pale penetrating spring sunlight there were no flaws in her near-golden skin; she continued reading for a moment, then put down the paper and smiled at him. He took her hand.

'I hope you haven't been waiting long?'

She shook her head. He could smell her now; it wasn't just her perfume, but the smell of cleanliness, the smell of the new cloth in her blue worsted suit, the smell of starch in her white frilled blouse, the smell, over it all, of a healthy woman. It was a smell he couldn't have found words to describe, but it was a smell he hadn't encountered for a long time. The women he met these days were clean enough, perhaps too clean – his wife bathed not once but twice daily – and were addicted not only to the most expensive scents but to potent preparations guaranteed to remove every body odour which could possibly cause offence. There was always strain though, a slight rankness which was even exciting. Exciting but not fulfilling, as Robin's smell was.

'I've booked for us at the Terrazza,' he said.

'Isn't that where all the film stars go?'

'Some of them,' he said. 'And directors. And writers. But

the food's good and it isn't an expense-account clip joint. I mean, most of the people there would still go if there were no such things as expense accounts.'

As he spoke, he knew that he wasn't saying what he ought to be saying and what he wanted to be saying. He was wasting time – her time too. There was none too much available today and at his age the supply wasn't going to be increased. He had more than enough of it when he first knew Robin; enough, he remembered, to give her lectures about architecture, politics, the arts; he had wasted time then and now he was still wasting time.

In the taxi he kissed her gently on the mouth and then leaned back, his arm around her. 'I love you.'

'I love you.'

'I've been thinking about you all week.'

It was a lie; he had long ago trained himself to look forward to nothing, to live only in the present, however lousy the present sometimes might be. If you looked forward to things they blew up in your face. And if you were frightened of them blowing up in your face then that was exactly what would happen. He had survived as long as he had in commercial TV because he'd learned this very quickly. In learning it he had lost something – sensitivity, spontaneity, the ability to respond. Robin was all of a piece; nothing had ever happened to her to mess her up. She wasn't a repair job, she didn't have to work out how to give herself, she just gave.

'I've been excited too,' she said. 'Imagine, a middle-aged matron like me.'

'You're not middle-aged.'

'I'll not see forty again.'

He kissed her. 'Neither will I; what the hell does it matter?'

'Everyone in the village says you like dolly girls. I'm not a dolly girl, am I?'

'They become very boring.'

'Don't middle-aged matrons?'

'You never bore me. You never have.' It was the truth this time; even when they weren't making love, he was never bored with her. Her reactions to everything about her were always fresh and delighted, she was never blasé; it was the dolly girls who were jaded, who'd seen it all before. And they were of the same generation, they had the same values, the same tastes, the same memories and, being so close in age, the same fears and the same intimations of infirmity. It was extraordinarily comfortable to be with her; they walked, as it were, at the same pace, he wasn't out of breath trying to keep up with her.

Not until they were going downstairs in the Terrazza did he reproach himself for wasting time, for treating her like a dolly girl who had to be impressed. They could have had sandwiches in the park, they could have had something at his house; but she enjoyed her lunch so much, was so impressed by the number of famous faces around her, that he knew he'd done the right thing after all. It didn't matter as long as he could give her pleasure and in giving her pleasure he gained pleasure himself of a kind which before he'd only tasted when taking his son to the circus or a football match or a Western or the Zoo.

'They all seem smaller,' Robin said in the taxi going to Kensington.

'Are you disillusioned?'

'Not really. It's what I expected. Film faces always seem smaller, I mean real film faces. You know an awful lot of people, don't you?'

'It's my bread-and-butter.'

'You don't write poetry any more, do you, Stephen?'

The question, or rather statement, took him by surprise. 'I don't write, period. Except articles, which I dictate. You outgrow it. Or maybe I just wasn't good enough.'

'I don't care. I don't care about anything except being with you as much as I can. Which won't be at all for the next month because I'll be in the play every night for ten nights and then I'm going to Denmark for a week with Clive.'

'I'll come to Charbury,' he said.

'It'll be a month at least. A whole month. Why couldn't you marry me when you had the chance?'

'Because I was a fool.' He was seeing himself more clearly than ever he had done. He wasn't sure that he liked it.

'So was I. If I'd known then what I know now, I could have made you marry me.'

'I was very cunning. I'd have had my will of you and left you.'

She started crying and didn't stop until they had reached his house.

With any other woman he would have seen it as a trick; with her, in an odd way, it brought them closer together. He sat beside her on the sofa, holding her head against his chest. The brooch which he'd given her was boring into his chest, but he was glad of the discomfort.

'I'm sorry about that,' she said. 'I'm not a very good mistress, am I?'

'Maybe I'm not a very good lover.'

'Oh, you are. You're marvellous.'

'Not *that*. I mean I shouldn't hurt you, I should be more careful about your feelings.'

A cloud had come over the sun; the room seemed dark and old and dusty but at the same time too tidy, too unused.

She sat up suddenly and took off her jacket and began to unfasten her blouse. 'I'll hate you if you're too kind,' she said. 'It's not kindness I'm short of. Clive smothers me with kindness.' She stood up and took off her skirt, then went into the bathroom.

Stephen took a bottle of Haig and two glasses from the sideboard and put them on the coffee table. He lit a cigarette and then leaned back, his eyes half-closed. There was the sound of running water from the bathroom. He felt totally contented: later there would be sadness, but now there was plenty of time before them. It had so happened that this afternoon had been one only for minor chores, ones which could wait a day; the next time she was able to get to London he mightn't be quite so lucky. In his position he had a lot of leeway, and there was always work he could do at home. But on the whole it was best to stay around the office, and two afternoons off within a month was over his limit. That unbelievably devious young bastard Hawkins was all too keen an assistant, learning office politics all too quickly. But how and when and even where he'd meet Robin in the future could be settled in the future.

She came back, all traces of tears removed from her face, and sat down beside him and accepted a glass of whisky and a cigarette. He put his hand on her thigh and felt the outline of her suspender.

'Fetishist,' she said.

'It takes me back.'

'I adored that scruffy old flat. I wish you could get another exactly like it.'

'They pull down houses like that now. They hate anything old.'

'If we could find somewhere cheap and old and shabby you could give up your job and write. I'd go out to work for you, so we wouldn't ever starve.'

'There isn't anywhere cheap and old and shabby. They'd send someone round and we'd be put in a high-rise block of flats at ten times the rent.'

'They don't like us, do they?'

'They hate us,' he said. 'But we'll go where they can't find us. There'll be just the two of us in a little shabby flat and we'll be in bed till noon and then we'll have sausages and black pudding and fried bread and then I'll write and you'll clean up the flat and then go to the market shopping. And every night we'll go to the pictures and hold hands. Or sit in an old shabby pub: I'll drink mild-and-bitter.'

'I'll drink port-and-lemon. Then we'll have fish-and-chips for supper.'

'And at weekends we'll do nothing at all. Would you like to do nothing at all?'

'Nothing but make love.'

She slid his jacket off and unfastened his tie. 'Do you make love to Jean very often?'

'About every other day.'

'That wouldn't be enough for me. We've missed so much. I worked it out once; you owe me six thousand' – she whispered – 'fucks.'

'I'll never be out of your debt, will I?' He took her hand

and they went into the spare bedroom. It was a small room with bare white distempered walls and a three-quarter bed with a hard mattress and small bedside table and small whitewood wardrobe which he'd never got around to painting; she wouldn't use the master bedroom because, she said, it smelled of Jean.

'I do love you, you know,' she said. 'I really would leave home for you.' She took off her slip. 'I'd settled down to being a comfortable middle-aged lady with a nice house. I didn't think anything more was going to happen to me—'

He'd been intending to take it slowly, as he'd done the first time they'd made love in this room, to wait until they were both naked, to be a marvellous lover in the way experience and the sex manuals had taught him, to care as much about her climax as his own; he had wanted to look at her naked body, he felt a great tenderness and he wanted to express that tenderness, but as he looked at her in her white brassière and pants and stockings it was as if his organ took over; he pushed her down on the bed as she was unfastening a stocking and tugged off her pants. As he penetrated her, he knew that she wasn't ready, that he was committing a kind of rape, but thrusting convulsively, knowing that he was hurting her, he didn't care.

It wasn't like the first time, because then she'd been ready, she had taken him; now he was taking her, now he was going beyond sensuality, not even assuaging a need but easing a pain. And he was releasing himself, breaking all the laws set up by the enlightened psychologists, treating Robin's body not as a delicate instrument but simply as a woman's body, not taking pride in delaying his climax but in attaining it as quickly as possible; and as for what she felt afterwards, whether she'd be satisfied or not, he didn't care.

These were the thoughts of his body rather than his brain; but after his orgasm they didn't dissolve into remorse but became more coherent. He was glad she hadn't made it, he was glad to have had a simple uncomplicated poke, to have got himself laid, to have thumbed his nose at the particular set of sexual conventions which enlightened people like him observed so meticulously.

Rather to his surprise, she was smiling. 'That was nice,' she said. 'You took me by surprise.'

He stroked her cheek. 'I'm sorry you didn't come.'

'There's five thousand nine hundred and ninety-nine times more to go. It doesn't matter very much about coming, you know. If I want it so badly, I don't even need a man, do I?'

'I think I love you,' he said.

'Only think?' She was still smiling. 'I don't think, I know. I do love you. But I'm not much of a conquest for you, am I?'

'I don't think of you as a conquest.'

'Do you remember that letter? *Thank you for being you...*'

'You never wrote me any letters.'

'I was engaged. And perhaps I didn't fancy having them read out to some other woman. What happened to that girl?'

'She got married. To that frightful shit who talks about sociology on TV. Old Compassion Carver, you must have seen him. I got him on TV in the first place, God forgive me. Or she did. She's in there, pushing him all the time.'

'I've never had to do much of that. I might have been rather good at it.' She touched his limp organ. 'There isn't much time. Do you think if I took off this silly bra and girdle it would help?' She pushed him down on the bed, taking charge of the situation, her breasts hanging heavily but softly against him. Her mouth left his, travelled to his chest, his belly.

'I think that was very good for a middle-aged gentleman,' he said as they were dressing. 'I must love you, mustn't I?'

'I wouldn't have cared if you hadn't been able to make it,' she said. 'Can't you see that?'

'Not all at once,' he said.

'I didn't expect you to,' she said sadly. She made her face up briskly with the mirror in her compact. It was gold, he noticed; like everything about her it was redolent of a solid prosperity. She was now the calm sensible middle-aged – no, mature – matron from the provinces; he was almost incredulous that only a few minutes since they'd lain together naked and moaning.

'You'll see me off?'

'I want to.'

'Doesn't your wife ever come home?'

'Not on a matinée day. Too frightened of not being able to get back to the theatre.'

'I don't want to go,' she said. 'If you asked me to stay, I would.'

'You'd regret it afterwards.'

'No.' She smiled. 'Don't look so unhappy, darling. I won't do anything silly. But I do love you.'

Looking at her smiling face he felt, alongside an unreasonable and heady exultation, a sense of foreboding; whatever came of this, he wouldn't escape lightly.

Eleven

Late one wet Saturday afternoon on the last day of the Hailton Players' production Clive was browsing in Ruth's bookshop. With its bright orange and red floor and bright orange ceiling and walls and the faintly erotic smell of new books it was precisely the place of refuge that he needed; he hadn't been for a fortnight, and during that fortnight the month's new paperbacks had arrived. It had been very busy all afternoon and Ruth had been on her own; but they'd managed to talk – not about books but about her family of all things – and had a cup of tea in the little office at the back of the shop.

Absorbed in a huge book about old cars he didn't realize that he was alone in the shop until she tapped his arm.

'We're closed, sir. I'm afraid you'll have to put that book back.'

'Can't I buy it?'

'Good gracious, no. I'll be reported to the union.'

She took the book away from him. 'But if you buy me a drink I'll consider it. I put the rest of your books in the office, if you're wondering where they are.'

He followed her into the little office. It was, considering the amount of objects – books, stationery, typewriter, electric kettle, magazines – crammed into it, extraordinarily neat. It was lit by a skylight, against which the rain drummed steadily.

'The car book's rather dear,' she said, a little breathlessly. 'I was going to reduce the price anyway. So you can have a guinea off.'

'That's very kind of you.'

She looked curiously abashed.

'It's nothing. I wish all my customers were like you.' She parcelled up the books rapidly. She was wearing slacks as usual – pale blue with a pale-blue reefer jacket and a black sweater and black display handkerchief but, like her trouser suit at the party, they were feminine in their cut and effect.

In the confined space of the office he couldn't be sure whether he'd brushed against her or she against him; but their bodies touched and he found himself kissing her. She threw off her jacket, her lips still on his, put her hand behind her and jerked it downwards impatiently, then took his hand and guided it upwards under her sweater. She was trembling violently. Her hand moved to his waist and pulled down the zip; it was all going too quickly, he felt almost as if he were being raped, taken by storm; he moved away from her and said gently: 'Don't be in such a hurry.'

Her hand continued to explore his groin. But there was nothing stirring; though the street door was locked and the door at the short passageway which led to the office was closed, he still felt all too much in the public eye. And he couldn't get Robin out of his mind. There hadn't been much sex between them these last few weeks; she was going through a phase again of being either unwell or tired whenever he made any overtures. But perhaps she'd guessed that he'd been involved with Vicky, if you could call it that, for he hadn't seen or spoken to her since the night he'd taken her home, much less rented a flat.

'What's the matter?' she asked. 'Don't you like me?' He pushed her hand gently away and fastened himself up. It wasn't any use, and he knew enough about psychology to be certain why it wasn't any use and why it wouldn't be any use with Vicky either.

'It's guilt, I expect,' he said. 'Old-fashioned guilt.'

'Guilt? Guilt what about?'

'Robin. Oh, don't think I don't want you, but it's that that's holding me back.

She laughed. 'Clive, darling, you're not serious.'

'Of course I'm serious.'

'There's no need for you to feel guilty, dear. Not a particle of guilt should you feel.' Her face seemed to wizen a little. 'Not about Robin.'

'What on earth do you mean?' He already knew what she was going to say.

'I wouldn't have told you, but it seems to be necessary. She's having it off with Stephen Belgard. You know, the TV chap.'

'I don't believe you.'

'Mary Hardrup saw them coming out of a Kensington mews hand-in-hand three weeks ago. They didn't see her.'

'Mary Hardrup? What, is that bloody woman everywhere?'

'It's a small country.'

'I know, but you'd think you'd be safe in London.' He felt almost sorry for Robin.

'Nobody's safe anywhere.'

'She could have been mistaken.'

'What, Mary? The keenest eyes in Yorkshire.'

'And the longest tongue. But why did she tell you?'

'Because she knows I fancy you. I believe she thought in a queer way it would hurt me. And in a queer way it does.'

'You fancy *me*? I thought that you and Norman—'

'Oh Christ, how little you know! Norman doesn't matter—'

'I don't believe it about Robin.'

'I'm telling you what Mary says she saw. I don't think there's any reason why she should make it up. Besides, he does live in Kensington.'

'There's still nothing proved. I've kissed you and I've felt your breasts, and we're still not lovers. Stephen's the sort who walks about hand-in-hand with every woman he knows.'

'You'll have to ask her then. Maybe she'll even tell you the truth if you pick the right moment.'

'I think I know why you've told me.'

'Oh, you do, you do. But from the look on your face I can see that I should have been a bit more devious. That's me all over, can't keep my big mouth shut. You don't like me now, do you?'

He tried to put his arm around her.

'No, Clive. We'll have to go back to where we were before, except that we can't go back now. But you can buy me that drink if you like.'

They sat in the snug of the Royal Sovereign, a small pub in an alleyway off the High Street, for an hour, and it was almost as it had been before. The conversation again and again returned to the same topic; he heard all about Stephen's early background, his marriages, his failures and his successes. And, listening to accounts of Stephen's early days, he started remembering, piecing things together from the time he and Robin were engaged and she was Stephen's secretary. He could remember those days well enough; he couldn't remember either her referring to Stephen very often or in any way manifesting involvement with him or any other man. Nor could he remember how she'd behaved with Stephen at the party, what signs there'd been of the beginning of the liaison; but that, of course, wasn't astounding. He'd been occupied himself.

'You're taking it very calmly,' Ruth said as she left him. 'Are you sure it's true now?'

He nodded.

'It won't work, you know.'

She lowered her voice; another couple had come into the shabby little bar.

'What won't work?'

'Getting your own back. You can't use it for that.'

'It?'

She glanced towards the couple, middle-aged and dull-looking, but obviously listening to every word.

'Don't pretend to be stupid.'

Out in the street, the rain now stopped, the wind blowing cold and fresh, she grasped his arm so hard that it hurt.

'One last word. I told you at the party about that goggle-eyed bitch. You watch out.'

'I'll see you to your car,' he said.

'No, you won't.' She kissed his cheek and ran across the road. He walked on towards his own car, feeling tired and empty, but free for the first time in years.

Twelve

Tower House seemed huge looming up out of the rain in the gathering darkness; he put the Mercedes away and went in by the back door into the kitchen where Petronella in blue jeans and a yellow polo-neck sweater was eating bread-and-honey. He kissed her; her cheek was soft and she returned the kiss twice over, her arms tight around his neck.

'I'm so glad you're back, Daddy.'

'Are you, pet?'

'Sometimes I like being here by myself and sometimes I'm frightened.'

'You should have invited someone in.'

'Olive was going to come, but she had to visit an old aunt.'

'That does her credit.'

'Oh no, I think she has expectations from the old aunt.'

'She's got all her buttons sewn on, has Olive. Is the tea hot?'

'I'll pour you some.' She took out of the cupboard the pint pot with the view of the Brontë parsonage on it which was called his piggy mug. 'Are you hungry, Daddy? I'll make you something.'

'I think I could eat a boiled egg,' he said. He sat down at the table with his mug of tea and lit a cigarette. 'When you were little, you always used to say that when you were grown up you'd look after me. It doesn't seem so long ago.'

'Don't sound so sad, Daddy.' She filled a pan with water, put it on the cooker, took out salt and pepper from the pantry, two plates and an eggcup from the cupboard and a teaspoon and knife from the cutlery drawer under the sink, almost all at once, her movements brisk and cheerful.

'I feel old, that's the trouble.' He did feel old; the feeling had come to him along with the sense of freedom he'd had when hearing Ruth's revelations.

'You don't look it. Gosh, you ought to see the fathers of most of the girls I know. Fat, wheezing, bald. They seem to let themselves go. But you don't. And Mummy doesn't.'

'No, Mummy doesn't.' He wondered how she would take it if he divorced Robin. Girls of her age were supposed to be nonchalant and matter of fact about such things these days, even to enjoy the excitement. But Petronella still seemed to him to be terribly vulnerable, to be dependent upon both her mother and father being around the place when she needed them.

'Olive says older men are much more attractive than young boys,' Petronella said.

'You're trying to cheer me up. Older men are more attractive because they have more money.'

'I don't care very much about money,' Petronella said, putting the egg into the pan.

'You will, love, you will.' Was this the most satisfying relationship with a woman that he knew? Neither side wanted anything from each other but companionship and yet there was no doubt about the force and intensity of their love.

'Don't be cynical, Daddy.'

'All right, I won't be cynical. But if you marry an older man, for God's sake let it be a *rich* older man.'

She giggled. 'We don't really meet anyone who isn't rich, do we? I mean, all your friends are rolling in it.'

'Not in the Players.'

'Ah, but they're a different category. They come here now and again but you don't go to their houses very much. Or dine with them.' Her tone was unexpectedly shrewd. 'They're not like the people you take out to do business with. Or bring here.'

'That's different.'

'Oh, I like us having money. But I know people who haven't got very much and they seem to have more fun. They don't weigh each other up so much.' She spooned out the egg and put it in the eggcup.

'You've thought a lot about it.'

'Oh, I'm not just a pretty face, you know.'

He thought that perhaps he would rather have had her just a pretty face; she wasn't in the least like her brothers who cheerfully accepted the world as it was, who would never look beyond the surface of things. So they wouldn't be hurt or, if they were, their wounds would heal quickly. Petronella could be hurt and was going to be hurt and there wasn't anything he could do about it but love her and be there when she needed him. Be there?

'I must change,' she said. 'Olive and I are going to the Young Cons dance. Are you going out, Daddy?'

He pointed to the parcel of books which he had put down on the table.

'I'm going to stay in and read.'

'I think you like that better than anything. You know, you've changed since you started reading.' She paused. 'Or is it the bookseller?'

He grinned. 'Naughty. Besides, you said older men were more attractive.'

'You eat your egg, Daddy. And you watch out with that, that *bookseller*; she's a dangerous woman.'

'They all are,' he said.

After she had left the room he made himself a fresh pot of tea and lit another cigarette. Then he unwrapped the package of books. They were the last he'd buy from Ruth. He could neither forgive her for stepping out of character and trying to seduce him nor for telling him about Robin and Stephen. He had thought about her much as he thought about Petronella, except that no love bound him to her; his visits to the bookshop had been both a relaxation and a stimulation, she'd wanted nothing from him but had taught him a great deal. She'd told him about Robin's affair for no other reason than to get him for herself and, since she was unmarried, she might well want him permanently.

He didn't look at the books, absorbed in his thoughts, aware that once he wouldn't have been capable of working things out in this way. There was a concrete satisfaction in it – not altogether too wholesome, he had to admit – and a mounting sense of superiority. What was rather singular was that he hadn't been greatly shocked or hurt by Robin's unfaithfulness. He had merely been annoyed. In over twenty years of married life there'd been plenty of chances; he'd turned them down simply because it hadn't seemed fair. He'd never been a jealous man; he'd always trusted her absolutely. Now he felt a fool. He didn't, strangely enough, hate Stephen. Stephen could die tomorrow, of course, for all that he cared; but he didn't hate him. It was Robin who'd made a fool of him, and he just as soon wouldn't have been told about it.

He got up and paced about the room. He wasn't having the conventional reactions; it made him vaguely uneasy. He might or might not confront Robin with her unfaithfulness when she came home, but he didn't want to hurt her. He wasn't sure whether he wanted to divorce her or not, though the idea of a fresh start more and more had its attractions.

He took the books to the study, put them down on the marble table in the centre of the room, put an ashtray on the table and moved the table adjacent to the sofa. He lay on the sofa and lit a cigarette. Now there was nothing more he needed. There was plenty of time to make a decision about Robin, or to decide not to make a decision. And then just as he'd opened the car book and was looking dreamily at a Pierce-Arrow limousine, a spasm of lust went through him. It went away again, almost hurting him in its going as well as in its arrival, then returned; he tried to continue looking at the Pierce-Arrow, but had to close the book. He hadn't felt like this since his youth; for some ten years now physical desire had been conditional on time and place, on gentle preliminary caresses becoming less and less gentle, more and more explicit; he was a complete man but he was a civilized man. He wasn't civilized now; he was in a state which drives men to rape or to whores. He pushed the table away, got up, and went to the phone in the hall. Before he picked it up he went up to the landing; from the bathroom came the sound of splashing.

He went downstairs again.

'Vicky? This is Clive.'

'You're a fortnight late. I ought to hang up on you.'

'I'll explain when I see you. Are you alone?'

'What do you think?'

'I'll see you in the Heckley Arms in about twenty minutes. Go in as for some cigarettes or something.'

'I'll think about it. I still think you're a rotten bastard.' She hung up.

He grinned and put down the phone very gently. As he ran upstairs to the bedroom he was working out the details of the assignation. He could meet Vicky as if by chance, and offer her a drink. Then he'd tell her to follow his car to Bixby Moor, some five miles from Throstlehill. She'd get into his car there, and leave her own; then they'd go to Eldwick. Then a quick drink and back to Bixby Moor. He washed his face and hands in the bedroom, cleaned his teeth, then shaved quickly and brushed his hair. Passing the bathroom he shouted, 'I'm going out, Petronella. Close the doors behind you.'

Petronella emerged in her dressing-gown. 'What did you say, Daddy?'

'I'm going out for a drink. Close the doors behind you.'

He noted that if she hadn't heard him from outside the bathroom door, she couldn't have heard him from downstairs; it was as well to be sure of these things.

'All right, Daddy. Be good.'

'I've no option at my age,' he said. 'Goodbye, princess. *You* be good, never mind me.' He kissed her and walked briskly down the steps; there was suddenly in the back of his mind a faint regret which as he got into the Mercedes began to fade away; it had come upon him when he was kissing Petronella and it was as if he were losing something.

An hour and a quarter later Vicky lay beneath him on the Reutter seat of the Mercedes, now fully reclined. The car was parked off the road near the reservoir at High Eldwick, some twenty miles from Throstlehill; there were better places in Throstlehill itself, but you never knew who mightn't be driving by in Throstlehill or worse still, taking a health-giving walk, even in the drizzle.

They'd driven to High Eldwick with her hand inside his trousers, so that once he'd stopped he'd had no inclination for preliminaries; but they hadn't been necessary, she was more than ready for him, moaning with pleasure almost as soon as he entered her. They had spoken very little on the journey and he'd been glad of it, because suddenly the idea of Robin in bed with Stephen had begun to hurt; now, moving away at last from Vicky, it didn't hurt any longer.

'That was nice,' she said.

'It'll be even better, when we get that flat.'

'Don't look,' she said, as he went back into the driving seat. 'I don't mind you seeing me take my pants off but I hate anyone watching me putting them on.'

He cranked up the seat back and she took out her

handbag. The smell of lipstick and powder began to compete with the smell of sex. He lit a cigarette, then cranked down the window. The air was fresh and cool on his hot face.

'This is really the first time I've done this,' he said.

She laughed. 'Darling, I can't say the same.' She took a cigarette from him. 'You're not upset about it, are you?'

'I enjoyed it.'

'It took you long enough to make up your mind. Struggle with your conscience?'

'Not exactly.'

'I don't think you need bother yourself. But I might be wrong ...'

He felt frightened for a moment; her tone was exactly the tone of Ruth that afternoon. It was as if, in the darkness, all women really were the same, as if he'd gone with Ruth after all; and if women were all the same, what about men? The sweep of the moors, black beyond the drystone wall, was the sweep of the moors at Throstlehill: where and who was he?

'I don't know what you mean,' he said.

'I'm guided by my instincts, honey. They never guide me wrong. I think Robin's up to something.'

'I'm sure not. I'm absolutely sure not.' He tried to put some conviction in his voice.

'I can't prove it,' she said. 'But if you're curious, ask her where she got that Victorian brooch from.'

'Did she tell you?'

'She didn't have to tell me. Listen, Clive, a woman handles a gift from her lover in a special way.'

'It's all rather – nebulous.'

'Just so.'

'Why didn't you tell me before?'

'You wouldn't have liked me for it, would you?'

'Not really.'

'But I wouldn't have wanted you to poke me just because your wife's being poked by someone else.'

'I wouldn't do that,' he said. He was surprised at how easy it was to be. When he came to think about it he'd gone through his whole life without lying except on that one occasion in the way of business; it wasn't that he was eminently virtuous, but there hadn't been any reason for him to lie before today.

'I hope you're not thinking of divorcing Robin,' she said sharply.

'I'd have to have proof, wouldn't I?'

'It wouldn't be difficult to get hold of. But don't get me involved.'

'You think I should just leave things as they are?'

'Things are always best left as they are.' She stroked his hair. 'We can be a great comfort to each other, Clive. As long as we keep our big mouths shut.'

Her eyes were very large in the dark; from one angle she was almost monkey-faced, from another almost beautiful. He did feel relaxed now, he had been comforted, he was able to stop thinking about Robin.

'I'll get a flat on Monday,' he said.

'Just like that? You must have lots of money.'

'I've never thought about it much,' he said.

'It's rather splendid to have a rich lover. Will you load me with gifts?'

'Dress lengths,' he said. 'In navy and beige. At cost price. How do you think I got so rich?'

'Treading down the workers, how else?'

'Chance would be a fine thing. The bastards tread *me* down.'

He felt enormously cheerful: here by his side was his new start, here was a woman with whom he could have a relationship which wasn't charged with emotion, weighed down by memories, he didn't have any responsibility for her and her children, every moment was a fresh discovery, the act of love itself was new, he felt younger because making love with her had had the same flavour as when he'd been younger. He started the car and they drove towards Dick Hudson's and the road to the village of Eldwick.

'Don't stop,' she said as he approached the pub.

'It's a nice pub.'

'So they tell me, but you never know who you'll meet in a pub.'

'You're frightened,' he said. 'We're twenty miles from Throstlehill.'

'Darling, you could be fifty miles away and still someone who knew you could see you. It's a small country.'

'I want a drink.'

'I tell you what. I'll phone you just as if we hadn't been out together. At about ten o'clock. And I'll invite you and Robin over for a drink. I'll say I'm nearly going mad all on my tod, my selfish sod of a husband being in New York. And then you'll say, Robin's bringing some people back from the show about ten-thirty, why don't you come to us? And I'll come, and you can look at me and think what we've done tonight.'

'I shan't be able to keep my hands off you.'

'All the better. Flirt with me like mad, and then no one will suspect anything.'

A Mini shot out of a side turning off the narrow winding road; he jammed the brakes on and the Mercedes went into a long skid; instinctively he released the brake and after a long three seconds felt the car right itself.

'Bastard,' he shouted after the tail-lights of the Mini. 'I'd have squashed him flat if I'd hit him.'

'You be careful,' she said. 'How would you have explained your passenger?'

'I'll be very careful,' he said. 'And I'll flirt with you like mad.'

She put her hand on his thigh. 'Promise to remember. Don't look away from me, don't be polite and formal.'

'I promise,' he said, laughing. 'I promise faithfully.'

'Faithfully,' she said, and started to laugh too. 'That's a very good word.'

Thirteen

No sexual relationship stands still. No sexual relationship is bound by common sense. No sexual relationship is bound by the will, any more than passion is. If at the beginning Clive and Vicky had talked about their affair to anyone else – which they didn't – they would have leaned pretty heavily on the word *comfort*.

Comfort was, in fact, something which they both needed. Though Robin still shared a bed with Clive, their love-making had become more and more mechanical, less and less frequent. They kept up appearances in public; love and a cough, the proverb says, cannot be hidden, but certainly the lack of love can. Robin, though no one told her, had a shrewd idea that Clive had found himself a woman : but she never voiced her suspicions. She was content as long as she could be with Stephen from time to time; any violent disruption in the pattern of her life would mean the risk of not being with him any more.

Vicky still shared a bed with Bruce when he was home, but he seemed to be away more often than not. His love-making didn't alter; it was quick, greedy, and without tenderness, something which, she felt, he saw simply as a right, bought and paid for. It was not unendurable or even completely unenjoyable, but she grew more and more dissatisfied when she compared it with Clive's.

Clive became increasingly important to her. She'd never had anything like this happen to her before; but then neither had she met anyone like him before. (Looking back, she came to the conclusion that all her lovers had been different editions of Bruce.) Clive was without ambition, for a start; this was curiously restful. He'd had everything handed to him on a silver plate; and yet he wasn't spoiled or conceited, but unfailingly sunny-natured and – there was no other word for it – sweet. And he was masculine too, quite apart from the physical side of it, far more masculine than Bruce, who'd reached his present position not only by hard work but by intrigue and cunning and ferocity. Bruce saw everyone as a tool to be used or an enemy to be destroyed, Clive never had a hard word for anybody, the idea of either using or destroying a human being was completely alien to him.

She began to fall in love with him. It didn't happen all at once; it was at first with him as it had been with all the others – a diversion, something to daydream about, a kind of absorbing hobby almost, a way of reassuring herself she was still desirable, a way of being one up over Bruce. They never talked about divorce – she'd done too good a job of persuading him against it at the beginning – but they did talk about love.

Talking together was in a way the best part of the affair. Despite all the books at Tower House she'd thought of Clive at first as being completely the rich woolman, with no interest in anything beyond the strictly material. He was, she was at first not entirely pleased to discover, rather better-read and better-informed than she was – she found herself listening to him with pleasure as she'd never listened to anyone since the university.

Clive, as he said he would, rented a flat in Inkerman Road in Bosworth Green, a northern suburb of Charbury. It was on the ground floor of a large Victorian terrace house; there were two other tenants above them, but they had a separate entrance at the back. The rent was paid by banker's order on the Lendrick Mill's account; officially it was for the accommodation of visiting customers. Clive had chosen it with some care; Inkerman Road was well away from the main road to the city centre and the district wasn't one which anyone they knew would have any reason for visiting. There was an unusually broad alley at the back and a garage large enough for the Mercedes; there was also a backyard open to the alley which comfortably accommodated four small cars. So both their cars were parked well out of public view. The other tenants, two Pakistani doctors from the Charbury Infirmary, and a middle-aged commercial traveller, kept themselves to themselves, as the saying goes.

The flat comprised a sitting-room with a new colour TV and a radiogram; a bedroom; next to it, a kitchen, and a bathroom. The rooms were all large with high ceilings and had been redecorated recently by the landlord; the patterns and the colours weren't what she would have chosen, being predominantly floral and blue in the sitting-room and bedroom, culinary and red in the kitchen, and marine and green in the bathroom. The colour TV and radiogram had been provided by Clive, the furniture and fittings by the landlord. There was little beyond the bare minimum – a table and four dining chairs, a three-piece suite, a bed, a Woolworth's coffee table, a whitewood wardrobe painted dark brown, a small gas-oven, a deal kitchen table and an unpainted whitewood cupboard, and two carpets. The oak stain on the sitting-room and bedroom floors extended exactly one inch under the carpets; the floors of the hall and the bathroom and the kitchen were covered with the same battleship-grey linoleum. The heating was with two rather battered old gasfires and three small Dimplex heaters and a gas-fired towel rail in the bathroom.

Over the months Clive added a bookcase, books, a gramophone record cabinet, gramophone records, a cocktail cabinet, cutlery, crockery, pots and pans and kitchen equipment. But neither of them was tempted to do anything more extensive to make it into a home. It was enough that they had a place where they could be alone together: what meant as much as what happened in the bed was the quiet evenings in the sitting-room, sometimes looking at the TV, sometimes listening to the gramophone, but most often just talking. They had meals there occasionally, but they were generally of the simplest – cold meat, salad, fruit, meat pies. Sometimes they would share a bottle of wine, but she didn't feel the need for alcohol when she was with him.

They managed somehow to be together every week if only for an hour in the afternoon; the evenings were more difficult. It was easy for Clive – he felt, indeed, that Robin was deliberately trying to make it easy for him – but Bruce had a bad habit of phoning on the nights that he was away from home. It wasn't an invariable habit and he always had a colourable excuse for phoning – documents to be posted, appointments to be arranged, a particular bill to be paid – but Vicky's instincts told her that for some reason of his own he was keeping tabs on her.

She had imagined herself in love before; but what it had been, she perceived clearly now, was a way of dignifying her passions, perhaps even of excusing her infidelity. The three words *I love you* had always some sort of magic about them; and magic, God knows, was what her life badly needed. She was accustomed to uttering the words early on in an affair, to introduce the magic as soon as possible; and to have their full effect they had to be spoken in bed or its equivalent, at the moment when one lost all identity – they were words to be whispered, wrung out between moans and sighs.

She told Clive that she loved him when they were at the flat one evening in early July drinking coffee and listening to *Cabaret*. It was growing dark and despite the season cold enough to have the gasfire on. They had been out of bed and dressed for more than an hour; there was a chance now that she might entice him back to bed, and one half of her was greedy for it and the other half was contented that he should be so contented, enraptured with Judi Dench's voice in the half-light, smiling across at her from his arm-chair.

> *Don't tell my mama!*
> *He comes here every night—*
> *You can tell my uncle, that's all right—*

The husky voice filled the room, every word clear, the tone erotic yet laughing at itself for being erotic; and then, if you listened properly, there was both loneliness and joy. Vicky knew that he was meeting the singer in his mind now, going away from her. She didn't mind; but she had to register her own claim. 'I love you,' she said loudly.

He turned off the record. 'What's that?'

'I love you.' She giggled. 'Do you know, that's the first time I've said that with all my clothes on.'

He knelt beside her. 'Are you quite sure?'

'Oh yes. It's not just that you're very lovable. One doesn't always love lovable people. It just came over me: I love you.'

'I love you,' he said. 'I must, mustn't I? I've never been so happy.'

'There is nothing we can do about it,' she said.

He put his hand between her legs.

'No, darling.' She pushed his hand gently away. 'That's delicious, but it isn't what I meant.'

'I could talk to Robin.'

'For Christ's sake, no! Leave things alone. She's not complaining, is she?'

'I think she knows something.'

'So do you.' She was imagining actually living with Clive, being Mrs Lendrick, going to bed with him every night and waking up with him, seeing him without mounting a kind of security operation every time and never – she couldn't help it coming into her mind – worrying about money again.

'And Bruce?'

'I don't know. I'm rather frightened of Bruce.' She went over to the cocktail cabinet and poured herself a vodka. 'Don't you want something?' she asked.

He shook his head. 'I love you. I love you. It's a long time since I said that. That's strange, isn't it? With the boys when they were little, yes. And always to Petronella. Quite a lot to Petronella. Not to anyone else. I wonder how it happened. It does change things, doesn't it?'

She had finished her vodka and was about to pour herself another. Seeing his eyes on her, she put the glass down and the bottle away. 'Yes,' she said. 'It changes things all right.'

The next day Robin went down to London. She caught the six forty-five from Charbury Central as usual; as usual

145

at that hour in the grimy old station among the smells of fish and coal smoke and oil and raw wool and dank stone she felt faintly sick. She would feel better as soon as she'd had her breakfast but at this moment she always found herself wondering if any man was worth it. She felt no better for having a quarrel with Petronella the night before; she was going to London ostensibly to see *The Canterbury Tales* and Petronella had asked tearfully why she never took her to London or, come to that, why Daddy couldn't take them both.

Clive had unexpectedly intervened on Robin's side, saying that he himself certainly couldn't afford a day off, and at this stage in her studies neither could Petronella.

What had upset Robin was that they were both telling lies. Clive could take a day off at any time he liked; and a day off now wouldn't do Petronella any harm at all. In fact, she'd have liked to have taken the child. The train reached King's Cross at ten; there would be time to take her to the King's Road for a shopping orgy. Most of the stuff there was rubbish, but girls of Petronella's age adored rubbish. And she and Petronella could have talked together. She took it for granted now that she'd never be near the boys again; but she had been near Petronella and now they were going apart. And none of this, she thought drearily, was relevant. She did love Petronella – love her, rightly or wrongly, more even than her sons – but Stephen, whom sometimes she saw only once a month, was real in a way Petronella was not.

As she got on the train and found a first-class smoker she began to rationalize. Petronella would eventually go to University, she would find new friends there, she would be less and less at home. It was more than likely that she'd want a place of her own, even though her home was so near and even though Clive would gladly buy her a little car to make the journey. And she'd get married, perhaps not even to a local boy – and then where would Robin be if she hadn't made a life of her own?

After breakfast and the first cigarette of the day she returned to her compartment and newspapers and paperbacks.

The worst part of the journey was over; now she'd shaken the sleep out of her system and could be quite happy with her thoughts. She'd look at the papers, but she'd save the paperbacks; having got them, she had no pressing urge to read them. It was only when you had nothing to read that you had the urge. She could think of Stephen now, she could look back right to the beginning and then to the last time they'd been together; there's be no phone calls, no appointments, nothing to do except to sit and to think of him. She could give herself, she could think of how she could have given herself in the beginning.

And that was something to think about. She'd been mean and begrudging and calculating when she was young: it was only now at forty-three that she knew anything about giving. Yes, young people ran off to Gretna Green, they were made wards of Chancery, they seemed to be the generous and the reckless ones, but these were the exceptions. Most were like Robin when they were young: they weighed up a man's income, prospects, stability. Sometimes they were lucky: the man measured up to their requirements and they loved him too. But the measuring up came first, not the love – *don't marry for money, but marry where money is.*

Did men think like this? No, they didn't. They fell in love, they imagined that because they were in love the girl would automatically measure up to their requirements too. They couldn't really love someone just as they were. And then when they found out that they hadn't got the person they had wanted – which was little wonder, since she'd never existed – the trouble started. Stephen was an intelligent man and he'd made this mistake twice. It appeared now that he was making it for a third time.

She didn't have any sympathy for Jean. If she wanted to keep Stephen, she'd have to be with him and not spend nearly all her waking hours in the theatre. In the true sense, she'd been with Stephen a hundred times more than Jean had in the last five months; and she'd been with Stephen just five times, counting this time, counting her chickens well before they were hatched. In twenty years she'd never so much as kissed another man except under the mistletoe or after Auld Lang Syne or now and again at a party and now she was going to see her lover as if it was the most natural thing in the world.

She caught sight of the middle-aged man who had got on the train at Bradford looking at her legs under cover of his *Yorkshire Post*. Her blue nylon dress was far from being mini length but it was well above her knees; unless she was very careful there was a glimpse of stocking top. She didn't move; there was nothing very terrible about the poor devil extracting a little harmless pleasure from the contemplation of the fraction of an inch of stocking material. It was a male fetish which she'd never been able to understand; she liked looking at the only two naked male bodies she'd ever seen, but their socks and underwear left her cold.

She must get Clive some new underwear; in nearly every pair of underpants he'd got the elastic was frayed, and two vests at least had small holes. But probably Vicky wouldn't notice, any more than she'd notice with Stephen. She'd phone the shop tomorrow; he'd never think of it himself, and she didn't want him to be uncomfortable as he would be with his underpantts bunched round his hips. She wondered sometimes about him and Vicky. She hadn't been in much doubt about their relationship since the night she'd come in for a drink and there the connexion had been between them, absolutely palpable. They'd even gone in for the oldest trick in the game, a jolly flirtatiousness, looking at each other openly, Clive putting his arm round her at every opportunity; it was very clever, but what Vicky had forgotten was that Robin had been married to Clive for over twenty years.

Apart from that, she'd known, from other occasions when she'd talked to Vicky, that Vicky was interested in Clive. It doesn't matter what words you use – *I hate him, he bores me, I've never thought of him in that way* – a flicker of the eyes, an inflection of the voice, a movement of the hand, tells a different story. You grew older, the lines came, you had to have a girdle and a really good brassière, you had to be careful about what you ate and drank, you had with increasing difficulty to steer the middle course between letting yourself relapse into the dowdy matron, comfortable Mum, always sensible, always neat, and being mutton dressed as lamb. No one seemed to make nice clothes for women in their forties; perhaps they thought that they didn't have any money or that their money was counterfeit.

You were in your forties and even if you'd found a lover – or found him again – you were already wondering if you wouldn't be replaced by a younger woman some day. It was of no consequence how old a man was; that middle-aged man, still peering at her legs from behind the *Yorkshire Post*, had most of his hair and probably all of his teeth, he was two stones overweight and had never been good-looking, but somewhere there'd be a dolly of twenty who'd be happy to have him. And a man like Stephen, clever and amusing, with all his hair and teeth, no belly at all to speak of, and a job in TV to top it all, would have his choice of dollies.

You were middle-aged and there were all these things to contend with, and the change of life looming ahead and old age and the grave not as far away as they once had been. But one advantage you had: you knew the score. If your husband had a mistress you knew without anyone having to tell you. You also knew why he'd taken a mistress. He'd never strayed before; although if she hadn't met Stephen again she'd have taken steps to nip his little friendship with Ruth in the bud. But Vicky had evidently done that job for her.

She wondered who'd told Clive about her and Stephen. For someone had told him: men never know until they are told. Their wives can stop sleeping with them, never be home at nights, neglect the house and the children, take to expensive coiffures and scent and underwear, and still they don't catch on. Of course, most men don't even notice whether their wife's hair has been done or not, and they can't tell the difference between Woolworth's scent and Chanel or nylon and pure silk. Or else it was that they simply didn't look at their wives, or even smell them.

Clive knew, though; and without a word they'd come to

an agreement. All those years together meant something, after all. But Vicky's husband hadn't come to an agreement, and he didn't appear the type who would. And she always forgot Jean. She'd only seen her on TV, and Stephen hardly talked about her at all. If she hadn't seen her on TV, she would have been a less shadowy figure; you could believe in the existence of someone you'd never seen, but you couldn't really believe in the existence of someone you'd seen in fictional situations in two dimensions. And the house seemed to bear no impression of her character; her real life, of course, was not lived there.

Robin dozed off and woke to find the train passing through the soft, tamed, almost edible landscape of Hertfordshire, the green of angelica, the brown of milk chocolate, and the dress which had been on the cool side in Charbury at dawn now a little too warm. Her skirt had ridden up to show her slip and she was certain that she'd been showing her pants too; the man behind the *Yorkshire Post* would have had an interesting journey.

She freshened up in the toilet, but her nap had left her with the beginnings of a headache. And she wasn't quite sure, looking at herself in the mirror, that the dress, a mid-blue with white piping, suited her. She could buy another and change into it, was in fact going to buy some dresses if she saw anything decent, since she wasn't meeting Stephen until one o'clock, but it might look rather strange when she returned. Why, she couldn't say, but it would. It wasn't Clive who would notice, but Petronella. And, she thought, feeling something like guilt for the first time, Petronella was the one person she didn't want to know.

But over a cup of tea in Peter Jones she decided to buy a new dress, change into it for Stephen, and then change back into the blue one. And she'd buy herself a new handbag too. And something for Petronella and – why not? – something for Clive. A neckerchief with a ring, in a dark colour because he was so fair. She had Stephen's gift already, the complete poems of Louis MacNeice; he'd lost

Plant and Phantom and *Autumn Journal* and hadn't got the later poems in any case.

Now in the sunlight the pale colours of the tearoom came into their own. There were a lot of women of her age there, passing the time by spending their husband's money, chattering away about clothes and children in piercing well-bred voices. She was to all outward appearances just such another, compensating herself for being middle-aged, buying what, to be honest, she didn't really need. But she wasn't compensating herself; this was an extra. She had what few, if any, of these women had; a lover she excited, and was excited by another human being, she'd soared away from the beaten track. No matter how long or how short a time it lasted, she was more than half-alive.

She lit another cigarette and then in the sunlit room, in one part of her mind already choosing a dress, seeing the colour, a sort of flame red, which she wanted, she was seized, ravaged almost by the thought of death. She didn't want to die, but for a second she saw death as a culmination: she now had had everything, more – even without Stephen – than most women ever had. She never, if she could help it, thought of death but if it came now, even at this very moment, she wouldn't go into the darkness having missed anything. And if Stephen this afternoon had to say it was all over, her heart would be broken, and she knew that hearts did break. But what she had had couldn't be taken away from her. At the beginning of the affair she'd been frightened that it could; now she wasn't frightened any more.

Lying with Stephen later in the bed in the spare room she tried to tell him some of this. It seemed important that he should share it with her, that more than their bodies should come together, that there should be no secrets between them; and in a way, because it had meant so much to her, because it had been the kind of thought one so rarely has, she wanted it to be a gift, like the volume of poetry, she even found herself hoping that he might start writing poetry again, that he might write a poem for her. She wouldn't even want a dedication: it would be enough to know that the poem was for her.

'I was thinking about death this morning,' she said. 'At Peter Jones.'

'That's no place to think about death.'

'I was so happy. I thought of all that I had. I couldn't have any more, could I?'

'We could be married. Or we could just go away and live together.'

'What would we live on?'

'I've got a little money saved up. I'd write. Maybe write a book.'

'But that's not now, is it?' She looked down at his loins, then put her hand very gently on his manhood. 'I think about *now*. I mean there isn't any more to want. I didn't think I'd see you again or that if I did I'd feel nothing. And it was better than before. Because when you're younger you're more easily frightened. And now' – she gently, almost imperceptibly, began to stroke – 'I'm not frightened of anything. I'm not asking the price any more. I'll pay it, whatever it is.'

He sat up suddenly. 'For Christ's sake don't talk like that, Robin. Death, paying the price, not being frightened – it's not, it's not – healthy. It's not *you*, don't you see?'

She smiled. 'Do you know who I really am, then?'

'Someone I've loved for a long time. Someone who's always the same, always happy, always calm, always a real woman. Someone who isn't a bundle of nerves – Jesus, have you seen all those pills in the bathroom cabinet? – someone who's not always in a bloody stew about her bloody career and her bloody looks and her bloody buggering sodding image ... Someone who doesn't talk about death.'

The yellow Venetian blinds, which should have looked gay against the whitewashed walls, suddenly put her in mind of prison. Since her last visit to London four small framed watercolours of sketches for stage sets had appeared on the walls and a big yellow nylon fur rug beside the bed, but the room was still austere – a prison cell in a progressive country, Denmark or Sweden or Norway, perhaps.

'You don't really want me,' she said. 'You want your idea of me. You don't really know me.'

'Don't be angry with poor old Stevie,' he said in a wheedling voice. He put his hand between her legs. 'What's this nice thing here? What is it? What do you call it? Tell me.'

'No. You're very well aware – I won't. I won't, I won't use that word. You're not fair. Oh God, yes.' She sat up and whispered into his ear. 'Dirty little boy,' she said, happily. 'You're just a dirty little boy.' She reached out. 'I'll show you the way, little boy. Are you lost, little boy?'

But at the moment when there should have been no thinking, the thought wouldn't go from her mind: he didn't know her, only her body and his memories of his youth. There would be no poetry except this simple physical collaboration: the chance for it to be born should have been taken long ago.

It didn't alter all that she felt for him; but when they were dressing afterwards with an eye on the clock, when she was putting the sheets in the laundry basket and putting on new ones (did Jean, she wondered, never concern herself with such mundane matters?), when he was sitting back in the taxi afterwards, his arm around her, talking all the time of divorce, of marriage, of living together if Jean wouldn't give them a divorce, of the contacts he had in journalism, of the books he was going to write, of actually working in TV as a producer and performer again instead of an *éminence grise*, she listened to him and smiled, she reiterated her love for him, she promised to come with him whenever he asked. But she couldn't keep the sadness out of her voice; and when he had left her and she was staring out of the window at the sweltering tenements outside King's Cross, she realized that never once had he noticed that sadness.

Fourteen

One of the reasons for the Hailton Players being very much solvent, with a healthy surplus every year and better equipment (including a brand-new lighting plot) and wardrobe and properties than most repertories was that, apart from having a central position on the High Street, they had, soon after they were founded just before the war, been able to buy the dance hall in the next street. Apart from the income from lettings for dances and other functions which this brought in, this meant that now they possessed what many other amateur theatres didn't, adequate rehearsal facilities. And of course they always had sizeable premises available for their own dances and meetings. The Atlanta Hall (it was now officially the Players' Hall, but the old name had stuck) was a single-storey brick building standing next to the Council car park. The car park was ample for the needs of the users of the Atlanta Hall and was in fact used by few others in the evening.

Atmosphere is something which it's difficult to define or account for, but indisputably the Atlanta Hall had a good one. It was respectable, to begin with: whether it was a Players' function or not, there never was any trouble there. It was clean without reeking of carbolic and scented disinfectant; and it was cheerful and bright. It was even trendy; much of the decoration had been done by the members, who included architects, art teachers, an interior designer, and two ex-professional producers. (They hadn't been big name producers, but they'd made their living in the professional theatre and had put by enough to retire in comfort in Hailton.)

What the interior of the hall reflected was taste and labour *con amore*. The chairs – and this is a minor item – were, for instance, ordinary Windsor chairs. But instead of being left in their original brown they were painted in different colours. The walls had been repapered with a very good golden and purple flock wallpaper which had been bought cheap from bankrupt stock. In the home it might have been rather overpowering; in a public hall it induced an atmosphere of opulent cosiness. The lampshades for the wall and ceiling lights were large and copper-finished; these again were bought cheap from bankrupt stock, and replaced the plain white original ones. At one end of the room was a stage for the band, at the other end a rather larger one with a bar and tables and chairs. The décor for the band stage was never allowed to remain for too long and was never stereotyped. On the night that Stephen came, the night that things started to move, the drapes at the back and sides of the stage were purple and violet and the cut-outs in front of each musician were painted silver.

The band was the Players' Ensemble, made up from Players' members. The pianist was an accountant, the drummer a bank manager, the trombone a lecturer in economics, the trumpet an assistant sales manager at Lendrick and Sons. This was a pretty fair cross-section of the Players' membership, except that there was only one teacher among them. Teachers tended to predominate in the Players because teachers have shorter hours and longer holidays than most people. From time to time there would be grumbling about this but, as the teachers were quick to point out, they were the ones who put the time in on the various committees, they were the ones who did the essential chores, they were the ones who kept the theatre going.

The Ensemble didn't try anything fancy. It was there to play for dancing and it belted the music out in strict dance tempo, loud and clear. No one in the Ensemble thought that he was going to be discovered, any more than anyone in a Players' production did. Though Stephen didn't analyse it, this is what gave the occasion its particular charm. Everyone was there simply to enjoy themselves; though many of them no doubt were interested in advancing their careers they didn't foresee their presence at this dance as in any way furthering that advancement. Stephen was used to frequenting circles in which attendance at any function whatever from public ball to private party was motivated either by the desire to improve one's position or the necessity to maintain it.

Heads had been rolling at the studios lately, consequent upon a shift in the power structure of the Board; he wasn't as yet quite certain as to whether his head would join others or whether he'd be promoted. There were periods when he'd wished he'd stayed with the BBC and this was one of them. With Auntie you played politics to get ahead, not to survive. If you left other people alone, they left you alone.

He squared his shoulders as he entered the dance hall. He was more tired than he'd been for a long time; he'd not thought about his problems in the drive up, the Jaguar running beautifully after its servicing and the sunshine roof open to catch the Indian summer, the best weather of all, warm but cool, smoky golden, aromatic and faintly, pleasantly sad. Now it was night and he was well over forty and last night he'd had no sleep thinking about his job and Robin and Jean. Jean had gone to bed early for her after dropping her bombshell; she hadn't stirred all night, but he, after trying to read himself to sleep, had stayed up sipping whisky and trying without much success to work out where he stood and what he was going to do.

It had been a well-ordered life he'd built up for himself, he thought, looking around the dance floor for Robin. Work to fill the day – and work which you did better and better as you grew older – and always plenty of invitations to fill the evenings. And free tickets for all the shows. The time when you didn't get free tickets – or free anything – was when you were young and had no money. And Robin to humanize his life, Robin with whom he could take off his armour. It had gone past being merely physical: with grown-ups you want something more. There had been the occasional dolly girl – twice, in fact – since he'd met Robin again, but recently he couldn't even be bothered to notice them. They were insipid, even when they tried to titillate the appetite with casual mentions of drugs and lesbianism and suicide attempts; it was too easy, all they had to offer was offered the very first time. And they'd accumulated nothing from the past, because they had no past, only hockey and A levels and a couple of seasons giving it away up and down the King's Road.

He would have said even before he met Robin that he had nothing to complain about. He got on well enough with Jean; she went her way and he went his. Or until last night he'd thought that she went her way. Now everything was changed.

He looked at the people on the dance floor with something like affection. Was it his imagination or were they more English, slower-moving, slower-talking, fresher-faced, than their opposite numbers in London? Was it his imagination, or was there a sort of innocence about them, young, old, middle-aged? They'd have their infidelities and their hatreds, their feuds and backbiting, their secret shameful weaknesses. But there didn't seem to be any sense of tension, if they had a rat race here it was more in the nature of a sporting event, with rules and regulations and penalties, a race in which sometimes the nice guys might even win. And it wasn't on tonight.

He caught sight of Robin in a rather fussy lilac dress dancing with a sandy-haired man in a dark-grey suit exactly like his own. He went over to her when the music stopped.

'Robin.' He kissed her lightly on the cheek.

'Stephen.' She stared at him. Then her face lit up. She might as well, Stephen thought, have told the sandy-haired man that this was her lover, there was no mistaking that smile for one of friendship.

She turned to the sandy-haired man, her eyes still on Stephen. 'Bruce, this is an old friend of mine, Stephen Belgard, Bruce Kelvedon.' She took Stephen's arm and led him to the bar. 'Let's all have a drink. What brings you here, Stephen?'

'I'm visiting my parents.'

The expression on Bruce's face was one of faint incredulity. 'That's nice,' he said. 'What are you having?'

Stephen gestured towards Robin.

'Sorry. What will you have, Robin?'

'Scotch, please.'

'Me too, please.' As he looked round for a table he decided that he didn't like Bruce. He himself wouldn't ever be known as a *gentil parfait* knight as far as women were concerned, but at least he liked them. Bruce didn't. He wasn't queer, and he probably needed them as much as any other man, but he just didn't like them.

'Why didn't you tell us you were coming?' Robin asked, as he took her to an empty table. The fussiness of the dress didn't matter; she was as excited as a child on its birthday. He loved her, and she would be his last love.

'A programme was cancelled. So I was free at an hour's notice. I phoned you but you weren't in. Then I phoned again and Petronella said you were here. So here I am.' He suddenly didn't want to speak any more, he didn't even ask to be alone with her, but only to look at her. And there was a moment now before Bruce came back with the drinks that he could look at her. He wouldn't ever want to look at any other woman so badly. He would never feel so safe again, or less lonely. He knew now what she'd been trying to say about death; because if he had to die tomorrow it wouldn't matter. There was nothing romantic about it; it was the plain unadorned truth.

Bruce returned with the drinks. 'Sorry I've been so long,' he said, a faint smile on his face. 'Must be an interesting job, yours, Stephen.'

'I'm really more and more of an administrator these days.'

'Well, I'm more and more of a salesman. It's the pattern of things today.'

'I'm not very happy about it. I'd rather actually make programmes than plan them.'

'Well, I'd rather potter about with graphs and equations than sell products. But we'd rather have more money, wouldn't we? And unless you're terribly creative the money isn't in making things.'

Speak for yourself, Stephen thought. He began to dislike Bruce even more. 'Oh, I don't know. We worry too much about money. The way taxes are, what good is more money, anyway?'

'You can do something with the money before the vultures close in,' Bruce said.

'Some people can. I can't.'

'Don't talk about money,' Robin said. 'Or taxes. It makes my head ache.'

'All right, I won't,' Bruce said. He gave Robin a social smile. He had had his serious conversation. Stephen thought: now he was going to relax.

'I'll tell you a dirty story,' Bruce said. 'A *mucky* story, as they say in these parts. It seems that the Pope was very ill. The best doctors in Italy couldn't cure him, then at last they summoned the greatest specialist in the world. He examined the Pope, then he said—'

Keeping his face in the correct listening expression Stephen concentrated on Robin. He'd heard the story a year ago at a party in Hampstead and a Catholic had told it him; he did it far better than Bruce, because he was consciously making fun of something which he held in awe and reverence. Robin smiled at him; he put his foot forward under the table and felt her catch it between her ankles and hold it there. The last time they'd been together, in September, they'd lain together for an hour after making love, not speaking, not caressing, their bodies touching but their arms at their sides, breathing together, quiet and tranquil, asking for no more. It was *that* he was going to remember.

'We'll get you a blind one, then.' Bruce's voice came to the front of his mind, then he switched off again. He would ask for nothing more than this: to be with her, to touch her very gently. But she had to live in Hailton; there would be sharp eyes watching and sharp ears listening, even in that crowded bar. He looked at Bruce and broadened his smile as if waiting for the pay-off.

'A blind deaf-mute with no arms? Are you sure you could fancy that?'

Bruce paused. 'And then he said' – he chuckled – 'then he said' – he deepened his voice and assumed a foreign accent – 'What's it matter so long as she has big tits and kinky boots?'

Stephen went through the motions of laughing; Robin smiled then gave a polite snicker. Bruce emptied his glass and leaned back. 'I often wonder who makes them all up,' he said. 'Someone must.'

'There aren't any new ones,' Stepehen said. 'The old ones are brought up to date, that's all.'

'But someone must bring them up to date.'

'We'll never know,' Stephen said. 'Perhaps I should do a programme about it. Track a joke down to its source.'

'You'd have a job on with that one,' Bruce said. 'A lady in New York told me it.'

'Shame,' said Robin. 'You told Vicky you did nothing but work in New York.'

Bruce smirked. 'Oh, travel has its compensations ... Another drink, Robin?'

'It's my turn,' Stephen said.

Robin's ankles tightened. 'It's time you asked me for a dance.'

On the dance floor, she whispered to him: 'You needn't be quite so circumspect. When do you go back?'

'Tomorrow lunchtime.'

'Where are you staying?'

'The Grand.'

'I'll phone you if I can. Look over to the right. No, don't let them see you ...'

He saw Clive and a woman in her late thirties dancing together.

'You met her at the party.'

'That was the hell of a party.'

'That's Bruce's wife. Clive's *friend*.'

Bruce came on to the dance floor with a thin young girl in a white crochet dress.

'What goes on there?' Stephen asked.

'That's Olive Villendam. I don't know what goes on there.'

'She's out of his age group.'

'She likes older men. She chases Clive sometimes.' She nudged him. 'Who are you to talk?'

'I'm a reformed character now. Look. Bruce's wife isn't pleased.'

Bruce was dancing cheek to cheek with Olive now; Vicky's face was set with annoyance.

'She's been dancing with Clive all evening. She should be glad Bruce is off her hands.'

'I've been thinking of what it would be like to live here—'

Her eyes filled with tears. 'Oh, don't, Stephen. You're here, and that's enough. Talk about the band or something.'

'It's a nice schmaltzy combo. Very good with the waltz. Do I waltz well? It's about the only dance I really know.'

'It's like the bands they used to have when we were young. Sweet and strong and very refined.'

'I didn't have much sense when I was young,' he said.

The music came to a stop; for a second there was the usual dazed expression on the dancers' faces as if awakened from sleep.

'Buy me a drink,' Robin said. 'Something long. I'm thirsty.'

When they were sitting with their drinks she looked at him in silence for a moment. His foot searched for her legs under the table but she drew them back.

'Why did you come tonight?'

'To see my parents.'

'No, you didn't. Something's happened. I knew as soon as I came here tonight. I knew even before I saw you.'

'I'll tell you tomorrow.'

'It's only good news that keeps.'

'Jean's leaving the show.'

'I can guess the reason. Is she pleased?'

He hesitated. 'Yes. Strangely enough, yes.'

'Are you?'

He did not answer.

'Are you, Stephen?'

'In a way. Oh Christ, I don't know. It alters things, I suppose ...'

'I'm not jealous,' she said. 'You only see me about once

a month and sometimes not even that. What will we do now?'

'I'll get a place. And I can come up here.'

'To visit your parents?'

'I could do a programme about the Players.'

'What a marvellous idea.' She waved across the room. 'Clive, Vicky. Come and have a drink. And listen to Stephen. You know Stephen, don't you, Vicky? Stephen Belgard. You met him at Clive's birthday party.'

'I'll get the drinks,' Clive said and went about the business of getting them with an efficiency which Stephen found himself envying. 'Now. Why do we have to listen to Stephen? Not that we're not delighted to listen to him. But why especially now?'

'I'm thinking of doing a programme about the Players,' Stephen said. 'In depth, as they say.'

'And that's not all,' Robin cut in. 'Jean's leaving the show. You know, Stephen's wife, Jean Velfrey. She's having a baby.'

Clive shook Stephen's hand. 'Jolly good,' he said. 'Now your troubles begin. It isn't your first one, is it, though?'

It sounded like a rather snide remark but, looking at Clive's open, smiling face, Stephen decided that it wasn't, that Clive was, in view of Stephen's age, making a reasonable deduction. 'Not my first one,' he said. 'My wife's, though. She's had a lot of trouble, you see.'

'I'm sorry,' Clive said. 'Really depresses a woman, that sort of thing.'

'Your poor wife,' Bruce's wife said. She wasn't bad-looking with a rather thin face but large dark eyes and a passable figure and a good complexion, and she had the rudiments of dress sense, which was more than most of the women here had. But there was something strained about her, her whole manner was over-dramatic.

'Come, come,' Clive said, 'it's a natural thing for women to have babies.'

'Oh, is it. If you knew what a miscarriage is like – it can *kill* you – or even what they call a normal pregnancy is like ...' She turned on Stephen, her voice shrill, almost accusing. 'How old is your wife?'

'Thirty-four.'

'Then it won't be easy if she hasn't had one before. You'll have to take great care of her.'

Stephen decided that he disliked her as much as he disliked her husband. And she'd had a drink too many; she wasn't drunk, but another two vodkas should do it. If this was Clive's taste in women, he didn't admire it.

'I'm sure Stephen will take great care of his wife,' Robin said. Stephen saw to his amusement that Robin didn't like Vicky either.

Clive laughed. 'Vicky, anyone would think poor old Stephen designed the human reproductive system personally. Don't be so fierce.'

'I *am* fierce. The poor girl – not only is she going to have the hell of a time, but she's having to leave the play. It's not fair.'

'Life isn't fair,' Clive said. 'What's the use of making a fuss about it?'

All right for some, Stephen thought: when have things not gone smoothly for you? Clive, even more than Bruce, was the sort of man he generally disliked at first sight. Pink-cheeked, healthy, clear-eyed, spruce, masculine enough to get away with a pink batiste tie and matching handkerchief and a gold identity bracelet, exuding cheerfulness, he was one of those upon whom fortune positively doted. *Clive has a nice nature. Clive would never do anyone a dirty trick.* No, of course he wouldn't; he'd never have occasion to. Nothing had ever happened to sour that nice nature, and probably nothing ever would. But through conversations with Robin, those long conversations about every subject under the sun, earlier he knew about Clive's eczema, about his aversion to cats and lobster, his passion for new bread and the indigestion which followed indulgence of that passion, occasional bouts of hypochondria during which he'd buy patent medicines and take huge doses of them until he imagined himself better. It was impossible to dislike a man whom you knew so well, because you couldn't see him as a type any more, he became representative of no one but himself.

'But what about this programme?' Robin asked. There was a spot of colour in each cheek. He'd never seen her like this before.

'It's only in the preliminary stages,' Stephen said. 'There's a lot of planning to be done first.'

'Research,' Robin said. 'I'll be your research assistant. I have albums of all the Players' productions right from the first ones; you'd hardly know me, I looked a bit like Deanna Durbin. And there's Clive. He looked a bit like Nelson Eddy. And then there's a gap for me, when I was having babies. And Clive disappears.'

'I was working too hard,' Clive said. 'To support you and the babies, darling.'

'And then you see me again,' Robin said. 'It's fascinating. Getting older and older.'

'You're never old to me, my dear,' Clive said, and bowed in her direction.

'Well, of course, you've grown old along with me, haven't you?' They were sitting near the edge of the stage; she glanced down at the dancers. 'Bruce is cutting a rug with Olive Villendam,' she said. 'If that's the right term. Why don't you cut a rug with Vicky, Clive?'

'I'm not sure whether I'm the right sort of build for it.'

'Give me a cigarette, will you?' When it was lit for her, she inhaled with an unmistakable satisfaction. 'Clive never was one for jiving,' she said. 'Too heavy.' She was now speaking to Vicky. 'He has to be very careful about his diet. Even then, he's fifteen stone stripped.'

'All muscle and bone,' Clive said cheerfully. All this is going right over your head, Stephen thought with something like affection.

'I think we ought to try it,' Vicky said in a hard voice. 'Will you excuse us?' She pulled Clive out of his chair.

'Darling, are you trying to stir up trouble?' Stephen said after Clive and Vicky had gone out of earshot.

Robin smiled. 'Yes. Get me another drink. Whisky.'

When he returned with the drinks she'd gone. She returned in five minutes exactly; the two little spots of colour had disappeared.

'I haven't been long, have I?'

'I'd have waited.'

'Gabby is looking at us.'

'Gabby?'

'Mary Hardrup,' she whispered. 'A neighbour of mine. Knows everybody's business. Would you really have waited?'

'All night.'

'I was frightened you wouldn't wait.'

'I do love you.' He mouthed rather than spoke the words. It was strange how happy it made him to do so.

'I love you too. Where are we going to go now?'

'In London?'

'In London.'

'It's a big city. I'll find somewhere.' They were still speaking in low voices. She smiled at him, quite composed now.

'We take what we can get,' she said. 'She's coming over.'

'Hello, Mary dear,' she said to the woman who approached. 'Do sit down. Meet Stephen Belgard. Stephen, Mary Hardrup.'

'Our local celebrity,' Mary said. She was a plump woman with a very pale skin and a round stolid face. Only the grey eyes were restless.

'Stephen's doing a programme on the Players,' Robin said.

'It's really just at the planning stage,' Stephen said.

'Oh, how marvellous.' The grey eyes went from Stephen to Robin then back again to Stephen.

'He'll have to do a lot of research first,' Robin said. 'A lot of research.' The two little spots of colour were showing again on her cheeks.

Fifteen

When they had gone home later that night Vicky had a one-sided quarrel with Bruce which culminated in her throwing a glass at him. The quarrel was one-sided because he sat in silence sipping whisky whilst she screamed abuse at him. The glass missed him by a yard, hitting the wall behind his armchair and landing undamaged on the floor; he watched it roll to a stop on the sheepskin hearthrug, his face not changing expression, then spoke for the first time since they had left the Atlanta.

'That just about finishes it,' he said. He pointed to the armchair opposite. 'Sit down. Have another drink if you must. I've something to tell you.'

'And I've something to tell *you*. Making an exhibition of yourself with that little teenage tart. Sneaking out with her—'

'My last fling. But it's really no business of yours. And you haven't much room to talk, have you?'

'What do you mean?'

'My dear girl, do you think I didn't know? Not that I give a damn. I haven't for a long time.'

'You're horrible. You're quite horrible.'

'Some people think not. But that's quite enough of that nonsense.' He went over to her and slapped her hard across the face. His expression didn't change but when he hit her his eyes widened. He returned to his seat and continued to sip his whisky.

She rubbed her face. 'You're a bully too. A cruel bully.'

He started to fill his pipe. 'I shall hit you again if you don't shut up. But this time much harder. Now listen. I want a divorce. I may add that the firm wants me to divorce you too. It isn't so much your drinking – on the whole you carry it very well – or your infidelities. It's just that you don't pull your weight as a wife. You're too unpredictable. And a bit too intense. You make people uncomfortable.'

She started to cry.

'Cry if you like. But not so noisily that you can't hear me. Otherwise I'll have to hit you again. I think I may, anyway.'

'Christ! You absolute *bastard*.' She got up. 'I'm going.'

He made no move to stop her. 'If you like. But it'll be the worse for you if you do. And for Clive.'

She sat down again. 'Go ahead then. Say what you have to say.'

He lit his pipe. 'I'm going to divorce you.'

'Just like that?'

'Just like that. Now, I'm a reasonable man. And Tracy is a reasonable woman.'

'Who the hell's Tracy?'

'She's the woman I'm going to marry. I met her in New York. We went out together a time or two then she came to England, ostensibly' – he smiled – 'on business.'

'Have I met her?'

'I took care that you shouldn't. Of course being a woman' – he smiled again – 'she's very curious about you. But obviously it's better that you don't meet her.'

'Oh, you're cunning.' There was almost an admiring note in her voice. 'You're very cunning.'

'Well now, let's get down to details. The last thing either of us wants is trouble. That is, Tracy and I. Tracy's a widow, a very rich woman indeed, and she doesn't like trouble in any shape or form. Besides, she feels rather guilty about you. I've told her she needn't, but she does nevertheless.' He nodded his head approvingly. 'So we'll be very generous. We'll buy you this house to begin with. And you can have everything in it. And your car. And on top of that I'll allow you four thousand a year—'

'And you'll cite poor old Clive?'

'I told you we didn't want any trouble. Nor do I want to be revealed as a cuckold. Tracy's a very sensitive woman. She understands that. I'll use a professional co-respondent. After leaving this place for good on Wednesday. That gives me time to pack.'

'Time to pack!' She started to laugh hysterically. 'God, I always knew you were a cold sod, but this beats the band. Tell me, how old is Tracy?'

'Thirty-eight. She's been a widow two years.'

'Has she any children?'

'A son of eighteen. That's not really a problem.'

'I suppose if he were you'd throw him out. What about our children?'

'We'll work out something. Or rather I will.'

'You haven't thought of the effect on them?'

'They don't see all that much of me. Or of you, come to that.' He frowned. 'Perhaps if we hadn't sent them away—'

'If we hadn't sent them away, you wouldn't have gone so far so quickly. What's your family life in comparison with that? Please, Bruce, don't be sentimental now, it's more than I can stand. Let's face it, you don't like children. Though you like young girls, don't you?'

Her head was aching and for a moment she felt the need for violence, not in return for Bruce's blow, but to prove that she had heard what she had heard, to prove that he was a human being, to drive away the fear of the future which was overwhelming her.

Sixteen

There are times when the gun is loaded, so as to speak, when every incident has a violently disruptive consequence. The gun must have the bullets put in; this is what Stephen did when he came to the Atlanta Hall that Friday night.

Bruce had been intending to ask Vicky for a divorce – or rather to force a divorce upon her – in any case. He wouldn't, however, have announced his intentions when he did, or have announced them quite as brutally, if Vicky hadn't got so drunk that night. And Vicky wouldn't have got quite so drunk but for the atmosphere which Stephen brought with him. It was an atmosphere of danger, of passion, of *change*. It's easy to say that this is romantic, high-pitched, strident, false, founded upon the odd notion that a sexual relationship with one particular person is all that is necessary for spiritual and physical fulfilment. It doesn't prevent people from being affected by it. Vicky was on the way to being drunk when she met Stephen; exposure to this atmosphere finished off the job.

Robin was affected in a more direct way. To begin with, she was, whatever she said to the contrary, jealous. She accepted, as a reasonable being, the fact that Stephen had sexual relations with Jean just as she had sexual relations with Clive. But as an unreasonable being, as a woman infatuated with Stephen, she hated to think of him even touching any other woman, demanded absolute faithfulness from him, and would have done even had they slept together only once a year. As long as she wasn't reminded of the fact it could be pushed to the back of her mind, she could even pretend that Stephen didn't sleep with Jean. His announcement of Jean's pregnancy made it all too real; worse, she was reminded that she couldn't give her lover a child. For, quite deliberately, she'd tried to do just this. She'd never used any precautions with Stephen. This seems incredible for an intelligent and sensible woman: apart from any other consideration her doctor had warned her the year before she met Stephen again that to have a baby was highly dangerous. But to be in love is not to be reasonable; for some women the act of sex, if they're in love with the man, is bound up with reproduction.

Besides this she foresaw, on a more prosaic level, that Stephen's house would very soon be not available. It would be a question of making love wherever they could – outdoors, in a car, in a borrowed flat, in a sordid hotel if they could find a sordid hotel. Twenty years ago it wouldn't have mattered, but she had long been used to comfort and privacy.

Not that this hurt. They would manage somehow as long as they really wanted to be together. What upset her was that now she would find herself matched against Jean and a child. Jean by herself she could have taken on; but there was no telling how Stephen would feel about the child. He was older now than when he'd begotten his first child: old enough to know what he'd missed by not seeing the child grow up, old enough to need to be loved by a child. She could understand this, she could even feel that she wouldn't want him if he could leave Jean and the child for her. But this was of no consolation.

Bruce and Vicky left before the dance ended, arguing at the tops of their voices. It was not quite a scene, not quite a scandal, but it had been noticed. Clive, his usual cheerful and unperturbed self, had invited Stephen back to Tower House for a nightcap. The nightcap, on Stephen's insistence, had been tea: he was, he went to some pains to tell her, leaving for London early in the morning.

Alone in the hall with her for a moment he said in a whisper: 'I'll phone you.' But Petronella had come out of the study at that moment and he left without telling her when. She was surprised to find herself glad to see the door close behind him.

But after Clive had locked up and emptied the ashtrays and they were going upstairs together she was visited by a huge desolation. At the door of their bedroom she stopped.

'I don't feel terribly well,' she said. It was an effort to speak. 'I'd rather sleep in the spare room tonight.'

'I'm sorry, dear,' he said. 'Can I get you anything?'

'I'll be all right.'

'I thought you looked a bit pale tonight.' He looked at her anxiously. 'Are you sure I can't get you anything?'

'No, no,' she said, holding back her tears. 'I'll be all right.' She ran into the bathroom and when she came out their bedroom door was closed. She cried herself to sleep that night, pressing her face into the pillow to muffle the sound, and she cried herself to sleep again on the Saturday night. But on the Sunday night there were no tears. She slept as soon as her head touched the pillow and on Monday for the first time in her life got a prescription for sleeping pills.

She continued to sleep in the spare room. Clive made a polite inquiry about her health every day, and then seemed to dismiss it from his mind. He did not refer to her decision to sleep apart after over twenty years of sharing a bed; she both resented this and was grateful for it, and on the balance gratitude outweighed resentment. She couldn't have endured any sort of quarrel, would have even gone back to his bed to have avoided it. She had once heard Clive talk of battle fatigue, when you came to the limit of what you could bear, when you literally could sleep standing up, and she now understood what it was like. Clive was outside what she felt now: she had no feelings about him. She didn't know whether she would sleep with him again or not; but in the meantime she forced herself to be very careful about the sleeping pills.

On the Wednesday morning following the Players' dance, Bruce left Vicky as he said he would. There was a quarrel, again one-sided: Bruce sat looking at his watch, not answering her, then left, putting a typewritten sheet of paper on a coffee table and weighing it down with an ashtry. He stood back and looked at the paper, whistling between his teeth, a habit of his when doing minor tasks, then carefully placed the ashtray so that it was dead centre. He left without looking at Vicky. She listened for the sound of his car engine and when it started up she poured herself a vodka.

At half past six she phoned Clive at Tower House. Robin answered.

'I must speak to you, Clive. I must—' Her voice steadied. 'This is Vicky. Could I have a word with Clive?' Each word was separated by a fraction more than was strictly necessary.

'Wait a moment,' Robin said, and went into the study. Clive had just poured himself a whisky.

'It's Vicky.'

'What does she want?'

'I don't know. Why don't you find out?'

When he came back into the room Robin had poured

herself a whisky. He noticed that it was a larger measure than usual.

'I'll give you a divorce if you want,' she said.

'Oh, Christ, Robin, leave me alone. I've enough on my plate as it is.' He lit a cigarette.

'You're smoking too much. Give me one, though.' There was no emotion in her voice. 'I can see there's enough on your plate. You might remember what I said, just the same.'

'I like this room,' he said. He went over to the big mahogany desk and looked at a mark on the front, frowning. 'Joan's done it again,' he said. 'She just *slams* the chair against the desk.'

'There's some stuff I got that'll shift the mark.' She sipped her whisky. 'I saw Ruth in Hailton today. She sent you her love.'

'Comfort me with apples, for I am sick of love.'

'Poor old Clive,' she said. There was feeling in her voice now. 'You only want a quiet life, don't you?'

Clive became aware that a decision had to be made. There was an escape route opening up, twisting and narrow and steep, scarcely visible through the fog, but feasible. But he needed a guide. He couldn't make it by himself. He looked enquiringly at Robin, but she looked away from him and down at her drink.

'I'm going out,' he said.

'When will you be back?'

'I don't know.'

'You haven't had anything to eat yet.'

'It doesn't matter.'

'You needn't tell me if you don't want to. But what's the matter with Vicky?'

'Bruce has left her.'

'It was always on the cards, wasn't it?'

He sat down heavily and took a drink. 'God, what a mess.'

'You'd better go to her, hadn't you?'

He didn't answer immediately, but finished his whisky and poured himself another.

'I like this room. I don't want to go out.'

'It's your choice.'

He stood up. 'There are times when I wonder just how much choice any one of us has.'

'Are you going to her or not? She needs someone, you know.'

'I didn't say I was going to her.'

She laughed. 'Clive, you needn't keep up any pretences now. I know you're all for a quiet life, but there are limits. Go round and see her now. Why don't you?'

He lifted himself out of his chair with an effort and walked slowly out of the room.

It could now be said that all the bullets had found their targets. Clive was the last one to be hit. Or perhaps the last one to know he'd been hit; a strong man can carry on for some distance before the wound begins to pull him down. Or perhaps he was too stupid, too complacent, too secure, to know that he'd been hit, perhaps the message had farther to travel until it reached his brain. But of all those who'd been affected by what had happened on Friday night he was the only one to realize that we don't have any choice in what happens to us, that once the bullet leaves the gun, there's no hope of dodging it.

Seventeen

Vicky was at the wheel of her car when Clive drove up. He brought the Mercedes to a stop with the bumper an inch from hers, ran out, and reached over her into the Imp and took away the ignition key.

'I told you to wait for me.'

He helped her out of the Imp; she stood there swaying a little. 'I wanted to get out of that damned house.'

'In the state you're in? Your first bloody stop would have been the morgue.'

The light was on above the porch of the house; her face contorted as she looked at it. 'Swedish style,' she said. 'Melodiously warm brick and glowing cedar harmoniously combining – it doesn't look like a real house at all.'

He held open the door of the Mercedes for her. It had been warm all day but now that the sun had gone in there was a cold wind, faintly stirring the poplars beside the road.

'Get in, for God's sake, Vicky.'

'Are you frightened of the neighbours?' She laughed. 'It's a bit late to bother about that now.'

'Fasten your safety belt,' he said as she sat down beside him.

'I can never fathom the damned thing, darling. Don't be so fussy.'

He fastened the belt for her. 'I once saw a face that had been through a windscreen,' he said. 'I don't want to see another.'

He was enjoying himself now: she was a little drunk, her eyes were red with crying, but she was glad to see him, she wanted him. The older houses on the road were set well back, some with high walls, some with hedges; their occupants wouldn't see him, but the occupants of the new ones next to Vicky's would. By tomorrow evening at this time everyone in Throstlehill if not in Hailton would know that he and Vicky had gone off together. Before another day had elapsed it would be an essential part of the story that both of them were blind drunk and after another day it would come out that Robin had run alongside the car weeping and cursing and trying to stop them.

And he didn't care any more; when Robin had asked him so calmly if he wanted a divorce he had seen himself not as a husband and a father and an individual, not even as an individual to be hated and resented and feared, but as something less than a man, as an object to be got out of the way. He had ceased to exist for her that night Stephen had come to the Atlanta Hall; and the worst of it was that he was beginning to wonder if he'd ever existed for her as

174

anything more than a signer of cheques, an escort when needed socially, and, of course, a reliably erect penis. He'd kept to the rules all his life, he hadn't had a day off work since he went to Lendrick and Sons from the Army, he'd never gone with another woman until she'd given him cause to; and now she'd written him off. He scarcely heard Vicky's convulsive sobs.

Then he smelt face-powder, and she said: 'I'm all right now.'

'Good.' He glanced at her; she'd recovered with extraordinary rapidity.

'We're burning our boats,' she said, almost gleefully as they took the Charbury Road.

'You can say that again. Why are you burning yours?'

'I told you. Bruce is leaving me. For a rich American widow I've never even met.'

'He'll be back.'

'Oh, no. That's the trouble. That's the horrible thing about him. He never changes his mind.'

'Did he find out about us?'

'Oh, that's not the reason. For a long time now he's gone his way and I've gone mine. But I was a help to him you see. Daddy was Bruce's professor, and he pushed him on and introduced him to people. And Daddy pays for the boys' education.'

'Where does a professor find the money?'

'Daddy's very clever at investments. Didn't I tell you?'

'No.' There were a lot of things they hadn't told each other; there would be plenty of time.

They were in Bosworth Green now; it seemed curiously empty. When he was a boy there always seemed to be plenty of people on the streets at night; now it was as if there were a military curfew. The old Electric Palace on the right was a Bingo Hall, the Carmel Street Methodist chapel further down a tyre storage depot, the little shops which had kept open late all seemed to have boarded-up windows, the supermarkets all closed at five-thirty, and it seemed that almost every day another block of buildings was torn down. Change had to come; but sometimes he had an unreasonable fear that the district wasn't being demolished for purposes of redevelopment but to destroy any cover in which the last remaining human beings – he himself would somehow be amongst them – might hide.

When they entered the flat in Inkerman Street it smelled cold and musty. Clive switched on the Dimplex and lit the gasfire; Vicky went immediately into the bathroom. When she returned the redness round her eyes had disappeared and she smelled of cologne. The mustiness and damp had vanished; the room had now become home.

'Just hold me for a moment,' she said. 'That's better ... I feel like a woman now.' She rubbed her cheek against his. She moved away from him and went over to the cocktail cabinet. 'Drink?'

'A small whisky.'

'I'll have a very small vodka. Then we'll just sit for a while and be kind to one another. Shall we always be kind to one another?'

'I'd like nothing better.' He sat in the armchair opposite hers and sipped his whisky very slowly, the warmth spreading inside him. He was savouring this as he had not savoured the last whisky he'd had: that had been to give him a quick lift, to steady his nerves, and this drink was an extra, a luxury on top of the luxury of looking at Vicky in her bright green wool dress. She was looking at him with warmth, she saw him as a man, there was no coldness there or, what was worse, cool pity.

'Shall we live here?' she asked.

'I think we can find somewhere more comfortable. With central heating for a start.'

'This will do,' she said. 'I'd settle for a tent the way I'm feeling.'

'Bruce seems a Grade A bastard, I must say.'

'I'm not so struck on Robin either.' Her voice had a sharp edge.

'She asked me if I wanted a divorce tonight.'

'Just like that?'

'Just like that.' He hesitated. 'Is Bruce going to cite me?'

'Does it worry you?' Her voice had a sharp edge again. 'The answer is categorically no. He's going to do the gentlemanly thing. As long as his widow isn't involved. Tracy. I can just imagine her. I bet they're well-matched. Tracy wants to be generous' – she fished in her handbag and handed him a sheet of paper – 'as you can see. Bruce is going to help her manage her business interests. But one of the reasons he was divorcing me, he was frank enough to say, was that I wasn't a suitable wife for a man in his position.' She got up and poured herself another drink, a large one this time. 'Oh, I speak well enough and dress well enough and know which fork to use, but I drink too much and I'm too indiscreet. So his seniors have informed him.'

The tears were coming to her eyes. This wasn't what he'd brought her here for, she was going to ask him for more than he had to give. Perversely he thought for a moment with real longing of Robin's serenity, of the way in which she kept her sorrows to herself. He looked at the sheet of paper. It was very neatly typed and consisted for the most part of figures and dates. There were half a dozen addresses and telephone numbers and one short paragraph written in the third person.

'He's being surprisingly generous,' he said. 'Financially, I mean.'

'It's Tracy who's being generous. Buying me off in fact. Not that Bruce has ever been bad that way. He's never kept me short.' She looked at her empty glass with an air of surprise and got up to fill it again.

'I love you,' she said. 'I was thinking about it today and I kept thinking: never mind, it isn't so bad, I've got Clive, and he's ten times the man that Bruce is.' She was talking to herself rather than to Clive; her eyes kept coming back to her glass. 'Do you know what Bruce did last night? He'd been sleeping in the spare room since Friday and then last night he came into my room and poked me. Never spoke a word. I thought I must be dreaming.'

'I'm sorry.'

'Oh, I expect I'll have worse than that to put up with before I die. I suppose he was getting his money's worth. If you're trading in a car, you drive it until you get the new one, don't you?'

Suddenly he realized in panic that she was a stranger. He'd mistaken her for someone else. He didn't know her, he wouldn't ever want to know her. There wasn't any love. He'd used her because Robin had hurt his pride, he had used her because Robin was more and more absent from his bed, in spirit if not in body; and now he was going to use her because even Robin's body wasn't there. Between them something did exist – he couldn't have made love to a prostitute, he couldn't, if it came to the pinch, have made love to a young girl like Olive Villendam. It had to be a grown-up woman, it had to be a woman he could feel some respect and affection for.

She'd said she loved him and soon he would have to say that he loved her. He'd said it before, but then it had been part of a game, it gave you a definite emotional kick, it gave the most *outré* variations a genuine panache, it swept away any hint of the sordid. Vicky had used him too, used him because she was lonely, because she was bored, had taken up extramarital sex as other women took up good works.

She left her chair and sat on the floor at his feet, her body warm against his legs. He stroked her hair then reached own and put a hand over each breast. As he did so a pain expanded inside his chest, holding him back against the chair; very slowly he lifted one hand to his chest and rubbed it and the pain had gone, not gradually, but as instantaneously as it had appeared.

He was left frightened as he'd never been frightened before, even in battle. In battle he'd not been alone, in battle it was plain to see what there was to be afraid of, in battle there was a set of technical problems to be solved, there was an overriding purpose.

Then he worked out the reason for the pain and the fear passed. 'I'm hungry,' he said.

She jumped up. 'Oh, my darling, I'm sorry. I'd better get used to looking after you, hadn't I?' She held out her hand. 'Come on, we'll see what there is.'

He sat down at the kitchen table with his drink and a cigarette as she looked in the refrigerator and the store cupboard. 'There's RyVita,' she said, 'and four different kinds of pâté, and soup, and tinned ham and tinned chicken. And eggs and butter and lard and frozen beefburgers and chicken joints. And a pie we'd better not risk. And four bottles of rosé.' She looked in the cupboard again. 'And tea and coffee and that everlasting milk stuff.'

'I've been stocking up,' he said. He had actually bought the provisions the day before on his way home from the mill, not quite knowing what impulse had led him to do it, except that he foresaw trouble and wanted to prepare a refuge.

'It's funny,' she said. 'When there was just tea and coffee there, this place was like a hotel. Now it's a home.' She kissed him on the forehead. 'Our first home.'

It was too easy, all too neat: he could read her mind. Her husband had left her, his wife had all but left him; they had been lovers for six months, therefore they would get married. She hadn't used the word yet, but she was working up to it.

'You're not talking much,' she said. 'Are you sorry you left Robin? You have left her, haven't you?'

'There isn't anything more between us,' he said. 'I don't think there ever was.'

'I'll make it up to you when we're married.'

'I know you will.'

'Get me another drink, will you, darling?' She held out her glass.

He half-filled his own glass then put a small one in hers and topped it up with tonic. He found himself glad even of the two minutes of solitude in the lounge. Gradually he was realizing that what he really wanted to do now was to sit by himself and be quiet, very slowly to get drunk enough not to care. He had always needed solitude; he had never needed alcohol before.

When he gave her her drink she scrutinized it wrily. 'Are you trying to make me taper off, darling?'

'I'll get you another.'

'Clive, I'm not an alcoholic. I drink too much sometimes when I'm unhappy, but that's all. I wouldn't have to if I were happy.'

He stared over her shoulder at the too-red apples, the too-yellow carrots, the too-green lettuces and cabbages on the wallpaper. That was why he didn't like the kitchen; the vegetables looked as if they were made of plastic. And the room was too bare, too cold; for a kitchen to come alive meals must be cooked there every day, there must be traces of flour, sugar, salt, and a few stains which can't be scrubbed off, the bottom of pans must be blackened, there must be odd cups and plates and a small knife, once part of a set of dessert knives which is especially useful for purposes for which it was never designed.

'You'll feel better once you're rid of Bruce,' he said. He took the tin of ham from her. 'We'll just have some of this and some RyVita. And some coffee would be a good idea.'

'I could make you an omelet.'

'Don't bother, honey. Just as long as I have something solid inside me I'll feel better.'

She threw down the tin. 'You mean you're feeling lousy? You mean you're feeling miserable? You mean you don't want to be here with me?'

It was as if the flat were really his home, as if he really were married; her voice grew loud and shrill, her face ugly with rage. He wanted to run away, but he couldn't think of anywhere to run away to; he got up and put his arm round her shoulder and said soothingly: 'Darling, I only mean I'm hungry. I love you' – he switched his mind off as he said the three words – 'and I wouldn't be anywhere else. Let's be kind to each other, pet, because nobody else is going to be.'

'I'm sorry,' she said. 'I've been through a lot lately. It was that damned typewritten list that finished me off. I wouldn't put it past the bastard to have had his secretary do it.' She straightened up perceptibly and started to move about the kitchen briskly and efficiently, gathering together pans, knives, bowls, forks, butter, eggs, salt, pepper. 'You're going to have a ham omelet,' she said, 'and we'll have some rosé with it. No, you needn't do anything except open the tin. Just have your drink and relax.'

He drank another whisky – a full glass this time – whilst she was preparing the meal. He had a good head for liquor normally, but normally he didn't drink this amount of straight whisky before a meal. Normally his wife didn't ask him if he wanted a divorce, normally his mistress didn't talk about marrying him. And then his mood altered rapidly: marriage to Vicky, even children, was suddenly a practicable and desirable idea. 'From now on,' he said, 'I'm going to please myself. I've never considered myself, do you know? We'll have a nice new flat to live in, then we'll look for a house. What kind of a house would you like?'

'A big old house.' She brought out a bottle of rosé.

'Robin can go to her bloody Stephen if she likes. If he'll have her—' He shook his head slowly. 'Mustn't say that, it's unworthy. Most unworthy.'

She laughed. 'Be unworthy if you like, darling. Because you're quite right. That affair's over, let's face it.'

'Poor old Robin,' he said. 'Poor old Robin.' He ate his omelet greedily, washing each mouthful down with wine.

'When shall we be married?'

'As soon as we can. I'll look after you. Do you know who the biggest shareholder in Lendrick and Sons is? Me. And I've always been careful, you know.' He took a large bite of RyVita; some splattered on to the table. 'Not mean,' he said. 'Careful. No speculative investments. Shall I tell you a funny thing? My sensible brother Donald is the one who likes a flutter. Not me. Yes, I'll look after you.'

'Always? You promise?'

'I promise faithfully.'

There was some part of him untouched, watching coldly even when afterwards they took another bottle of rosé into the lounge and sat on the sofa together, the light off, the slightly unsteady but soft light from the gasfire taking ten years off Vicky's face. For a while he sat in silence with her, stroking her hair and her breasts very gently.

'You know that story of Hemingway's?' he asked her. 'We've declared a separate peace.'

'I don't know it, darling. But it's a lovely idea.'

'Peace,' he said. 'That's all – all I've ever wanted.' He pulled up her skirt slowly. She had white nylon pants through which the pubic hairs showed; he stroked the smooth material for a while, the cold part of his mind sneering: this was a return to adolescence when the words *knickers, suspenders, stockings*, were exciting in themselves, he was being a voyeur, not a man; he disregarded the message and pulled down her pants and for a moment was enraptured. Vicky sighed, but did not speak; then suddenly that cold part of his mind had taken over and he felt nothing at all.

She got up suddenly, kicking away her pants, and led him to the bedroom. Like the lounge, when they had first entered the flat it smelled cold and musty: he lit the gas-fire, switched on the Dimplex in the far corner and then automatically began to undress. When he saw her naked, desire suddenly returned; but he had no sooner entered her – or rather her eagerness being so great, had been drawn in by her – than it was over.

'Goddam you,' she said harshly. 'Have you finished already?'

'I can't help it.' His head was beginning to ache. He turned his back to her. This had rarely happened to him before; but never had any woman used that tone to him.

'You never were like this before. Have you got someone else on your mind, then? That bloody Ruth?'

'Ruth? I haven't seen her for months.'

'Don't think you can deceive me. I saw her at that birthday party of yours. And I saw you.'

He climbed out of bed and took cigarettes and matches from his pocket. He put two in his mouth, lit them, gave one to her, and went back to bed. He heard her voice from a distance but he was thinking of Ruth. He'd not thought of her because it would have unsettled him too much to think of her. If he'd thought of her, he might have remembered that his happiest moments with any other human being had been spent with her merely talking. He might have remembered too that at that same birthday party she'd warned him about Vicky.

He felt a fist strike him in the back.

'You're not even listening, you cunt.'

'I've told you, my head aches.' The obscenity affected him more than the blow; it wasn't just that she used it, but the tone in which she used it.

'Get yourself some aspirin then.'

He dragged himself out of bed, went over to the wardrobe, and put on one of the two old beach wraps he kept at the flat. The beach wrap was of cotton towelling, worn thin by washing, but there was a certain comfort in being covered up.

In the bathroom he doused his head in cold water, and then took two Alka-Seltzer and brushed his teeth. He sat for a moment on the edge of the bath, his head in his hands, waiting for the Alka-Seltzer to begin working. The effect of the drink was already beginning to wear off a little, enough for the cold part of his mind to take over.

He returned to the bedroom to find Vicky sitting up in bed in the other beach wrap with the bottle of vodka beside her on the bedside table.

'Christ, haven't you had enough?' he said. He yawned as he said it: he was tired to the bone, a phrase he'd never really appreciated until now.

'Don't worry about me. You don't anyway, do you, leaving me high and dry like that?'

He looked at his watch. It was midnight. He hesitated, then climbed into bed. Lighting a cigarette that he didn't really want, he said, 'I've never seen you like this before.'

'Well, this is me. This is how I get to sleep when Bruce is away. *Got* to sleep when Bruce *was* away.' She looked at him appealingly. 'There are two glasses here.'

'My God, no, I've had enough.'

'You could stop me.' She put a hand inside his beach wrap.

183

'Sorry. I'm forty-seven, not twenty-seven.'

'We won't do for each other, will we?'

He turned his face away. 'Will we?' she insisted. He still didn't answer. 'Oh, Christ,' she said, 'we really won't. How did I miss it?'

'We might have done,' he said.

'But for this—' she indicated her glass. Her tone was now detached, almost amused, but her voice was becoming more slurred. 'Funny you didn't notice before.'

'Perhaps I didn't want to.'

It was almost impossible to resist sleep now.

She leaned over, took the cigarette out of his hand, and put it out.

'Sorry,' he said. He sat up in bed. 'I think I'll go home.'

'You know what I dream about? Some man who'd know what I was and would still love me. And who could help me.'

He only half-heard her. He shook himself like a dog emerging from water. 'I'd better get home.'

'Stay with me till morning.' She pushed him back gently on the pillows; he fell asleep almost immediately.

'It's not much to ask, is it?' she said to herself. 'Nobody else ever will. Not ever again.' She emptied her glass and poured out another. When the bottle was empty she got out of bed slowly and took a cigarette from the packet by Clive's side. She lit the cigarette and sat on the edge of the bed by him, smiling as she looked down at him. When she had finished the cigarette she put it out very carefully and thoroughly on the big blue ashtray and, slowly and laboriously, holding on to the bed for support as long as she could, walked over to the gasfire. She did not stagger, but every time she brought her feet up it was as if she were dragging them up out of a bog. When she reached the gasfire she supported herself against the wall for a moment to draw breath. Then she knelt down.

Clive wasn't frightened at first of the man who was trying to push him through the open trapdoor in the floor of the aeroplane; he was too small, scarcely five feet, though he

184

had broad muscle-packed shoulders and long arms which appeared to be growing longer and were, he saw now, fighting to keep his balance as the aeroplane suddenly climbed steeply, growing thicker too, filling the cabin. He couldn't see the man's face; he pushed forward against huge cold hands, hands which now forced him back until, sickeningly, swoopingly, slowly he was falling through darkness, to awake sitting on the floor with a sharp pain in his back where it had scraped the bed frame. There was, coming through more and more painfully with the smell of gas, a scraping sensation inside his lungs; he spent what seemed like a quarter of an hour but was in fact three seconds struggling against the desire to fall on the bed (something inside his head assured him that if he let go the scraping sensation would be taken away) and then staggered over to the source of the hissing sound in the fireplace and turned down the tap. 'Across,' he said thickly in between convulsive coughs and retching. 'Across, you stupid bastard.' He made his way, painfully and slowly to the window and moved the catch. It was an old-fashioned sash window with a cord that needed renewing; it was either fully up or fully down and always descended with a bang; it crashed down now and the cold night air came in and he sagged against the window-sill, the scraping sensation inside his chest still pulling him down.

Then he realized as the fresh air came into the room that he was alive and vomiting; he straightened up and walked across to the bed, where Vicky was lying breathing stertorously; she was half across the bed, her legs on his side of it, which probably explained how he'd fallen out.

He pulled her out of the bed by her arms; she landed with a thud on the floor and moaned once and then slumped down; he dragged her to her feet and out into the passage and into the kitchen. Still holding her he let down the kitchen window and felt her stir in his arms.

'Oh God,' she said. 'Who're you? Go away. *Go away.*' Then she vomited violently into the sink; the vomit smelled of alcohol.

'That's handy,' he said, and ran the tap.

'Jesus,' she said, holding on to the sink, 'I'm going to die. I'm going to die.' She vomited again, then sat down at the table, holding her head between her hands, her hair falling across her face. 'I'm going to die,' she said thickly, 'I'm going to die.'

Clive ran the tap again to clear out the sink and then filled the electric kettle.

'You're not going to die,' he said. He switched the light on; she covered her eyes with her hands. It occurred to him that if it hadn't been a moonlight night he probably wouldn't have found the gas tap; he'd only just been able to find it as it was.

'What happened?' she asked. 'What happened? Oh God, I feel so awful. You tried to kill me. That's what it is. You tried to kill me ...' She relapsed into muttering; he saw that she wasn't yet quite sober.

'You tried to kill us both,' he said. He would have been angry if he hadn't been, now that his head was clear, so glad to be alive. The kitchen, he realized, was beautiful, the heat from the Dimplex was beautiful, the steam from the kettle was beautiful, the electric light and its plain white coolie hat lampshade was beautiful; his mouth was acrid with vomit, his head and his chest ached, but that too was beautiful, because he wasn't going to die.

'The fire went out,' Vicky said in a whining voice.

He handed her a cup of coffee. 'It didn't, you know. Gas-fires don't go out.'

She sipped the coffee, holding the cup with both hands. He felt an unexpected twinge of pity noticing how thin and small her hands were. There was a little colour in her face now, but those large dark blue eyes seemed to have become almost grotesquely larger, a darker blue, almost black, and the thin face still thinner. 'It must have gone out. And then come on again.' She was speaking with great care, but the thickness was leaving her voice. She was sobering up quickly, which wasn't surprising.

'The fire was on when we went to bed. You kept on drinking, and then you turned it off and turned it on again. You wanted to kill us both.'

His coffee was washing away the taste of vomit, warming his stomach, easing the ache in his chest; never in all his life, even in the Western Desert, had he enjoyed any liquid more. But now he was beginning to feel angry with himself as much as with her.

'It was an accident,' she said. Her eyes filled with tears. 'Why can't you be kind to me? You used always to be kind to me.'

'You're lying,' he said. 'You forget, I wasn't as drunk as you. I saw that gasfire on as I went off to sleep. It didn't turn itself off and it didn't turn itself on again.'

She rummaged in the pocket of her beach wrap for a handkerchief, found nothing, and wiped her eyes with her sleeve. 'Get me some aspirin, or something, will you?'

He brought her the tube of Alka-Seltzer from the bathroom, half-filled two glasses with water, put in two tablets in each glass and handed a glass to her.

'The boozer's friend,' she said, looking at the fizzing water. 'Polo mints help too. And black coffee. And arrowroot biscuits. Then if you're sick, you've something to be sick on.' She went to the cupboard and returned with a RyVita. She began to nibble it. 'This'll have to do.' She shivered. 'Do you think we could have that window closed?'

'Wait a moment.' He went into the bedroom and sniffed. There was no trace of gas, only the reek of vomit. It was now simply a large room with a high ceiling, a double bed with tumbled sheets, two bedside tables, a wardrobe, a Windsor chair and two piles of clothes on the floor. The bronze-painted gasfire was simply a rather old-fashioned heating appliance, no longer an instrument of death. There was an empty vodka bottle and two glasses on Vicky's bedside table. It was no longer a death chamber; he looked at it without fear. But as he picked up the clothes from the floor he knew that he would never spend another night there.

'It's safe now,' he said to Vicky. He put the clothes on the kitchen table, closed the window with an effort, and spread out the clothes on the Dimplex. 'It's no use escaping death by gas only to get double pneumonia.'

'Sometimes I hate people like you,' she said.

He found an unopened packet of Benson and Hedges King Size in his jacket pocket.

'Do you?' he said, grinning. 'Then I won't give you one of these cigarettes.'

'You needn't, but you could make some more coffee.'

'A pleasure,' he said. 'Give me your cup.' He rinsed out the cup and his own, filled the electric kettle and plugged it in, then turned to her smiling. 'Do you know, I feel as if I were drunk. It's almost worth being nearly gassed for.'

'That's one of the reasons why I hate you,' she said, in a matter-of-fact tone. 'You see, you *can* get drunk without liquor. I've got to have liquor to get drunk. And then it's always the same after. I wake up feeling dreadful, and then I just drink black coffee and nibble biscuits and take Alka-Seltzer and suck Polo mints until bit by bit I come back to life again.'

'What, every day?'

'Oh no, not *every* day. Otherwise even you would have spotted it. Of course, when we used to come here and Bruce was away, I wouldn't settle down to serious drinking until after I'd got home. And even then I'd be careful. Tonight I didn't have to be careful. No need to go home, no need to drive home even. No Bruce. No children. If he did go away when the boys were home, he had his sister Elspeth stay. To give me a hand, you know. You met her once when she was here this summer. She's a widow. Ex-nursing sister. Very Scots and sober. The boys adore her. I've a feeling she's going to take over more and more.' She wiped her eyes with her sleeve. 'Give me a hankie, damn you.'

He passed her the red silk Paisley handkerchief from the breast pocket of his jacket.

'I'll keep this,' she said. 'It's a very good one. That's what I first noticed about you. Everything you have is very good. You didn't bargain for me, though, did you?'

'I was glad enough you came along when you did.'

'Someone else will, and I think I know who that some-one else is. Or you'll go back to Robin. You'll get by. I got by, myself, until the boys went away to school. There was always so much to do. You grumble about it at the time, but you don't realize how happy you are ...' She beat her fist on the table. 'Oh, God, I wish I'd had more children and they'd been girls ...'

He found the tears coming to his own eyes.

'You're crying,' she said. 'You'll not be able to get by any more if you weep at other people's sorrows.'

'I'm sorry,' he said. 'Only I can hardly endure listening. It's too much—'

'Too much? Yes it is. I almost wish you hadn't turned that damned gas tap off.'

'Oh Christ,' he said, shocked. 'You can't mean that.'

'Listen, I'm going to be by myself now. I haven't a husband, I haven't a lover, I *know* I'll lose the children. I'll be by myself. *And I can't bear myself.*'

'You mustn't do it again—'

'Don't worry. I said *almost* wish. I can't remember exactly what I did. But I do remember, just remember, trying to wake up.'

'I ought to take you home now.' Suddenly there seemed nothing more to be said.

'I won't spend another night at that house!' Her voice rose to a scream. She put her hand over the table and clutched his. 'Let me stay here. I don't even want you to take me home. You can get me a taxi as soon as it's light.'

'What will you do then?'

'My brother lives in Surrey. I'll stay there until I find somewhere.'

'Do you need money?'

'No, no,' she said impatiently. 'That's not a problem.'

'You should check, just the same.'

She left the room and came back with her handbag.

'There. Thirty-five pounds and my deposit book. And a banker's card and an American Express card and a Barclaycard. Do you want to look at the deposit book?'

He shook his head.

'You really are kind,' she said softly. 'But it's rather like being kind to animals, you do it out of a sense of *noblesse oblige*, don't you?'

'You'd better get some rest.' He went over to his jacket and took out the Imp key. 'You may need this.'

She took the key from him and gave him the key of the flat. 'That ends that, doesn't it?'

'It's a long way to Surrey,' he said. 'You really do need some rest first.' He took the clothes off the Dimplex. 'I'll move this into the sitting-room and then you should be warm enough. Put these clothes on and you can wash in the morning.'

They dressed quickly, their backs to each other by unspoken agreement, and went into the sitting-room. 'Where shall I sleep?' she asked.

'On the sofa.'

'I don't want any of the blankets from next door.'

'I'll bring the rug in from the car.'

When he had brought the Dimplex and the rug in, she lay back smiling. 'I'm warm and safe now,' she said. She stroked the rug. 'Lovely soft colours, all the colours of the rainbow, and so soft, so soft. Everything you have is very good ...'

'Go to sleep,' he said. 'It'll soon be morning.'

'Don't go away, Clive.'

'I'm only going to switch the light off.'

'Keep it on. *Please keep it on.*'

He pulled up his chair closer to the sofa.

'Don't fall asleep,' she said drowsily.

'I won't fall asleep.'

As her eyes closed she reached out her hand for his, clutching it tightly.

Eighteen

'I won't ask you where you've been.'

Robin's voice was not so much cool as patronizing, slightly amused. Clive's head was aching again and his face was smarting. He kept a razor at the flat, but it didn't suit his skin as well as an electric shaver; he'd be very lucky if he didn't come out in a rash.

'Don't ask me where I've been,' he snapped. 'I never ask you, do I?'

'Do you want to come home?' There was not even a hint of pleading in her voice.

'I'm going away.'

'With Vicky?' For the first time her voice betrayed concern.

'By myself. To think things out.'

There were two panes missing in the call box and the wind drove the rain in, soaking his trouser leg.

'I think you're doing the right thing. Are you telling me the truth about Vicky?'

'For God's sake, why should I tell you a lie? Vicky's going away. For good.'

'I never thought it would last.'

'I'm not as faithful as you are.'

'Clive, you needn't rub it in. I'm not trying to reproach you, I'm not blaming you for anything. If you're upset, I'm the one to blame. Just tell me what to say to people.'

'Say I've gone away on business.'

'And Donald?'

'I'll deal with Donald. And I'll ask Walter to take care of the money side.'

'Clive?' Then there was a silence and he thought he heard a sob.

'Yes?'

'Don't – don't do anything foolish.'

'I wasn't thinking of it,' he said. 'Goodbye.'

He hung up and went back to the Mercedes, feeling both unaccountably guilty and unaccountably elated. For twenty years at this time on a Thursday morning he'd been either at Lendrick and Sons or out on Lendrick and Sons' business; if there had even been an occasion when he was off ill he couldn't remember it.

He had tried four call boxes before he came to one in working order; he hadn't been before to the part of Charbury where he was now. It was a district of new housing estates as far as the eye could see: they all seemed to be semi-detached and pebbledash with red roofs and mean little porches with half the ground floor of each taken up by a garage, the windows on the door the same size as the other windows in the house, suggesting rather disturbingly that whoever designed the house thought of cars and human beings as being equally important. He wondered idly what it was like to live in one of these houses; he had lived in a small house, older than these, and with no conveniences, during his childhood but he could bring few of the details back to mind.

There was a terrace of shops in the same pebbledash and with the same red roofs as the houses on the estate on the small concourse where he was parked; he got out of the car and went into a newsagents. Buying a *Yorkshire Post* and a packet of Gold Leaf – there were no king-size cigarettes stocked, the middle-aged woman behind the counter said with an air of fierce resentment – he realized that he was merely delaying the moment when he'd have to make some sort of decision about what to do with his freedom.

There was a young woman in the phone box when he went out of the shop. He settled down to wait in the car. He had smoked two cigarettes before the woman came out. She stared at him as she went into the baker's next to the newsagents; the stare was a hostile one.

Donald's voice was aggrieved. 'What the hell are you up to, Clive? You know damned well Holmonroyd's coming at ten. It's nearly that now—'

'Listen. I'm taking some time off. I'm probably going to see a specialist. I haven't had any time off in twenty years. I'll let you know when I'm coming back.'

'Oh, all right, but why didn't you tell me before? Why didn't you tell Robin? Why all the mystery?'

'I've an appointment now, Donald. Let's just say that I'm tired. Christ, did I ever complain when you were off all those months?'

'That's all very well, but what'll I'll do about Holmonroyd?'

'You'll think of something, or one of those bright young men about the place'll think of something. Tell him I'm not well. It'll surprise him a bit because evidently every bugger at Lendrick and Sons down to the bloody office boy can go off sick but me. But he'll have to like it or lump it.'

'Clive, you're not in trouble, are you?'

'When have I ever been in trouble? Don't worry, Donald. I leave everything in your capable hands. I'll keep in touch with you through Walter.'

'Why not Robin—'

He hung up and went back to the car. The young woman who had been in the phone box was still staring at him as he came out, and the woman at the newsagents had moved to the door to get a fuller look at him. He considered thumbing his nose at them as he drove away, but thought better of it.

He switched on the radio as he drove on away from the city through a metropolitan-rural landscape in which old stone farmhouses and fields seemed to alternate with new red-brick estates with almost mathematical regularity. He took the turning for Harrogate more out of impulse than any conscious plan, and an hour and a half later phoned Walter Fareland from the Old Swan Hotel.

'I'm going away for a while, Walter,' he said. 'Reasons of health.'

'I'm sorry to hear that. You looked fine the last time I saw you.'

'Well, I'm having a certain amount of – let's say difficulty. You needn't noise it around. No doubt it can be cleared up. Will you pay all the bills and pay thirty quid a week into Robin's bank? I'll settle up with you every month.'

'It shall be done. Where can I get in touch with you if anything comes up?'

'A message to Ruth Inglewood at the bookshop will reach me,' he said to his own surprise.

'Will it indeed? You may recall that I foresaw this particular illness some months ago.' Walter's voice was cold.

'You needn't do all this if you don't want to,' he said.

'If you're going to make a fool of yourself it may as well be a friend of yours who eventually picks the pieces up.'

Clive laughed. 'Aren't you going to dissuade me?'

He heard Walter snort. 'A waste of time. A standing prick has no conscience. Goodbye.'

Clive, smiling, picked up the phone again. He felt curiously lightheaded. It was of no consequence what mattered now. There didn't have to be any plans. He could go away with Ruth or not go away with her; he might even, if it came to it, return home and say nothing. Norman might present a problem but it wasn't a problem which had weighed very much with her that day they'd kissed in the little office at the back of the shop.

'Ruth,' he said, 'this is Clive. I've left home.'

'So I've heard. What do you want me to do about it? Put you and your girlfriend up?'

'Just me.'

'What about her, then?'

'She's gone away. For good.'

'It didn't take you long to find out about her.' Her voice seemed to be a shade less cold.

'No. I made a mistake there. Haven't you ever made a mistake?'

There was a silence. 'So you're coming to me. There's nowhere else you can go to.'

'That's it. Nowhere else.'

'You're a rotten sod, Clive. I want you to understand that some women would tell you to go to hell. But I'm grown-up enough not to bother about my pride. Not if it gets in the way of what I want.'

'I won't ask you to forgive me. It would be wrong for us. Wouldn't it?'

'Quite wrong,' she said.

There was a pause. 'All right. Have you got a pen? Good. Here's my home address and telephone number.'

She gave him a Charbury address and phone number and brief business-like instructions on how to get there. He recognized the address as not being very far from the old flat and for a moment was seized by fear and a longing for Tower House.

'I'll see you there at half past six, darling. Au 'voir.'

The 'au 'voir' was an invariable affectation of hers, he found it endearing though he wouldn't have done on the lips of any other woman.

'Au 'voir,' he said, and walked out of the phone box almost into the arms of a middle-aged blonde woman who had hold of Bruce Kelvedon's arm.

The sight of Bruce brought back the memory of awaking to gasp for breath, of the long agonized stumbling to the gasfire, of the long moment when he couldn't remember which way to turn the tap; if he'd followed his instincts he'd have turned and run out into the rain and the cold untainted air; instead he took Bruce's proffered hand and the choking feeling passed.

'Mrs Van Greer, Clive Lendrick,' Bruce said, with a proprietorial air. Clive had the feeling, so obviously proud was Bruce of having captured her, that given encouragement Bruce would have given her vital and financial statistics and stripped her into the bargain.

'You're here on business, Clive?' Bruce said. There was a difference in him already; his face was not quite as tense, his gestures smoother, self-satisfaction radiated from him.

'In a way,' Clive said.

'I'm just stealing an hour or so. Tracy's got a flat near the Stray.'

'It's a very beautiful little town,' Tracy said. She appeared to be a genuine blonde with that faint peach-blossom fuzz on her face which only American women seem to have. Her voice was deep and resonant with the faintest of accents.

'Have you time for a drink, Clive?' Bruce asked. There was now an almost suppliant tone in his voice.

Clive nodded.

'Fine. We'll go in the Wharfedale.'

When they were sitting with their drinks – Clive noticed with amusement that Tracy had ordered a tomato juice – a signal seemed to pass between Tracy and Bruce. She stood up immediately.

'I must leave you for a moment, gentlemen. No, don't get up.'

'Marvellous woman, that,' Bruce said almost before she had left the room. 'I'll tell you something. She's like a young girl – *tight*.' He lowered his voice. '*Special operation*.' He looked sly. 'Then they talk about the French ... But this is serious, you know.'

'You're in love with her,' Clive said gently. As he said it, he was puzzled with himself for understanding that even Bruce, whom he still didn't like, whom he could never bring himself to like, could be genuinely in love.

'You can't live without it,' Bruce said. 'Or some semblance of it.' His tone changed. 'How is Vicky?'

'She's gone to her brother's in Surrey.'

'Let's level with each other, as Tracy would say. You're not interested in her any more, are you?'

Clive shook his head.

'I think you know why.'

'Poor bitch,' Bruce said. 'I bet I've been painted as the worst villain under the sun, haven't I?'

'I wouldn't say that,' Clive said uncomfortably.

'You needn't spare my feelings, old boy. The truth is, I'd have stuck it out, tried to get some help for her – and I *did* try, but I dare say she didn't tell you that – but I got fed up of it. There were the boys to consider too.' His smooth face suddenly was crumpled then pulled itself into shape again.

'I can understand that,' Clive said gently.

'My father's generation, now, would have stuck it out,' Bruce said thoughtfully. 'We don't, do we? Because when a man gets to be forty he realizes that he's only one life and half of it's over. And people don't change.'

'I've come to realize that.'

'You're having your own spot of complication, aren't you?'

'How do you know?'

'One hears things. But that's your own business, of course.'

'It doesn't matter. I was thinking about your boys.' It was one of the worst moments in his life; he had to speak, but he couldn't help remembering Vicky's hand in his – *I'm warm and safe . . .*

'My boys?' Appallingly, Bruce's face turned white. 'What about them?'

'Don't have them stay under the same roof as her, that's all.' His sense of betrayal grew.

'Oh, she's back to her old games.' The colour came back to Bruce's face. 'It was aspirins last time.'

'Games can become serious. It's only through sheer good luck that I'm alive.'

As he recounted briefly what had happened the night before – or rather, to be accurate, that very morning – he had the sense of being manipulated by a force outside himself. He was telling Bruce that he had cuckolded him; he was also telling him that his wife was unfit to be left in charge of his children. He was also putting himself in Bruce's hands. Being in someone else's hands wasn't a sensation he was used to or one which he particularly relished.

'It might have been an accident, of course,' Bruce said when he had finished. 'But that's just as bad.' He stood up suddenly as Tracy entered; Clive automatically stood up with him, but as he got to his feet was attacked by dizziness and had to support himself with his hands on the table.

'Do sit down, please,' Tracy said. Clive fell, rather than subsided into his chair, and mopped his brow.

'You look real sick,' Tracy said.

Clive recovered himself. 'I'll be all right,' he said.

'It's the after-effects of gas,' Bruce said.

'Gas?' Tracy's face was puzzled.

'Coal gas.' Suddenly the bar started too fill up, mostly, it seemed, with women in elaborate hats.

'You ought to lie down,' Tracy said. 'In fact, my good man, you're going to be made to lie down. Bruce, we're going to my flat. Right now. We'll have a bite there, there's plenty in the icebox—'

She was in her element, completely in charge of the situation, brushing aside Clive's protests briskly but kindly.

Out in the fresh air the dizziness passed and he made a last attempt to break away. 'Really, Mrs Van Greer, it's very kind of you but I'd better—'

The thin jewelled hand on his arm was surprisingly strong. 'You'd better rest. If you had an accident now, why, I'd never forgive myself.'

He found himself in the back of Bruce's Rover with her beside him, her hand still grasping his arm. Over the smell of her perfume he caught intermittently her personal smell, violently, fanatically clean, all natural odours banished. He leaned back, his eyes half-closed: he was going out of the battle-line, this was like that moment in the ambulance at Benghazi before the morphine took hold.

Tracy's flat was a blur of beige overstuffed furniture, all apparently one size larger than normal with a great many flowers for that time of year; it was full of little tables, and cabinets and had a large TV and a Grundig hi-fi taking up almost the whole of one side. There was a glass-fronted bookcase with half a dozen books in. He ate cold ham and salami and liver sausage and a salad which was mostly fruit and drank a glass of hock and three cups of strong coffee, answering Bruce and Tracy in a daze and then was shown to a small room with a single bed covered with a pink satin eiderdown. He took off his trousers, folded them neatly over a chair, put on the dressing-gown which Tracy had given him, lay down on top of the bed, and fell instantly to sleep. His last conscious thought was that the dressing-gown, a voluminous affair of purple silk, was too big to be Bruce's.

The sun was going down when he awoke and the rain

had stopped; he opened the window and breathed in the smell of wet grass and the clean cold air. The flat was empty; he had a shower, shampooed his hair, and had a Listerine mouthwash. The bathroom was large and almost too warm and the bathroom cupboard full of bottles, sprays, and boxes arranged with finicking neatness. He took two Alka-Seltzers, dressed, and went into the lounge. Everything was clear now: he was warm, he was clean (though he would have welcomed fresh underwear and socks) and his system was free of poison. It was as if Robin and Vicky didn't exist. He didn't know what he was going to do in the future, except that within two hours he'd be with Ruth. Whatever that conjunction might imply it wouldn't, he was pretty sure, imply his awaking choking to death; nor would she ever look at him, as Robin had done so frequently lately, as if he weren't there.

He heard voices outside and Tracy and Bruce entered, laden with parcels. Tracy handed three parcels to him. 'There you are, honey,' she said. 'Toothbrush, toothpaste, undershorts, socks, shirt, handkerchiefs.' The gesture caught him at a vulnerable point. 'It's so kind of you' he said. 'Really thoughtful – I had a shower, and that's just what I was wanting—' He stopped, afraid that he was going to cry. 'I'll change now,' he said, and half-ran from the room. Putting on clean things in the bathroom, he did cry; it wasn't painful, as it was always said to be with males, but it somehow diminished the sense of freedom he had been experiencing.

He hesitated for a moment before he pressed Ruth's doorbell. The house was a large square one set well back off the road with a well-kept lawn and flowerbeds, bordered with laurels. There were four cars parked on the tarmac in front of it, among which he recognized Ruth's white Mini Traveller. The house wasn't very far from the estate where he'd stopped that morning but when it was originally built the road would have been part of a small exclusive residential suburb with a clear view, situated as it was on a plateau some thousand feet above Charbury, almost to Harrogate on a clear day. It was a good solid house with no trimmings – unless one counted the bay windows and dormer windows as trimmings – and if the exterior were well maintained so would be the interior. But he didn't want a big scene with Ruth; he wasn't sure that he could take any more violent emotion. Already as he stood with his finger above the bell-push he could hear the sound of his own heartbeat, so loudly that his ears almost ached. He pressed the bell at last and when he saw Ruth's face, found his heart steadying.

'I've come to you at last,' he said, kissing her.

'You could have come to me at any time, you idiot,' she said.

The room she took him into was large and as untidy as the room he had been in at Harrogate was tidy. There were two large bookcases crammed to overflowing with books, on the top was a medley of boxes, statuettes, aeroplane and car models, and knitting wool and needles. Two walls were almost entirely covered with pictures, posters, and pages torn from magazines; the furniture was old and battered, almost tatty, with the exception of a large red-and-black studio couch, and the red fitted carpet beginning to show signs of wear. An easel and canvas stood in one corner and on a long deal table by it was a confusion of paints, brushes, pencils, sheets of drawing paper, and tins of Polywog paste; next to it was an upright piano and a violin case.

'Have a drink, darling,' Ruth said. 'You're going no farther than here tonight. It's whisky, isn't it?'

He nodded. 'Look, honey, there's something we must get straight. What about Norman?'

'Norman?' She handed him the whisky, kissing him. '*Norman?* What has he to do with us?'

'Well, you live with him—'

She laughed. 'Really, darling, I thought you knew. Norman isn't my lover. He isn't anyone's lover. I don't believe he's ever had sex with anybody or anything in the whole of his life. He's quite contented.'

'Won't your living with him put men off?'

'It hasn't put you off, has it?'

'Where is he tonight?'

'Gone to a concert. He's no trouble anyway. He spends most of his time with the gramophone in his own room. He's got a portable TV too. Now *his* room's really lovely, not like this. But he keeps his paints and stuff in here, cunning little devil that he is ... Oh, there's no mess in Norman's room – and he decorated it himself – believe me, he's better than most professionals. But sod Norman. What about you?'

'It's simple. I left Robin and went to Vicky. Bruce is divorcing her. I was sorry for her—'

'Beware of pity, darling. Go on.' Her blue eyes were fastened unblinkingly on him. Or were they sea-green? He decided they were sea-green.

'She got drunk and damned nearly killed me. Gas. Then I realized what a fool I'd been.'

'I thought you would eventually,' she said calmly. 'Does Robin know where you are?'

'She knows I've left her.'

'I thought you wouldn't put up with it indefinitely. Is she going to Stephen?'

'I don't think so. His wife's having a baby.'

'Poor Robin.'

He raised his eyebrows.

'She really does love him, you know. Just as I love you. But she's the marrying type and I'm not.' She hugged her knees. 'I suppose it'll be awful when I'm old. But I'm not old yet.'

'You'll find someone.'

'Oh no, Clive. I've already found someone. You're the someone. I don't know why, but as soon as I first met you I was certain. There won't be anyone else.' She stood up. 'Come on, we'll eat.'

They had steak and salad and Burgundy in the large kitchen – a room curiously like the kitchen at Tower House with a large pine table and a stone-shelved pantry off it. Afterwards she washed up whilst he sat and drank his coffee.

They spoke very little. Had he been of a religious turn of mind the word *sacramental* might have occurred to him of the meal, but it didn't. He only knew that here and now he was happy. Pride – once again he had revenged himself on Robin – had nothing to do with it, and sensuality surprisingly little. He wanted to make love to her, but it could wait. She had somehow given him all the time in the world.

Sipping brandy in the living-room, the feeling continued. They were not separate persons, he thought: as they sat there opposite each other something was growing between them, quietly and strongly and inexorably. He had needed to be jolted out of his routine to see it, he had needed to see in action the very sort of love he couldn't cope with, he had needed even to be near death.

'You know,' he said, 'people in films and novels are always saying they're tired of running away. My trouble is that I haven't run away before.'

'As long as you've run to me it doesn't matter. I used to dream about this, you've come here tonight for the hundredth time, not the first time.' She came over to him and sat at his feet, her head against his knees. 'I always put you in that chair, the one you're sitting in now. When I heard about Robin and Stephen, I was so glad – isn't it awful of me? So I overplayed my hand. It's all right now, though. It's all right even if you go back to Robin tomorrow.'

He stroked her hair. 'I shan't ever go back.'

'You will, darling, you will. Because our lives aren't just other people, they're things and houses and places. You'll go back to Tower House. You'll go back to Lendrick and Sons. I could make my life just you, but you couldn't make your life just me.'

She was wearing a polo-neck jumper; he reached down, unfastened her brassière, and cupped her breasts in his hands. Sensuality was still absent; if he'd been asked to put it into words, he would have said that he was getting to know her. She put her hands over his, pressing them hard; they stayed like that for ten minutes, the only sound in the room the very faint hiss of the electric fire. Then she jumped up suddenly. Still not speaking, they went into her bedroom.

When she was naked he saw why she always wore slacks. Her legs were long and smooth and straight but extremely thin. She saw him looking at them and, for the first time in their acquaintance, blushed. 'I'm a cheat,' she said. 'Very nice upstairs and like something from Belsen down below. Have I put you off?'

'Don't be silly,' he said. 'I love all of you.' The skinny legs, like the short chestnut hair and boyish face, were another reason for tenderness; suddenly he found himself trembling and tears coming to his eyes.

When they were in bed the trembling became violent, and the tears began to flow fast; this time they were painful, seeming to go through his body convulsively, to leave his eyes smarting, to sting his cheeks. 'Oh God,' he moaned, 'I'm sorry, I'm sorry, I can't stop, I can't stop—'

'Have your cry out, my darling. There's nothing to be sorry for.' She pressed his head into her breasts, stroking his back very gently. 'You've been through an awful lot, my darling, you can't help it.'

And then the weeping diminished into childish snuffles and he was suddenly overwhelmed by sleep, a black pillow forcing him down, a black pillow he punched holes in, letting a grey light through, aware fleetingly of Ruth's face, then only of someone else beside him, then of more light, more and more light and his eyes prised open gently by the light to hear birds singing outside and to see Ruth sitting up in bed smoking a cigarette.

He took the cigarette from her and put it out in the ashtray on the bedside table; his mouth against her cheek, he searched between her legs, heard her draw in her breath, felt gratitude for the moist welcoming smoothness around his fingers and dimly and far away but sharply a brief disappointment that it was as it was, that he wasn't, now never could be, the first; and now they were together and staying together and hurrying on a journey together, hurrying towards an end they wanted and did not want, clinging together at the end as if in agony, transfixed by the same spear, carried off into sleep to be awakened by Norman in pink pyjamas and a turquoise dressing-gown carrying a tray.

'Good morning, my dears,' he said. 'Here is some refreshing tea.'

'God bless you, Norman,' Ruth said, sitting up and yawning.

'Drink it whilst it's hot,' Norman said. 'I don't want to rush you, Ruth dear, but we've a lot to do this morning, and time's pressing.' He seemed completely unaware of Ruth's nakedness.

Ruth poured out a cup of tea, her heavy breasts swinging forward, and passed it to Clive. 'Hasn't Jack an appointment with us this morning?' she asked.

'And that nice old girl from the College too. That's why I said we'd a lot to do. So get a move on. Breakfast's up in ten minutes.'

Ruth lit two cigarettes and passed one to Clive.

'It's a bad habit, but I adore it,' she said. 'When Norman says ten minutes he actually means twenty. He's an awful old fusspot. Keeps all the clocks half an hour fast.'

'Are you sure he's not queer?'

She laughed. 'Well, I'm sure he's got complexes that even Freud never heard of. But he's just not – *anything*.' She smiled at him. 'I've never been happier,' she said.

'I wish you didn't have to go to the shop.'

'So do I.'

'I'm sorry I broke down like that last night.'

'There's nothing to be sorry for. It's worse if you bottle things like that up. You might have died, after all. You're not still bothered by her, are you?'

He shook his head.

'That's good. I'm not a jealous type, but I wouldn't share you with a loony like that. She's got the death-wish and it rubs off on to other people ... Do you like my room?'

It was half the size of the main room, with the floor covered with straw matting and a large pink nylon rug each side of the bed. There were two bookcases each painted scarlet. One corner was curtained off with tangerine curtaining matching the window curtains; the dressing-table and chest of drawers and the wardrobe and the pelmet matched the pink of the bedside rugs. The bed-head was covered with scarlet plastic quilting; only the wallpaper, of a pale biscuit colour with an open-weave effect, didn't quite match anything. But the walls had so many pictures on them that it didn't really matter, any more than it mattered about the two dark-brown hospital-type bedside tables or the battered Windsor chair by the dressing-table. Sooner or later the whitewood beneath the layers of paint would warp, the plastic quilting peel, the plastic handles come off: in the meantime the total effect was bright and frivolous, a long way removed from the careful and solid elegance of the Tower House interiors.

'I like it,' he said.

'It was really dingy when we came. Various shades of dark brown and red. Norman's the genius responsible.'

She got out of bed and drew the curtains of the recess.

'The bathroom's next door,' she said. 'There should be plenty of hot water. Norman takes a cold tub every morning, would you believe it?'

Clive lay back watching her at the washstand, the curve of her back dappled with sunlight. He got out of bed as she turned, drying her face.

'It's a lie when they say women don't get a kick out of looking at naked men,' she said. She touched the wound across his belly. 'What's this?'

'Shrapnel.'

'It's terribly sexy. I'll make it better—' She kissed it. 'No, Clive. No. Quick then, quick—'

After Norman and Ruth had gone Clive went into the living-room and looked through the bookshelves. He took *The Soldier's Art* to the studio couch and lay down with a cushion under his head. He read for half an hour, then put the book down and lit a cigarette. There was a smell of turpentine in the room which he'd not noticed before, and in the morning light its untidiness verged on the scruffy. But he was content to be there, it was his destiny to be there, to let himself go, be a kind of beatnik at the age of forty-seven. There was nothing to stop him. He sat up and took an envelope from his pocket, resting it on the book, and made hasty calculations. There was enough for him and, he supposed, Robin, and his father had taken care of the children's education a long time ago. In fact, when he added it up in pounds, shillings and pence, he was doing what everybody said they did, working for the Inland Revenue.

He put the envelope and the pen in his pocket and as he did so was gripped by a pain in his chest. It expanded inside him, forcing him back against the studio couch, his hand still grasping the pen and the envelope; then with his left hand he rubbed his chest and the pain went as quickly as it had come. Walking very slowly, he went into the kitchen and brewed himself a pot of tea; after two cups he put the pain firmly out of his mind.

He read until one o'clock and then lunched off bread and cheese and a can of lager, reading with the meal, a pleasure in which he rarely had the chance to indulge in what he already thought of as his old life. After lunch he slept for an hour on the studio couch, then drove into Leeds. There he bought a suitcase, a briefcase, a Selectromatic cordless shaver, and some two hundred pounds' worth of clothes. He could have collected all that he needed from Tower House; but this was a way of marking the beginning of the new life. The clothes were all brightly coloured and casual, of the kind which he never wore at the mills; they were in fact, weekend clothes. His new life, however long it lasted, was going to be a weekend life. He didn't know as yet what pattern it was going to take, except that it would include Ruth, but work or any kind of responsibility wouldn't exist any more for him.

He wasn't frightened of the possibility of being bored as long as he could read or visit the cinema or the theatre or buy the sort of gramophone record he liked; and in addition he had known for some time that he could be absolutely contented doing nothing at all as long as he did it in physical comfort. This was partly sheer indolence – an abandonment to the deadly sin of sloth, if one wanted to look at it in that light – but more a genuine fondness for contemplation. If his father had not been a rich man, if he'd been forced to make his own way he'd have been simply a lay-about. If on the other hand he'd been more of an intellectual turn of mind he might have been an original thinker. For what he contemplated – or began to contemplate, slowly and with difficulty but with a kind of joy – was the nature of existence. Ruth's attraction for him was that she was one of the few persons – perhaps the only person – he knew who could understand this.

That day set the pattern for his life with Ruth. In the afternoon he arrived at the flat an hour before her, had a bath, his second that day, and changed into brown slacks, brown suede shoes, bright orange socks and shirt, a match-ing yellow tie and handkerchief, and a turquoise and scarlet and lemon checked hacking jacket. The combination of bright colours had the the effect not of making him seem less masculine but more masculine. And the effect was of cele-bration of his new relationship with Ruth also, as if he were the bridegroom in some simpler society where men are as dominant as peacocks. His putting on the new clothes was as much a gift to her as the bottle of champagne and bunch of red roses he had bought.

And, that evening being a Friday, it was the evening on which she always met her friends. It was not always the same friends, nor was Friday evening the only time when she met them. But if you were a friend of Ruth's you'd know that on a Friday evening she was always to be found at the Bulldog Inn on Carpenter Street in the centre of Charbury from about half past eight to closing time and after that it was open house at her flat.

The Bulldog was a small pub built in 1901 with two large blocks of office buildings of the same period at either side. It was separated on the left by a narrow passage just wide enough for two people walking abreast and on the right by a broader passage. The passages led to an expanse of waste land on which before the war there had stood a maze of tenements and back-to-back houses. It was now a free car park but very few people used it; the notice indicating it was badly placed and the ground was rough and stony and murder on the tyres.

The pub had been in biscuit-coloured stone originally, but now was sooty black. The two square bay windows downstairs were of stained glass in the upper panes and the curtains were lace and red velvet. There was a small taproom with a sanded floor and dartboard and sets of dominoes, a tiny bar parlour behind the bar, and a saloon bar, a large square room, to the right of the bar. The taproom was, for some reason, much used by steeplejacks and demolition workers, the main bar, which occupied the largest space, by the majority of the customers, and the bar parlour by the oldest regulars. Ruth and her friends used the saloon bar. Seating throughout was benches against the wall, of wood in the taproom and red cloth upholstery everywhere else. The tables were ironwork with marble tops; there were a few wooden chairs but they weren't very comfortable. There were a great many pictures of dogs on the walls, put there by a previous landlord on the strength of the pub's name. But the Bulldog never became the special haunt of dog-fanciers; indeed, it was unusual to see a dog there.

Why Ruth had selected the Bulldog in the first instance she'd long since forgotten. But when she and her friends began to use it gradually it became an artists' pub, using the term in its broadest sense to indicate those who practise or wish to practise any of the arts – and also those who are interested in any of the arts. It could not have been said that every night in the week the saloon bar was crammed with this sort of person; but if you were at all interested in any of the arts you would sooner or later find company at the Bulldog.

It was not a pub that Clive had ever been in; he didn't in any case frequent pubs very much. He never said as much, but the truth was that he didn't like the proximity of anyone who was poor and unwashed. It wasn't from any feeling of class hatred or because he was frightened of catching anything; it was simply that it upset him too much mentally and physically.

So when Ruth announced after dinner – grilled halibut and chips cooked expertly by Norman – that they were going to the Bulldog to meet her friends he wasn't very pleased.

'Couldn't we have a quiet drink here?'

'Not on a Friday,' Ruth said.

'I don't particularly care for pubs.'

'I can see you don't. But this is quite a nice pub really. And I want you to meet my friends.'

'They may not want to meet me. I mightn't be clever enough for them.'

Her fingers drummed impatiently on the kitchen table; already he recognized this as a sure sign of irritation.

'Oh, come off it, Clive. You're a very clever man, and you're certainly better-read than any of them. You don't choose your friends for their cleverness, anyway.'

'Don't you?' he asked shrewdly.

She flushed. 'All right then. I just want to show you off. It's a sort of taking one's young man home to tea. You can just sit silent and look handsome in your smart clothes.' She came over and stood behind him, her arms round his neck.

'I do love you, Clive. I'm not ashamed of it.'

'I must phone,' Norman said, 'Excuse me, dears.' He took off his blue striped apron, folded it up neatly, put it away in a drawer beneath the table and hurried out.

Ruth kissed Clive's forehead. 'He really must phone, that's all.' She moved away from Clive and sat down opposite him and took out a packet of cigarettes. 'Darling, let's get this clear. Norman doesn't have any feelings towards me or any woman. Think of him like an old nanny – one of the family, that's all. He rather likes it when there's a man about the place, just as an old nanny does. But there's no sex in it.' She blew a smoke ring. 'People have got to get by as well as they can in this world,' she said, half to herself. 'You find relationships that help you through life, and to other people they seem pretty bizarre relationships. They're ramshackle, they're twisted, they're tied together with string and wire, but they work, and they're yours, the only ones you've got. I couldn't do without Norman and he couldn't do without me, but that doesn't affect you.'

'I believe you.'

'You can always believe me, because I don't tell lies. You'll tell me lies, though, because you're very soft-hearted. And you like to please. But try to tell me the truth always, won't you?'

'I love you. I don't want anyone else.'

'Oh, *that's* a lie.' She laughed. 'I don't care, darling. But you're going to want Robin again, and she's going to want you. You'll work something out.'

'No. It's over.'

'That's what you think. But it doesn't matter now. Take things easy, darling.'

Norman came back into the kitchen, rubbing his hands. 'Darling, Jack and Lucy are coming tonight. They're up here on a visit. Clare says they look *terribly* prosperous—' He looked at his watch. 'I do think we ought to be going, children. Just imagine, Jack and Lucy! I've missed them, you know.'

His smooth face suddenly wrinkled; Clive recognized his sincerity. He saw what he hadn't seen before: it was only one side of Norman that was, so to speak, uninhabited. The grief behind the last words was love speaking; not Eros, but another kind of love, and no less real.

'It's early yet,' Ruth said. 'No need to rush.'

Norman looked angry. 'I want to see them first,' he said. 'Otherwise I won't get a look in. They always come early.'

'All right, Norman, we'll go now,' Clive said gently.

He had a better evening than he'd anticipated. Ruth's friends weren't of a type he'd had much to do with before. They were all under thirty and two of them, a boy and a girl with identical long hair and jeans and sweaters and canvas shoes without socks, were under twenty. He didn't sort them out immediately; he was generally good at names and faces, but half his mind was slowly and with increasing astonishment sorting out what Ruth had said earlier.

When he'd come within distance of sorting it out, he was still faced with the fact that he wasn't sure of anything any more; he was beginning to get rid of the feeling of being directed from outside, he was moving, or having grounds for hoping to move, under his own power.

He blinked his eyes in the tobacco smoke and dreamily listened to the conversation around him. The young couple from the Art College were arguing with an older couple with more conventional hair and clothes; the older couple – all of twenty-three, he thought with amusement – were Eric and Jacqueline. He'd seen them at the Hailton Players; he had an idea that they knew Robin. Eric was a reporter with the Charbury Gazette who wanted to write plays and Jacqueline was a teacher who, from the way she looked at him, wanted to be Eric's wife. Eric, from the way he looked at her, wanted to poke the young female art student, who had large dark eyes and radiated a fierce energy. The art students were called Nicky and Kim; Nicky was the girl.

'Nakedness is part of it,' Kim shouted. 'Without that shock, what you have is just anecdotal, a series of crappy little puzzles, don't you see?'

'Bloody jargon,' Eric said. He had a thin face with an incongruously broad nose. 'A cunt is a cunt is a cunt. It's just a matter of stage directions—'

On looks alone he'd lost; Kim was almost as pretty as Nicky, with regular features and bright blue eyes. But it wasn't always looks that counted with a woman; once Kim had used up his jargon Eric might be far more articulate.

The librarian Teddy – that was easy, since his open brief-case bulged with books stamped Charbury Public Library – had buttonholed the novelist, Jack Byrock, a rather plump young man with a pink shirt and bright blue suit. 'You've sold out,' Teddy was saying. 'You should be bloody ashamed of yourself.'

There didn't seem to be any answer to that; the novelist merely grinned, and said something to Norman that Clive didn't catch.

'You too,' said Teddy to the BBC producer Harry – or was it Larry – a pink-cheeked young man in a green corduroy jacket and red polo-neck sweater. The producer grinned too; like the novelist, Clive reflected, he had made it. He passed Teddy a packet of cigarettes. 'Wouldn't you like to be me, though?' he asked Teddy.

'Yes,' said Teddy, showing white teeth. 'There's nothing I'd like better. But I wouldn't sell out. I'd revolutionize the medium—'

After a while Clive gave up trying to disentangle the conversations and relaxed in the corner, perfectly happy. Now and again he caught Ruth's eye and they smiled at each other; eventually Teddy and the novelist's wife, a small dark girl with a ponytail, talked about books with him, looking at him with a barely concealed wonder as at an exceptionally intelligent performing animal, as it was revealed that he could hold his own, in some respects more than hold his own, with them.

Somehow everyone was transported to Ruth's flat and he drove there arguing with Teddy about Iris Murdoch and listening at the same time to the argument between Eric and Kim in the back and from Nicky's silence coming to the conclusion that Eric was winning.

When the party ended – for eventually, spontaneously, it had become a party, bringing in guests who hadn't been at the pub – Clive found himself slightly drunk. It seemed to him that these were wonderful people: whether they had always talked good sense or not, whether or not most of them were ever going to do more than talk about their ambitions, whether or not he liked their politics, they had talked about something other than the usual party topics of cars, sports, jobs, clothes, money, children, money. There had been no small talk, no awkward silences; and no one as far as he could see had got more than slightly drunk. At most of the parties he'd been to there hadn't been anything else for it but to anaesthetize oneself with alcohol and sex, or rather the promise of it.

He told Ruth something of this as he and she and Norman emptied ashtrays and stacked glasses in the sink and empty bottles in the larder.

'I'm so glad, darling,' she said. 'I was afraid you were going to feel out of it.'

'Would you have thrown me out?'

She ran hot water into the sink. 'I'll never throw you out,' she said quietly. 'You'll leave when you want to leave and come back when you want to come back. I was going to go away if you hadn't come to me, but now I'll always be here.' Her tone was one of absolute finality.

Later as they were on the verge of sleep, she said drowsily: 'I won't ever marry you.'

'All right, darling.' He only half heard the words.

'Listen.' She nudged him in the ribs. 'There never seems much time with us, there's so much to say. I can't marry you.'

He sat up, yawning.

'Are you married already?'

'No. I'm just not the marrying type. I can't help it. Sometimes I wish I were. Do you understand?'

'It doesn't signify. I've heard you.' He smiled sleepily. 'Let's take things as they come.' He lay down and went straight to sleep, but she continued to sit upright in the bed, wide awake, her face a little puzzled.

He was to meet more of her friends during the next three weeks; it was never again quite like that first occasion, but now he was drawn into her circle and into a new pattern of life.

One evening he saw Gerry Sindram at the bar of the Bradford Alhambra. Gerry didn't recognize him at first, then stared at him coldly. Clive was wearing his turquoise and scarlet and lemon check jacket and red-brown slacks and brown-and-white shoes, a new pink polo-neck sweater and matching handkerchief.

'Christ, you look like a circus horse,' Gerry said.

Clive flushed. 'What the hell's up with you?'

'What's up with you?'

'Mind your own business.'

'If I were Robin I'd know what to do.' Gerry didn't bother to lower his voice. 'You're cunt-struck, aren't you? Often happens at your age.'

Clive turned away, but Gerry grabbed his sleeve, looking towards Ruth.

'A bit of young stuff, eh? I hope you can keep up with her.'

Clive wrenched his sleeve free. Ruth ran up to him. 'No, Clive, come away.'

'I'll go,' Gerry said. He looked at Ruth as if about to spit. 'Whore,' he said. Fiona rushed up, her normally pale face pink, and took Gerry by the arm; he allowed himself to be taken out of the room. Fiona didn't speak; but as she passed Clive she put her hand lightly on Clive's shoulder, looking at him appealingly.

'I'm sorry,' Clive said to Ruth.

'It isn't your fault.'

'I can't understand him.' His head began to throb. It was not actually painful, but it was as if his head couldn't contain it. He swayed against the bar.

'What's the matter, darling? What's the matter?'

He straightened up; the throbbing had diminished now.

'Nothing. I'm upset. God, he talked as if he hated me.'

'We'll go home. I'll make you better.'

In the car, he said thoughtfully: 'I'd have said he was the last person in the world to behave like that. There must be a reason.'

'Outraged morality.'

'Not him. Oh, he's clean living enough, but he's no moralist.' He rummaged his memory. Dining at Tower House, dining at his home, running across him at parties, drinking with him in their bachelor days; he'd known Gerry longer than he'd known Robin and he'd always been the same, pleasant, tolerant, easy-going, always glad to see you. Robin liked him perhaps the best of all their friends. Had done even before they married: Gerry had introduced him to her at the Players in fact. Then suddenly he understood. 'I see it now,' he said. 'Poor sod.'

'You're sorry for him?'

'I know why he was angry. I should have seen it before. It's because of Robin. You see someone else throwing away what you want but can't have, and you blow your top.'

'You frighten me sometimes.'

'Why?'

'You're growing so quickly.'

'Not growing,' he said. 'Understanding a bit more.' They were nearly at Lister Park Gates now, in a district of large old houses so like the district round Ruth's flat that for a moment he had a sensation of time and distance contracting upon him like a mailed fist.

'Don't understand too much,' she said. 'It mightn't be comfortable.'

'I've had a very comfortable life,' he said. 'Too comfortable perhaps. Now I sit down and think, and I remember all sorts of things ... I've lived in a fog all my life. Now it's beginning to clear.'

That evening was an exception in their life together because its enjoyment was marred by the incident at the bar. In the five weeks which followed they saw five plays and five films, went to the Bulldog on five Fridays, went to two parties, gave a party themselves, and stayed in London one weekend, taking a suite at the Royal Garden. If he'd been asked once he'd have said that he'd not be able to fill the time in without going to work; but whilst he lived at Ruth's the days didn't seem long enough. There was always a book he wanted to read or a record or radio programme he wanted to listen to during the day; sometimes he'd go out and buy presents – frivolous underwear, scent, flowers, china, gramophone records, fruit out of season, champagne, a new liqueur – for Ruth, but most days he was content to stay in the flat. Invariably he had cold meat or cheese and coffee for lunch reading as he ate, and afterwards would lie on the studio couch, sometimes sleeping but most often trying to penetrate the fog which, as he'd said, he'd lived in all his life.

Walter forwarded on his letters; he opened none of them. He made no attempt to get into touch with Robin and she made no attempt to get into touch with him. Donald phoned him twice; on the first occasion he cut him off short and on the second occasion said that he was willing to hand in his resignation at any time and then hung up. Every week he phoned Walter to tell him no more in effect than that he was alive and not interested in making decisions of any kind. He did not think of the future, though more and more often he thought of the past, not with regret but with a real intensity.

One afternoon in early December the phone rang. He was lying on the studio couch half-asleep. Outside the sky was iron grey with the approaching snow. A strange stillness seemed to emanate into the room, as if the earth were holding its breath. Generally only Ruth rang during the day, and that very rarely: he swung his legs off the couch and stumbled yawning to the phone.

It was Petronella's voice.

'Daddy, don't be angry with me.'

'Of course I'm not angry, love.'

'Mummy said I hadn't to phone. But I had to talk to you.'

He felt a constriction in his chest. 'Is anything wrong?'

'Oh, Daddy. I'm so miserable! It's awful in the house without you.'

He rubbed his chest. 'I'm sorry, darling. I can't expect you to understand—'

'Oh but I do, Daddy. How old do you think I am? I know about her and that bloody, bloody, bloody Stephen—' He heard her sob. 'She was on the phone one day, and I picked up the extension. I shouldn't have listened.'

'Don't worry about that.' He was fully awake now. Outside it was beginning to snow.

'Can't I come and see you, Daddy?'

'Of course you can, sweetheart. I should have thought of you before.' He gasped; the pain in his chest was growing.

'Oh Christ, I've been selfish—' The pain was filling his chest and now it was a tearing pain, he was being ripped apart. He moaned and fell forward; the telephone crashed from his hand on to the table and then slid off it on to the floor.

Nineteen

Some psychologists would assert that Clive willed the heart attack. For he could not have continued indefinitely in the sort of limbo he inhabited with Ruth. Sooner or later his letters had to be opened and answered, decisions had to be taken about his marriage, about his position at Lendrick and Sons, about his relationship with Ruth (whatever she might say about not being the marrying kind), about his future in general. The heart attack, you might say, took the decisions for him.

He went back to Robin and to Lendrick and Sons, and, perhaps most important of all, back to Tower House. There were no recriminations; neither of them was in a position where recriminations could be made. But when Clive came out of hospital they arrived at an agreement. They were alone in the house one snowy evening going through their Christmas present list when Robin laid the list down.

'We'll have to work something out,' she said. 'About us.'

'We'll leave things as they are.'

'We've got to agree about that. I can't not see him some-times. Even if it were only just to *see* him.'

'Are you sure you're not going to run off with him?'

'Oh God, no.' She started to cry and he came over to her and put his arm around her. She clung to him, letting him wipe her eyes and when the tears had stopped still remained within the circle of his arm. 'You know what's happening there, don't you?'

'I'm sorry, love. These things run their course, don't they?'

'Yes, they run their course. And you *stay* the course, the whole bloody course.'

'I'd help you if I could.'

'You do help me. You've altered so much since—' she bit her lip. 'It's no use. It's unfair, but sometimes I resent her because I need you so much. I was going to be civilized ...'

'I'm not going to run off with her,' he said a little sharply. 'I'll only ever have one wife. Let's leave it for now. There'll be another time.'

There was another time; and what the agreement amounted to was that she continued to see Stephen and he continued to see Ruth. It was as much an unspoken agreement as a spoken one, and somehow or other it worked. Whether it would work in the future, or not, bearing in mind particularly that Ruth was of childbearing age, would have been something for them to worry about, had either of them been the kind to worry about the future. But it's the young who worry about the future, not the middle-aged.

Eventually the scandal died down. Neither of them was, of course, socially ostracized; this doesn't happen these days on account of straightforward sexual irregularities and ones, moreover, not affecting young children. (Petronella was content that Clive was home again and his sons seemed to take it in their stride, looking at their parents with – or so Clive fancied – a half-incredulous respect.) On the contrary, they discovered that as far as a surprising number of people were concerned, they had joined an inner circle. They had broken away from convention, they had desired and had been desired, they had been figures of romance, they had acted out their dreams.

In a sense Clive and Robin were not only figures of romance, but figures in a stock situation of romance. Clive's heart attack brought him home; Robin once again became a good and dutiful wife, meticulously obeying the doctor's instructions, gently but firmly making sure that he took his medicine, did his exercises, ate and drank rigorously according to his diet, kept regular hours, didn't overwork and, as far as she could ensure it, didn't worry. And once again they shared a room. 'I don't forbid sex now,' the doctor had said when Clive's convalescence was over, 'otherwise what's the point of your husband getting better? But take it easy.'

They took it easy; and perhaps precisely because of this their marriage was better than it was before. When he was ill she had for the first time visualized her life as a widow, and had been able to do so all the more vividly because of his two months' absence from her. But theirs was not quite a stock situation; it was not until the June following Clive's heart attack that she decided not to see Stephen again. She told Clive her decision: they now hid nothing from each other.

'You don't have to for me,' Clive said. 'You can't help these things.'

'Don't be frightened,' she said. 'I shan't expect a *quid pro quo*. Anyway I don't expect I shall give him up. It's more a question of him giving me up.'

'We wouldn't have talked like this once,' he said. 'Most people never tell each other anything.'

'You have to say if you mind,' she said anxiously.

'I don't mind anything very much since I was ill,' he said. 'I don't mean that I don't care. I'd rather you did break it off with Stephen, because if you don't, you're going to get hurt.'

'I'll get hurt one way or the other,' she said.

'Yes,' he said. 'One way or the other.' They were sitting in the back garden; the day had been unusually hot for June in the North. A cold breeze sprang up: he drew in a deep breath. 'You can smell the roses,' he said. 'Sometimes I'd give anything for a cigarette, and then I realize how marvellous it is not to smoke.'

'I should have given him up a long time ago,' she said. 'When you came out of hospital.'

'If you had done then, sooner or later you'd have blamed me for it.' He grinned. 'It's strange, now I can see outside myself.'

'Some people would say we were immoral,' she said. 'But they don't have to live our lives, do they? We've got to come to arrangements without making too much of a song and a dance about it. In the end all we've got is each other.'

'Yes,' he said. 'And a home.' He glanced behind him at the house. 'I'll not leave here till they take me out in my coffin. Ruth said once—' He stopped.

'Go on.'

'She said she knew I'd never stay with her because I'd always be wanting to come back here. Do you know Norman's leaving?'

'*Norman?*'

'He has the offer of a partnership in a shop in Surrey.' His voice became fretful. 'I hate change. I want everything to stay the same.'

'Is Ruth leaving too, then?'

'Not that I know of.'

'I don't think she ever will. Don't ask me how I know it but I do.'

'Do you mind me still seeing her?'

'You keep asking me that. No, I don't. I like her, in fact. She gives you something you need. That's what I'm jealous of, not the physical side of it. But if I didn't like her, I wouldn't ever see her. Much less invite her to tea.'

'As long as nothing changes,' he said. 'That's all I want. You're happy about things as they are, aren't you?'

She put her hand on his for a moment. 'Perfectly happy.'

Ruth walked through the garden towards them. She looked pale and tired, as she always did on a Saturday. 'Hello, my darlings!'

They stood up. She kissed each on the cheek.

'It's turning cold,' Robin said. 'You'll be longing for tea, Ruth.'

Clive sat down again. 'I think I'll stay five minutes more.'

'We're going inside,' Robin said firmly. 'You know what the doctor said about avoiding chills. Tell him to get up, Ruth.'

Ruth held out her hand.

'Come on, darling.' She pulled him out of the chair.

As they went towards the house, Clive between them, each woman took an arm. They grasped his arms with affectionate firmness; it looked somehow like a patient between two nurses or a prisoner between two warders.

JOHN BRAINE

Life at the Top

Joe Lampton is a success – or so it seems. He's married to a rich man's daughter, has a well-paid job, and now belongs to the wealthy class he used to envy. But after ten years of affluent living he faces a crisis in his life. Once again his restless drive towards other women and material success begins to assert itself, and Joe is ready to break out . . .

The Pious Agent

Introducing Xavier Flynn, fervent Catholic and ruthless professional killer. The enemy is FIST, a secret revolutionary group – their mission is sabotage, their target one of Britain's best-established industries. Grappling with a ferment of intrigue, counter-plotting and violent death demands the ultimate degree of razor-sharp wits and ice-cool experience. But Xavier is a born survivor – with one eye fixed on heaven and the other on the nearest desirable woman.

'Mr Braine is a highly welcome newcomer to the spy story scene.'

Francis Goff, *Sunday Telegraph*

More top fiction from Magnum Books

	Michael Kerr	
417 0206	The Kutzov Haul	95p
	Ken Kesey	
417 0459	Sometimes a Great Notion	£1.75
	Dan Lees	
417 0231	Zodiac	70p
	Donald Lindquist	
417 0388	Berlin Tunnel 21	£1.50
	Ronald Lockley	
454 0004	Seal Woman	90p
	Jerry Ludwig	
417 0314	Little Boy Lost	95p
	Phillip Mann	
417 0251	Candles in the Sun	95p
	Baron Moss	
417 0380	Chains	£1.50
	Timeri Murari	
417 0385	The Oblivion Tapes	£1.10
417 0333	Lovers are not People	95p
	William Murray	
417 0328	The Mouth of the Wolf	95p
	C. Northcote Parkinson	
417 0549	The Fireship	90p
417 0548	Devil to Pay	95p
417 0246	Touch and Go	95p
417 0361	Dead Reckoning	£1.10
	Derry Quinn	
417 0187	The Limbo Connection	90p
417 0237	The Solstice Man	90p
417 0338	The Fear of God	95p
	Howell Raines	
417 0332	Whiskey Man	£1.25
	Bob Randall	
417 0245	The Fan	90p
	David Rogers	
417 0540	The In-Laws	95p